PREACHER STALLS THE SECOND COMING

Carry on!

PRAISE FOR THE EVAN WYCLIFF MYSTERIES

NINE BOOK AWARDS, INCLUDING BOTH GOLD AND SILVER IN NYC BIG BOOK MYSTERY IN THE SAME YEAR (2020)

This is literature masquerading as a mystery. Carefully yet powerfully, Gerald Jones creates a small, stunning world in a tiny midwestern town, infusing each character with not just life but wit, charm, and occasionally menace. This is the kind of writing one expects from John Irving or Jane Smiley.

— MARVIN J. WOLF, AUTHOR OF THE RABBI BEN MYSTERIES, INCLUDING *A SCRIBE DIES IN BROOKLYN.*

As anyone who's spent time in a small town in the American Midwest knows, there's a lot more going on behind the scenes than you'd expect. Or suspect. And there are plenty of suspects in the latest Evan Wycliff mystery by Gerald Everett Jones. *Preacher Fakes a Miracle* haunted my dreams as I read it, in the way that a good story about a bad situation should. I'm looking forward to reading the next installment of the Evan Wycliff mystery series.

— PAMELA JAYE SMITH, *MYTHWORKS,* AWARD-WINNING WRITER-DIRECTOR-PRODUCER

This is not your mother's preacher. Gerald Jones has created a character who can discover a corpse, kiss a girl, solve a crime, and get back to his trailer in time to say grace over Sunday dinner.

This time the Preacher digs even deeper, faster, and funnier than his prize-winning debut. It's just what you'd expect, except everything you expect is wrong because the Preacher, in the very talented hands of Gerald Jones, is always at least a step ahead in this very satisfying second time out of the gate.

A fast-moving mystery with twists and surprises that take you in unexpected directions. Jones is adept at creating unique and fascinating characters. His mystery sleuth is a part-timer with lots of heart who splits his time between religion, skip tracing and sometimes the metaphysical. The hero's search for a missing girl and his interactions with various eccentric individuals in the small town make him both sympathetic and compelling. A bit of a shock to learn what's really going on with the abducted young unwed mother... and amazing how it relates to real stories in the news today.

A smart, thoroughly entertaining, and suspenseful mystery novel, which is not so much a who-done-it as a how-and-why. The characters are universally well-drawn and quirky, and the relationship between Evan and Naomi is fresh and romantic.

I loved it.

Preacher Finds a Corpse is an absolute pleasure to read. Reminiscent of Charlaine Harris's mysteries and Barbara Kingsolver's early novels like *Animal Dreams* and *The Bean Trees*, it's full of quirky characters who animate the small town in which they live. Evan Wycliff is a complex and compelling protagonist, conflicted and lost in his own life but nevertheless fiercely dedicated to uncovering the truth about his friend Bob Taggart's death.

Jones manages to infuse a deceptively simple story with suspense, angst, and whimsy, as well as surprise. His command of setting, history, and behavior is beyond exceptional. I can't wait for the next book in the series.

From the secret contents in a rusty tin fishing box to clues that lead Evan further into danger, Gerald Everett Jones weaves a tense thriller peppered with references to Evan's ongoing relationship to God and prayer.

When the clues boil down to a final surprise, will forgiveness be possible?

Jones does an outstanding job of crafting a murder mystery that romps through a small town's secrets and various lives. His main protagonist is realistic and believable in every step of his investigative actions and setbacks; but so are characters he interacts with; from his boss Zip to a final service which holds some big surprises.

With its roots firmly grounded in an exceptional sense of place and purpose, Jones has created a murder mystery that lingers in the mind long after events have built to an unexpected crescendo.

Murder mystery fans will find it more than a cut above the ordinary.

— D. DONOVAN, *DONOVAN'S BOOKSHELF*

The constant shifts in trust and tidbits of new information kept me guessing until the end who was friend or foe and the 'need' to find out kept the pages turning.

Many of the common stigmas, questions, and feelings suicide deaths leave in their wake were also addressed in a responsible way, which will help the conversation around suicide in general.

— RUTH GOLDEN, WRITER-PRODUCER, *THE SILENT GOLDENS: A DOCUMENTARY ABOUT SUICIDE* AND *TALKING ABOUT SUICIDE WITH MARIETTE HARTLEY*

PREACHER STALLS THE SECOND COMING

AN EVAN WYCLIFF MYSTERY

GERALD EVERETT JONES

LaPuerta Books and Media lapuerta.tv Email: bookstore@lapuerta.tv

The novel in this book is a work of fiction. Names, characters, places, and incidents either are products of the author's imagination or are used fictitiously. Any resemblance to actual events or locales or persons, living or dead, is entirely coincidental.

Throughout this book, the author has attempted to distinguish proprietary trademarks from descriptive terms by following the capitalization style used for the brand by the mark owner.

Trade paperback ISBN: 979-8-9860953-8-7

eBook ISBN: 979-8-9860953-9-4 ASIN: B0CRCFGLDP

Library of Congress Control Number: TBD

LaPuerta is an imprint of La Puerta Productions lapuerta.tv

Cover and interior design by La Puerta Productions

Cover photo Silver Sword by tomertu from Getty Images licensed from Canva Pro

Editor: Jason Letts

Author photo by Runkee Productions

Epigraph quoted from *The Expulsion of the Triumphant Beast*, translated by W. Morehead from *Jordano Bruno's Spaccia Della Bestia Trionfante*. United Kingdom: n.p., 1713. [PD Google Books]

To Phil Enoch

Sophia. *So that if there was no Change in Bodies, no Variety in Matter, and no Vicissitude in Beings, there would be nothing agreeable, nothing good, or nothing pleasant.*

Saul. *If the Case be so, then there is no Pleasure without a mixture of Pain; and a Change from one State to another, partakes of what pleases, and of what disgusts us.*

- from ***The Expulsion of the Triumphant Beast***

"Reverend Wycliff, much of what you believe in your Christian faith is true, but not for the reasons you believe."

The grizzled old man at my door was muttering in heavily accented English, but his message was unmistakable. It didn't help my perception that I was severely hungover, having spent most of the night alternately guzzling cheap bourbon and praying.

It was a spring morning, only slightly chilly, promising a day that might be perfectly fine. I was clad in my habitual sweatsuit, which might well have reeked, but I'd grown so accustomed to my own stink I wouldn't know. I worried he did, even though his outward appearance was no more respectable than mine. He was dressed in a black business suit, but it wasn't his size and looked rumpled and dirty, as if he'd been sleeping in doorways.

I'd finally managed to drop off to sleep moments before a polite knock on my door, and I was having trouble keeping my eyes open.

"You've made coffee?" he asked with an approving sniff. It wasn't so much a question as an insistent hint. When I had prepared with undue optimism last night to crawl into bed, I'd set the automatic drip machine for precisely this hour.

It seems I have no choice but to invite him in.

I still hadn't greeted him or said a word yet. I simply opened the door to my humble cube-sized trailer home and waved toward its shabby interior.

On the narrow counter where I undertake food preparations often no more complex than opening a can, I could only find one crusty mug. As he jostled behind me and sat in the only chair, I rummaged in the wall-mounted crate that housed dinnerware, condiments, and pharmaceuticals. I was delighted to find a second cup, this one emblazoned with the logo of Twin Dragons Casino. I couldn't remember the last time I'd needed to use it, but it looked reasonably clean.

I filled both cups from the steaming carafe, turned to offer him his, and before I could finally manage to speak to ask his preferences, he blurted what sounded like, *"Kine krim, kine sook.* Trying to quit *zucker."*

German, I realized. Or perhaps his accent was of some other Eastern European extraction, and he was telling me he'd be more comfortable if I shared his other common language.

I sat down on my cot and blew out a puff of exhaustion, doubly fatigued after my long, dark night of the soul and the presumably unpleasant surprise of this intrusion on my unenviable privacy.

We both sipped, reverently it seemed.

He smacked his lips before he sighed and said, "I took long time finding you. Fortunately, your neighbors are shameless gossips."

I took another restorative sip, cleared my throat, and asked gruffly, "To what do I owe the pleasure, Mister …?"

"Doctor Hans Gropius. Forgive the similarity in name to the famous historical person, but no relation. The surname not my choice, of course. People assume I must be from family of architects." He sipped again, this time long and noisily, then added with a chuckle, "Although I stand in awe of the grand design."

Somehow I caught the hint. My brain was waking up. There had to be a reason this fellow had taken pains to seek *me* out. So I asked, "Design? Physical or spiritual?"

He chuckled again. "Insight, you have! I knew I was in the right place. I simply toss out phrases that suggest scheme of Creation, and you jump on it. Clever fellow. We are going to be friends, I am sure of it."

I cautioned him by displaying the upraised palms of my hands. It occurred to me he might think I was intending to show him stigmata or perhaps pre-Parkinson's tremor, which might seem crazy, but based on his behavior so far I had no reason to expect he was sane either. "When you talk about what I believe, I don't know how you'd know. I will say I'm not an agnostic, although certainly I've been accused of such. I insist I am a man of faith, but faith in what mostly defies definition, depends on the day and my mood."

He smiled, explaining, "I was faithful listener to your broadcasts until you went off the air. The news of your resignation from your ministry was also upsetting."

"I didn't resign. I was kicked out, but the result is the same. I suppose my tumble downhill began when my wife left me. Turns out being a minister's wife is an even heavier cross to bear than being a pastor. And as for my show, I tried to speak truth to power one too many times."

"Do you believe in afterlife?" he asked quietly.

At that moment, I wished the coffee were bourbon and I could stiffen myself with a shot. I began to worry he might be a journalist or some emissary from church leadership sent to chastise me, but I decided I might as well answer as honestly as I could. "I don't believe in resurrection of the body — as a living, breathing, human body. But reincarnation? Transference of consciousness from one being — or state of being — to another? I won't say it's impossible.

3

I worry it's not, but because I have an obsessively curious intellect, I worry a lot."

"My dear Evan," he began then stopped himself to ask, "May I address you so? I feel I know you so well, you see."

His manner was amusing, endearing. "Go ahead," I allowed. "Please tell me more about myself than I know, and I'll gift you another cup of coffee."

He loved this. Grinning broadly, he teased, "You are, of course, aware of virtual reality?"

"Sure," I said, "but can't say I've indulged. Not games for kids anymore, I understand. Frankly, it's scary."

"And you know work of physicist Nick Bostrum?"

"I do," I admitted. "Not in depth, but I believe he's famous for speculating we don't live in what's termed *base reality.*"

"Just so," the visitor said approvingly. "We say now we live in post-information age. Soon we live in post-reality. Dreaming, waking — who can know the difference?"

"What are you trying to tell me, Hans?"

"My dear Evan, you are a man of faith. You believe what you cannot see. We scientists, we say seeing is believing. I'm here to tell you that seeing means nothing anymore."

2

Even though it required an effort on my part to get cleaned up, I resolved to take him to breakfast. No question he needed a meal. I asked him to step outside while I doused myself beneath the weak trickle of my improvised shower. I put on a fresh shirt (yes, I had one), a clean pair of jeans, and my navy blazer. I resisted the temptation to brace myself with a shot of whiskey then realized there was nothing left in my only bottle.

I surveyed myself in the mirror made blurry by either my eyesight or its smudged surface and decided to add a tie. The extra touch of respectability might put over the impression that here was the pastor, back on his feet, counseling a poor homeless man.

Who am I to counsel anybody now?

I counted a wad of bills and reasoned there was enough for coffee and pancakes as long as we didn't spring for seconds. Miraculously, the car keys were close at hand, and I had a dim memory of stopping on the way home to put two gallons in the tank.

More than the clothes, my oddball vehicle signaled the preacher was in town. It was a robin's-egg-blue Cinquecento — an Easter egg on wheels. It was the cheapest car Zip Zed would let me buy off him, but any rube less desperate would know otherwise he couldn't give the thing away, maybe even as a service loaner. Not in farm country where the F-150 of any year is standard issue.

Dr. Gropius couldn't stop grinning, which perhaps I should have cautioned him to since it revealed yellowed teeth with a gap where he'd lost an eye tooth and emphasized his shabbiness. I knew Coralie would serve us, but she's not the owner of the C'mon Inn, and not even a man of the cloth can always brook the wrath of management.

"YOUR EYES IS BLOODSHOT," Coralie muttered disapprovingly as she poured coffee from the Pyrex pot that seemed perpetually welded to her hand.

"I'll go and sin no more," I replied, avoiding her gaze as I bent down to empty a pack of instant Folgers into her brew. She wasn't offended I like it syrupy and inky with generous spoonfuls of sugar, not the worst of my vices.

Gropius was already slurping his down gratefully. "*Kine krim, kine sook.*"

He beamed up at Cora, his angel, whose family name was Angelides. Shouldn't make those Greeks angry. They throw plates, or so I've heard.

"Nice place you have here," he told her.

"And where do you hail from, my man?" she challenged.

"Born Romania. Most of my life, Germany. Hence, I have accent."

She chuckled, "Yes, hence, of course." She looked over at me. "You're having the flapjacks. You got enough to cover him?"

"Sure," I said after taking a noisy, approving sip of my custom-mixed breakfast bracer.

"Ecks!" my guest declared, adding, "You got kosher beef? Anything?"

"Eggs, we got," Cora assured him. "But the nearest deli is somewhere in Springfield, I'm told."

"Scramble rye toast butter," he rattled off. It sounded like *scrimple*.

Cora looked back at me. "Four eggs for him, scrambled. I'll charge for two, two on the house." She turned, took two steps to the next booth, and immediately poured coffee for them.

Now the doctor's grin was aimed at me. "Friend of yours, this nice lady?"

"Yes," I admitted. "I married a cocktail waitress instead and made her a minister's wife. A wiser man would've done different, but Coralie is in what they call a committed relationship. He's a good guy, helped get me off oxy. Many things could have gone the other way."

"Not easy," the doctor nodded.

"I started taking it for this pain in my back. Turns out, the other ways to suffer are worse. At least pain lets you know you're alive."

"Ah, yes," he said. "I know about your work, about your struggle. As I say, I am fan, admirer. You built big church, go on TV, had a following. When you speak, people listen. Your word touches hearts. You speak truth to power."

"Whoa. Hold off on that true-believer stuff. I never preached a sermon I didn't think was honest, I never asked for money, and at no time did I ever claim to heal the sick."

"You were and are genuine, no doubt," he said solemnly. "Fly too close to sun, your wings come off. Old story."

Coralie came with our meals, a hot plate on each forearm, her Pyrex still affixed to her right hand. She set the plates in front of us with her left then untucked a bottle of syrup from her underarm. She'd been trying to get me to try the sugarless Keto monkfruit goo

7

instead but this time, perhaps sniffing self-pity in the air, had brought the genuine maple.

Gropius's plate held the promised eggs and toast, accompanied by a generous, ice-cream-sized scoop of butter. She must've figured he needed the fat. A farmwife frets about any man who doesn't have a tummy. I believe it has to do with keeping something in reserve for when you're laid up and poorly.

I didn't get as much butter for my pancakes, and I had a sneaking suspicion mine was margarine. I wasn't ready for the ways that woman wanted to change my life.

Talkative as the little fellow was, he said not a word as he tucked into his food. I did note a slight bowing of his head when he closed his eyes briefly, and his lips moved silently. I was ashamed he was saying grace and I hadn't bothered. I should have offered to pray for us both, but perhaps he was.

His eggs were gone before they got cold, and he was slathering a slice of rye as he said offhandedly, "You know Second Coming, also a thing?"

Halfway through my short stack (conserving on both calories and expense), I looked up and smiled. "I don't know where you're going with this, but I've thought about it. The Second Coming will be an awakening of consciousness, a dawning of awareness in humans all over the planet of the Christed essence in ourselves. And as for it being real, we have the evidence of the Internet. Worldwide digital consciousness was invented just when we need to think globally to save the planet. I'd say that glass is at least half full, despite how drunk we got on it for starters."

"Amusing," he said as he chomped on his toast. "And poetic, metaphoric. You might have something there. As to the real thing, that is."

"What else?"

"I'm talking about *phony* Second Coming. A stage show. Strategic false-flag operation. You never heard of it the first time?"

"In the Bible?"

"Hardly. Nineteen sixties. Crazy plot to bring down Castro. Submarine in Guantanamo Bay sets off fireworks, gigantic bullhorn announces Savior has come. I don't know, maybe they project some picture on clouds. Observant Cubans who worship in secret pee in their pants when they realize they serve Antichrist — that bugger Fidel. They rise up because bullhorn says communism evil, they must bring him down. And then mob guys move back to Havana with hotels and casinos. Just like God wants."

"Is this in some novel, or are you making it up?"

"An actual plan. Remember this was time when another way they get him was exploding cigar. It's all in the Church Commission report — the parts they let us read."

Until now, his wild speculations had been tinged with reality. He was clearly a student of science as well as religion.

But this? Right out of some Tom Clancy thriller, isn't it?

"Are you telling me, seriously, they'll try it again?"

He summoned patience. He really was a dear but aware he might seem pompous. "Remember, we talking about VR. How silly does such plan sound with twenty-first-century technology?"

He isn't only talking about VR. He's hinting all of life is an illusion. Or, at least, can't be proved otherwise. Not exactly new. Wittgenstein.

Something occurred to me. "And if the government is doing this today, I assume the target won't just be Cuba."

He shrugged. "All I'm saying is, someone will try it. It's inevitable. Probably soon — before the real thing could steal the show." Cora had dropped off a jar of marmalade, and he was smearing it liberally on his last piece of bread. Before he could take a bite, he patted the vest pocket of his coat. "No smokes," he grumbled.

I didn't want to encourage him, but I felt I had to tell him how far I'd go. "I'm buying your meal. If you want cigarettes, that's on you."

He stood up abruptly, now patting his baggy pants pockets. "I pop across street. Don't let her take my plate. We get more coffee, I tell you what I know." He muttered in afterthought, "*The Expulsion of the Triumphant Beast.* I will lend you this book!"

And he was out the door.

Three seconds later, he was dead.

Or perhaps he simply stepped out of the movie.

If I meet him in some other reality, I'll ask him how that works.

3

I hadn't been on my feet fast enough to restrain Gropius from running into the street. I stood with Sheriff Chester Otis at the curb. Despite the circumstances, I was otherwise glad to see him. Deputy Griggs used to be the one to show up on these calls, and back then we were not on remotely friendly terms. But since Griggs had moved on, Chet was breaking in a new officer, one Della Crandall, who stood behind him.

I told them, "He got up from the table, telling me he was headed across the street to Taggart's to get cigarettes. I heard brakes screech, a thud, tires squeal, and I raced out. There he was, sprawled in the middle of the street, and the truck was speeding away — west. I was calling nine-one-one as I ran to him, but there was no hope."

"You make the truck?" the sheriff asked.

"White F-150, older model. I didn't get the plate."

I'd just described half the vehicles in St. Clair County. The others were either black or red.

Chet turned to Deputy Crandall to order, "Get an all-points on the truck."

She strode toward the squad car to call it in. He squinted to watch the paramedics loading the covered body onto a gurney and into the ambulance.

He asked me, "Friend of yours?"

"He knocked on my door about an hour and a half ago. Never saw him before."

"So he's peddling door-to-door, and you decide to buy him breakfast?"

"He wasn't selling. He was a storyteller, unless you'd call that selling."

"Stories about his ex? Enemies? Grudges? Debts?"

How can I tell him and make it sound sane?

"He was a student of religion and science."

My friend the lawman got a kick out of that. "No wonder you treated him. Who else is gonna shoot that shit with you? He sang for his supper." Then, serious again, he asked, "So, a drifter? No friends in town?"

"He didn't mention anyone. And if Cora didn't recognize him, he was a stranger for sure."

"Crandall says no ID on him."

I offered, "Dr. Hans Gropius. Born in Romania and lived in Germany. No relation to the founder of Bauhaus."

"I'm supposed to know what that is?"

"A famous school of architecture. Came up between the two world wars. Modernism, clean lines, no frills. You see it everywhere here now."

He huffed. "Maybe you do." He called over to Crandall, "Have forensics get prints and DNA. You get to do the paperwork on this one."

He shot me that exasperated look of his. Not enough budget, not enough time. Shit happens. New recruit, diversity hiring. Bet she wouldn't dare throw a punch. People blame us.

And always making matters worse, being a black man and

trying to hang onto a position of authority in this part of the world had never been easy.

He squinted again as he looked at me. This time maybe it was skepticism. "Evan, you back in the game? First time I've seen you in a month of Sundays."

"I'm not going back into the ministry anytime soon, if that's what you mean."

"Except for counseling the homeless over a stack of pancakes."

I hung my head. "I knocked back more than a few last night, and I'd had every intention of sleeping through the day. This guy shows up, and I had to get my act together if I wanted to be presentable in town. If I'd showed up in my sweats with him looking that way, I wouldn't blame Cora for refusing to serve either of us. And I was as hungry as he was."

He sighed deeply. "This looks like a hit-and-run. Unless there's a witness who got the plate or a good look at the driver, I got nothing. He was a mysterious little fella, but unless he poured out his life story to you, again I got nothing. Maybe he wanted to end it all and stepped in front of the truck. Maybe his mom didn't tell him to look both ways."

"Or maybe it was vehicular homicide."

"Did I say that? You got some evidence?"

It was a risk to my credibility (if I still had any) to say anything more. But I did say, "I got that he was something of a conspiracy theorist."

"Shut up!" Otis exclaimed. "We got none of them around these parts! We got only sensible folks here. Proud Boys? Antifa? We kicked all them clowns out long ago." I know how it sounded. The sheriff was jerking my chain. He added, in a mocking conspiratorial tone, "Rev — if I may still call you that — unless his ID comes back with a criminal record or a warrant — I'm gonna tell young Crandall to shove her file in the drawer and send her out for donuts.

"But I know you. Inquiring minds want to know. You go sneaking around, who am I to stop you? God knows, ever since those casino boys showed up, it isn't only jealous husbands committing crimes in here. But if you get a sniff — if you get so much as a speck of something looks wrong — you come to me and no one else. Say you understand."

I mocked him back. "We're besties, Chet. Always will be."

He almost smiled. "You're trouble, Rev. Always will be."

4

IN RURAL GEORGIA, YEARS AGO...

Freddie Trucco was devoted to his sister, Ireenie, who was a
year younger. She was the only person in his life he cared
for. He had no friends, was so scrawny the other boys
bullied him, and was always the last picked on any team if he was
allowed to play at all. Girls shunned him because of his pinched
face and geeky looks, along with his habit of delivering know-it-all
answers whenever he was asked about anything.

Freddie's job was to shield her, as he'd done diligently since they
were toddlers. When he was three and she was two, their birth
parents broke up. Their father Hugo had some cash, so he took
them to live with his girlfriend Tamara in an old farmhouse in rural
Georgia, gaining custody not by law but by force, then abandoning
all of them on frequent sales trips. Freddie hated him because, when
he was home and often angry, he punished them with a belt,
woman and children alike. The boy and his sister overheard their
parents' heated arguments, and when Hugo began to whip his
woman, Freddie would take Ireenie by the hand and lead her away

through any open door. He was not yet tall enough to open them by himself.

Their circumstances were always poor, their meals meager, and their lives loveless. Tamara was more of an inattentive babysitter than a stepmother. By another man who was nowhere in evidence, she'd had two boys of her own, Charles and Nelson, both years older than Freddie and Ireenie. They were abusive to the little kids whenever they had the opportunity and their mother wasn't home or wouldn't care.

Tamara wouldn't discipline the young ones. When Hugo was away, she'd tell her boys to do it. They didn't spank or slap. Pinpricks, handkerchiefs rolled up as tourniquets, and burning cigarettes were their instruments of choice. Freddie valiantly volunteered to take punishments meant for Ireenie then regretted it. Her transgressions weren't as blatant as his, more like refusing to eat when they were served some disgusting food, which was sometimes spoiled but more often burnt because Tamara couldn't be bothered to watch the stove.

The boys became eager to let Freddie take Ireenie's punishments because, when they'd pushed him to the limits of bearability, they felt justified in giving him more until he fainted. Once when Tamara was out, they had used pliers on his fingers. Freddie's screams that time were so loud it brought a concerned neighbor, who was told the boy had mashed his own hand in the refrigerator door.

In their grade-school years, neither of them had much of an education. Hugo was hiding out, even though without a custodial order he might not have been charged as a kidnapper. He didn't want neighbors to know the kids existed, pretending when asked that, following their devout mother's wishes, these two were being home-schooled. Apparently, the authorities in the backwoods community never inquired. There were no books in the house except a Gideon Bible that Hugo must have taken from some motel room — for reasons God only could know.

The other source of information was the TV. When no one was at home to watch the younger ones, as when Tamara was off with the boys buying them school clothes, she'd lock Freddie and Ireenie in the basement. Their guardian was Buck, an old German-shepherd mix that was big but no longer muscular and wouldn't have so much as barked on encountering an intruder. The dog alternately slept or relieved itself on the concrete floor, so the cold basement stank of mold and dog waste. Unfortunately for the children, intruders never came. Someone might have taken an interest.

They shared a mattress on the floor and a horsehair blanket. Freddie read the Bible and watched TV. Ireenie pretended to watch the set as well, but when her brother looked over at her, her eyes were glazed or closed as if she were sleeping sitting up. Later in life, she'd tell him she was in meditation and could project her soul anywhere on the planet, to all those places on the TV where he yearned to go.

Perhaps because of her vulnerability, Ireenie was clever in ways Freddie couldn't grasp. He'd studied bullies, imitation, and intimidation but was careful to stay out of trouble, learning to rely on her to tell him what to do next in any situation. Outwardly, she was quiet and shy. She was pretty and knew it, was as sharp as her brother, but she hid her personality like some fearful hedgehog curling itself into a ball.

When Tamara finally grew tired of the chores of minimal child-care, without consulting Hugo, she enrolled the children in the new county public school, to which they would be bussed so she needn't be bothered to drive them. They were both admitted into the first grade even though they were years behind. As Ireenie matured, the older boys were always hitting on her. The ones her age teased her just to get a response, which would trigger the next joke.

As they grew into their teens, they began to be seriously abused

17

by their peers, but Freddie realized Hugo was a meaner bully and a greater threat than any of them, especially to Ireenie as her body began to fill out.

Freddie would eventually learn, when he was old enough to understand, that Hugo was not a traveling salesman — he fenced stolen goods, typically by the truckload. All during the kids' childhood, he'd had wads of money, none making it home.

When Freddie was sixteen, Hugo was apprehended in Birmingham and was rumored to have died in a knife fight in the city jail. Tamara's boys had left home by then, and she took the opportunity to track down Bettina, the kids' birth mother, who was living alone in Doraville and was almost as poor as the rest of them but working a steady job as secretary to the minister of a Pentecostal church.

Living with the kind-hearted Bettina, who hadn't had the resources to try to have them tracked down in all these years, Freddie and Ireenie were both enrolled in a high school equivalency program, and they began to attend Sunday school regularly.

Until that time, Freddie's notable accomplishment was knowing the Bible, chapter and verse, testaments old and new. He picked up other academic skills quickly, and although he never learned to write well, he got work dictating sermons that his mother would transcribe for Reverend Woodall.

Freddie came to dote on Bettina so much that Ireenie became jealous. He ran errands for her, managed her household expenses, and tended her when she was bedridden with her chronic migraines. But Ireenie never lost faith in him.

"You will do great things, my precious son," Bettina assured him as he laid a cold compress on her forehead. "God has put you through trials to test your spirit and your will. You know your Bible well enough to understand that's how the Almighty tempers the metal of righteous swords."

Like Bettina, Reverend Woodall was kind-hearted and fair-minded. Neither the church nor he personally could afford to sponsor Freddie to attend divinity school. But after encouragement, the boy completed a correspondence course, culminating in a mail-order certification to officiate at weddings and funerals.

One Saturday evening, Hugo showed up at their door. He was stinking drunk and reeling, had survived the fracas in jail, and was furious with Bettina for daring to take charge of his progeny. Shoving Bettina aside after bitter words, he moved to attack Ireenie. Before he managed to rape her, Freddie slit his throat with a kitchen knife.

Bettina's building superintendent, who was fond of her and needed no explanations, cleaned up the mess and, with Freddie's help, put the body in a dumpster. Perhaps refuse collection disposed of Hugo's putrid remains. No one cared.

No way they could stay in Atlanta. Freddie and Ireenie moved to Florida, where he assured her they could make a fresh start. To facilitate their new beginnings, they took the names Frank and Ida Trusdale. Frank became a persuasive preacher, able to salt his sermons with parables. As he gained confidence, his speaking voice deepened, and his delivery became more emotional.

He and his sister were inseparable. People probably assumed they were married. She was his helpmeet, always at his side, guiding his steps with her cleverness, loyal to him because the world without his protection had always terrified her.

The bond between Freddie and Ireenie was unbreakable, but if he had ever truly loved anyone, it was his mother.

5

The night of the accident that killed Gropius — if it was an accident — I sat holed up in my trailer intent on my laptop. I know some people used their phones for everything, but call me old school, I needed a keyboard. Chet was right to accuse me of compulsive data drilling. After my twin collegiate studies of divinity and astrophysics flamed out back east and I returned home to Appleton City, I did casual labor for Zed Motors as a skip tracer. I tracked down borrowers who'd missed more than a few payments on their cars, trucks, or tractors.

I got a rep for finding deadbeats quickly and rarely had to do a repo. I often negotiated win-win settlements that mostly pissed off Mr. Zed because he hadn't thought of them himself and nevertheless owed me commission on the recovery. My understanding search engines and knowing how to use a spreadsheet saved a lot of legwork.

I'd promised to share anything suspicious with Otis, but likewise I'd requested he let me know if any kinfolk or colleagues of the ill-fated doctor showed up. I'd offer my condolences, but just as important I'd want to speak with anyone who might know why he'd sought me out. From his crack that my neighbors were gossips, I expected he'd asked around.

But you'd think the first place he'd inquired would have been the C'mon Inn, and Cora insisted she'd never met him. Zed's son ran a gas station over on Route P, so that could be a place to ask. The doctor didn't seem to have a car (I'd heard none pull up that morning), and it was amazing in these wary times that anyone would dare to pick up a hitchhiker. A trucker might, but those guys were mostly passing through and might have no information about either passengers or locals.

I wasn't about to share with Chet that the eccentric doctor might have been killed to silence him about a secret government plot to fake the Second Coming of Christ. Weed was still illegal in Missouri, and he'd wonder how I'd come by whatever I was smoking.

Doctor of what? I began with an identity search and found an answer right away. Deputy Crandall would have, as well, if she'd bothered to undertake a simple search.

I found this brief biographical note in the *Journal of Concerned Scientists*:

Gropius, Hans Lichtenwort (1945 -), research scientist and engineer. Retired from Los Alamos National Laboratory. Author of white papers on battlefield simulations. Deacon in the Dutch Reformed Church. Also wrote the controversial treatise, "Why There Is No God and I Still Have Faith." Since his retirement, repudiated for his extremist views advocating false-flag operations. Guest speaker at Q-Anon conferences then reviled by the movement once they'd heard his opinions. No public appearances or publications after 2019. Last reported residence: Lee's Summit, Missouri.

My searches couldn't bring up much more on him. I drilled into the wiki article to find its authors and editors, but there was only one, and the link on the avatar-handle was dead. The article had only one footnote — a link to his theological paper, which debated recent scientific speculation that a godless universe could arise spontaneously. You'd think his research would have been published somewhere, but there were no links and no other search results. I tried Google Scholar, the National Science Foundation, and DARPA, among others, but got no hits, which was doubly surprising since the metaverse was one of the hottest topics in physics.

Lee's Summit was the location of John Knox Village, an assisted-living facility, making it a reasonable guess Gropius might have been living there. It was where several of my now-deceased friends had spent their twilight years. Among them had been attorney Angus Clapper. We'd played his last game of chess. The retirement home was about seventy miles to the north, an hour and a half on the interstate. Not an unlikely place to begin my inquiries.

And then there was the crusty Arthur Redwine. I ministered to him on his deathbed, and he gifted me and my new family with his farmhouse. We both knew and understood abandonment by our dearest loves — his, decades earlier — mine, once before then and another since.

Before I dropped off to sleep, I risked phoning my friend and unofficial collaborator, Special Agent Leon Weiss.

Having not seen me since he'd invited me to help on a prior investigation that quickly went cold, he considerately asked after my health.

"Still happily pickled," I told him. "Nicely preserved but at risk of turning wrinkled and green."

"How can I help?"

"Tell me about Dr. Hans Gropius. Paid me a surprise visit then stepped in front of a truck and got himself killed."

"Oh my."

I asked him, "Know the name?"

"Not personally. Notorious nut-job. Few took him seriously anymore. But at one time he had clearance, so of course he was never off our radar. He made a lot of noise in the community."

I began, "He was going to tell me about a false-flag operation…"

"Evan? Know what? My bowels are in a twist, and finally there's some prospect of relief. Gotta go — literally. I'm off the grid for a few days. Don't call me, I'll call you." Before he abruptly ended the call, he added, "Forget this guy. All due respect."

6

_____

I often worried I'd become numb to emotions, particularly sorrow and grief. Four years ago, when I found my friend Bob Taggart's body in that frozen cornfield, I'd already lost both of my parents and my fiancé Naomi, of beloved memory. I've never served in the military, but her death in a war zone connected me with soldiers who can hesitate only briefly over the fallen and then must carry on. More recently, during Covid when I foolishly thought I could manage as a full-time pastor, visiting the sick and the dying took its toll on what was left of my compassionate reserves.

Then my dog Murphy succumbed to what the vet said could have been an airborne virus. Gropius had been full of life, delight, and humor. He'd predicted we would become friends, and I bought into the hope. It was time I stopped my closeted moping. He'd gotten me to clean up, hadn't he? When he was struck down in the street, it was as if my arm had been torn off by the twirling round of an assault rifle.

I'm ashamed I felt nothing at the time.

And then I was overcome with guilt. I felt I'd lost my humanity.

How could I now presume to counsel anyone, much less rebuke the wayward in a sermon?

After I phoned Leon, I slept fitfully. A wounded warrior as well, he was encouraging me to do nothing. Perhaps his was wise advice, but it gave me no comfort. He knew me better than to tell me to ask no questions, and I sensed he was speaking about caution for my sake, not morality. Or justice. Whiskey might have helped to knock me out, but I had no cash to buy more, and sinking into a stupor would do nothing for my self-respect.

When I woke from a fit of REM that had me playing cards with Murphy, I prayed for Gropius, recognizing at the same time that I held no belief in the bondage of Purgatory or the lamentations of ghosts. I should've prayed for his loved ones, for divine consolation in their distress. On the last day of his life, I might have been his only friend.

And I feel I don't deserve my own prayers. Silly to fret that I should have walked him across the street. If only — the obsessive thought of the bereaved.

I'd BEEN present enough to set the timer on the coffeemaker, and when I heard it begin to gurgle awake, I decided I might as well do the same.

When I'd taken Gropius to the diner, it had only been yesterday but seemed like a year ago.

I was sitting on my cot, dressed in the jeans and white shirt from yesterday and downing my second cup of coffee when I heard the hiss of car tires on the gravel outside, followed by an insistent knock on my door.

I had the bewildering thought Gropius had returned, no doubt to chastise me for my lack of tears. A likelier possibility was either Sheriff Otis or Deputy Crandall had come with follow-up questions. I might as well tell them what I'd learned. They'd take it from there. It took an effort to stand, but for once I wasn't dizzy and my head wasn't throbbing. I was plain exhausted.

I opened the door on Leon Weiss, looking every bit the federal operative in a neatly pressed gray suit.

"I thought you told me to forget about it," I said groggily.

He shrugged. "Did I? Since when do you take orders from the likes of me?"

7

S orry about your friend," Cora said. "He was your friend, right?"

I answered, "He promised we'd become friends. That was enough for me."

Leon had been going on about how much he'd hankered for breakfast. The flapjacks at the C'mon were good, but I didn't think it was a secret recipe. (A touch of buckwheat? Shortening with lard? I didn't want to know.) Maybe he had a thing for Cora, as most of the other healthy males in town did. There was something about a caring woman who barked orders at you. No doubt a mommy thing.

As Cora waltzed away, Leon advised in a low voice, "We best take the conversation about your friend outside."

"You said he was a nut-job. Conspiracy quack."

Leon grinned as he swallowed a wad of syrupy cakes. "Truth can sound stranger than fiction. Lots of what I see in case files, you couldn't make that shit up. Now, as we finish off this feast, let's talk about your personal state of affairs and how to shore up your finances."

I told him I had an open offer from Zip to go back to chasing deadbeats, a term I only used with those professional colleagues, the car salespeople, who referred to themselves as *ironworkers.* They lived by the principle: "My money is in your pocket. You just don't know it yet."

All of Zed's sales staff were men. No doubt there were female ag students who knew a lot about tractors, but they must have been huddled in GMO seed-stock research labs because they weren't looking for work around here. Whenever I ventured into auto dealerships in KC or Springfield, I'd see classy ladies dressed in designer clothes on the sales floor. They sold luxury sedans and sports cars to horny rich guys who wanted to show off super-mechanical pricks.

Hey, if I had the money? I don't expect to drive it through the Eye of the Needle, but until then how could a spin with a classy lady be amiss?

I shared the salesman joke with Leon, who said he hadn't heard it. Then I figured, since he'd forbidden discussing the thing that worried me most, I might as well regale him with more car-biz lore.

"Okay, what's the difference between a salesman's promise and a lie?"

"None?"

"Nope. When a salesman makes you a promise, he *hopes* you'll get it. But he doesn't feel responsible in any way for its delivery."

No surprise, Leon has no jokes to share about federal agents.

After breakfast, he finally agreed to a serious conversation, and he wanted to know where we could go for a chat out in the open. I suggested the sports field at Appleton City High, where I sometimes went to watch the teams practice.

He instructed me to leave my phone in his car, and he did the same with his. It was one of those unmarked, full-sized staff vehicles with a blown V8, the kind no one seemed to drive except for undercover cops who sometimes needed to overtake bad guys in high-speed chases.

We strolled around the perimeter of the field, occasionally stopping to marvel at the sight of girls slinging a rubber-coated hardball at each other in a spirited contest of lacrosse. As far as I knew, the indigenous natives who lived in this area as recently as two centuries ago didn't know the game. But I wondered whether the new Missouri academic curriculum would permit any history lessons based on racial origins.

It's a game with a history. Isn't that worth knowing?

I told Leon what I'd learned about Gropius, which I assumed he already knew, including my guess about the fellow's recent residency at John Knox.

Leon nodded as if he knew, but he challenged me with, "You're intending to go up there, aren't you?"

"Seems a logical next step, about all I have to go on. I know the place. I visited Angus Clapper there. He passed on that night, natural causes. I began to think I was the angel of death, and here I go again."

"At the weapons lab, Gropius was assigned there to work on perimeter security. Sensors and displays. Not exactly advanced research. More like a way of keeping him employed. And watched."

"Sounds like a righteous effort. And a position of trust."

"He got sidetracked. Somehow he convinced his managers he could do more in another area. He was fascinated with virtual display technology. Started with battlefield simulations then got into designing VR for warfighter combat training."

"So how would he know about this false-flag operation? Something he read on the Dark Web?"

Leon took a moment to study his shoes. "Evan, I don't know that there *is* an operation. People believe all kinds of things, even scientists who should know better. Gropius was pulled off his projects, debriefed, and he retired. Three years ago."

I insisted, "You must have your suspicions. Why did you cut me short on the phone and hurry out here if you didn't think there was something to what the guy told me?" Leon looked up to search my eyes when I added quietly, "Maybe someone wanted him dead."

"Do we know that? Of course not. Are we right to worry it wasn't an accident? Sure. When anyone who's worked in a sensitive area dies in suspicious circumstances, it's an agency matter. You can bet we're not the only ones fretting about it. But it's not your problem to solve. As to whatever he thought he was working on, he couldn't possibly have had current information on anything that's classified."

"You're not on the case?"

"I couldn't say if I was, but I'm not. There is no case. No, my worry is about you."

"Me? I thought I'd already hit rock bottom. You might say I'm beyond salvation, but the gospels say otherwise." I meant it as a self-deprecating joke, but Leon didn't seem amused.

His tone became downright professorial. "Let's assume for the sake of argument that this guy wasn't mentally deranged. First off, I'd worry that if he was murdered, your life might also be at risk because he confided in you. But on reflection, that's not likely. You don't know enough. A secret — something that's for-real, actionable, protected information — isn't some rumor you could write on the back of a napkin. In my world, secrets are documented. A secret in this case would be a plan. It would be detailed and in writing. He didn't give you anything like that, did he?"

"No, only what I told you."

"If he came here to give you something, he didn't succeed, and maybe you have no reason to worry. That brings me to my second conjecture. What if he came instead to warn you? You told me he was something of a fan, followed your broadcasts and your ministry."

"Yes, he implied he was a Bible scholar."

"If this is a real operation, I think we can be certain its objective is not to subdue the entire population of the Earth. The people who would be convinced by such an event are a small fraction of human beings. They'd likely be Evangelical Christians — and among those, they'd have to be scriptural literalists, believers who are waiting, maybe even eager, for the Apocalypse."

"You're describing a few people in my congregation. Not including me."

He continued, "Which means, I would suggest, those people wouldn't be behind the plot. They'd be the targets, not the perpetrators."

I followed his logic, but it wasn't the only explanation. "And yet a lot of conspiracy theorists have claimed to be Christian. If they don't know the thing is fake, maybe they'd be the most easily persuaded."

He frowned as he said, "That old intelligence op to dupe the Cubans seems laughable these days. And if that was the only version of the story, it would be a minor footnote in some history book. But the plot got resurrected in the early nineties as Project Blue Beam. It's a book by a Canadian journalist with all the elements of the aborted plot against Castro, but now the nefarious fakers are alleged to be NASA, the United Nations, and shadowy actors in the Deep State. It's a favorite trope of present-day, anti-government militias — domestic terrorists. Along with chem trails, black helicopters, intentionally lethal vaccination side-effects, rigged elections, and feasting on babies."

"What do the conspiracy folks think the purpose of Blue Beam would be?"

Leon shrugged. He feigned a smile, but his tone was serious. "Inspiring blind obedience to whatever the fake god says next?"

"Maybe Gropius had gone over to the wackos or went off the deep end? He predicted we'd be friends, so perhaps he was trying to pull me into whatever scheme he had going."

"Evan, that's why I'm concerned. Okay, you fell from grace, but you had a sizable media following and credibility. You wouldn't be the first televangelist who made it back big time from a personal scandal." He chuckled. "Like you say, sin and redemption. That's the story, isn't it?"

Coming from someone else, his remark would seem sarcastic and mean. But this guy was my departed fiancé's brother, and I'd adopted him as mine, as I had the late Bob Taggart, my ill-fated boyhood friend. If I was about to get exploited, I'd want Leon as my protector.

"You're worried that, whoever they are, they want to use me."

He shrugged. "As I say, I'm out of the loop. If something's going on in my world, I haven't been read-in. As far as I know, Blue Beam is a fantasy. But after you called me, it didn't take me long to see why I had to show up. As it stands, we don't know whether Gropius was trying to warn you or recruit you. I'd worry either way."

"But how could anyone think I'd go along with such a crazy scheme?"

"Anyone who knows you knows that plying you with cash won't work. And even when you were on your way to becoming a household name, you didn't exactly lust after personal power."

"So what's the worry?"

"The other ways they get you are blackmail ... or they threaten your family."

8

The same afternoon Leon and I had our heart-to-heart as we watched the lacrosse match, he drove off in his staff car, perhaps on assignments I wasn't cleared to know about. It was reassuring that he didn't think my life was in imminent danger, but I was disappointed he wasn't about to enlist me in some new adventure. His involvement in my own concerns seemed passive. He was all too ready to leave it to nameless investigators to find out whether Gropius had met with foul play.

Nevertheless, he hadn't warned me not to go driving up to Lee's Summit to question the late doctor's caregivers and friends. And Leon was sharp enough to forbid me explicitly if he had preferred I shouldn't. I had to find out whatever I could, so I'd pursue the same unofficial agreement I had with Otis. He could always deny he'd given me his permission to inquire, but if I uncovered any evidence, I couldn't withhold it.

I didn't often have a reason to travel to that retirement home, even when I was doing visitations as pastor. Most of our members couldn't afford managed care, and when they became infirm it would fall to family members, not necessarily to take them in, but at least to pay them regular visits at home to take them groceries and medicine. If they needed daily help, they might be able to engage a practical nurse or at least a volunteer caregiver.

Our church's Loving Embrace committee saw to these needs, and it was a chore Loretta seemed happy to undertake. I didn't usually offer counsel in such matters, but she had one suggestion that always proved helpful: Get one of those pill dispensers, visit at least once a week, and count out their meds. Then you'll be sure they're remembering to take them — except for the ones who cheat — but Loretta would advise the caring relatives that you can't help someone who doesn't want help.

It wasn't caring for the sick that drove Loretta away. No, I think it had to do with the pressure of pretending to be someone she feared she wasn't. I never held her to some higher standard, but it was a role she must have felt obligated to play.

I looked forward to the drive because the route on the interstate passes by the village of Peculiar, self-proclaimed to be notable for its lack of momentous achievements. Its welcome sign boasts that here is "Where the 'odds' are with you," and a historical marker in its only public park informs visitors that nothing remarkable happened there during the Civil War, when the surrounding countryside was a no-man's land, strewn with the bodies of fallen Jayhawkers and Bushwhackers.

Venturing into a settlement of oddballs held appeal to me, first of all because of the appearance of my car. I fantasized that I'd find a town buzzing with multicolored metal ladybugs, where my little bulbous Fiat would blend right in. There the streets would converge at odd angles to accommodate the seemingly random zigging and zagging of our mechanical bugs. In an ideal town that was indeed peculiar, all those enterprising insects would eventually get quietly and safely where they are going. There'd be no white trucks careening about carelessly, no accidents without benign purpose.

Here was where the wizened fortuneteller Granny Longacre had failed to predict my demise, much less my presently disappointing circumstances, as well as where she had gifted me with her faithful canine companion Murphy, a nickname for Morphia, the drug that sank you into blissful oblivion. Murphy was not only a gift but a godsend, having cared for Luke and Melissa on their cross-country motoring adventures then seeing them safely home.

When I have companions, I fret less about myself. There's a blessing devoutly to be missed.

The other attraction for me on the route north was stopping at Merle's American Tavern, where I'd indulge in whatever was the blackboard special. Leon had given me a wad of cash. Regaining my appetite would be an encouraging sign I was recovering from my days of purposeless lethargy.

But I found Merle's closed for renovations. Not knowing where else to go, I drove back to the convenience store at the Flying J Travel Center, where I bought a readymade peanut-butter-and-jelly sandwich and a carton of chocolate milk. It amused me to think I'd be feeding my inner child. Without Loretta's guidance, my dietary habits were less than exemplary. If I wasn't careful, I'd grow a gut more ample than the modest pudginess Cora encouraged.

I probably looked downright gaunt. A minister was supposed to look prosperous, not overpaid but someone at least favored with glowing health. No one wanted their spiritual counselor to look like a guilty monk who was fasting in repentance for unspeakable sins.

Gropius's suit hadn't fit him, and my assumption was he'd come by it in a thrift store. But now I realized that my habitual sport coat was too big on me, hanging like a sack. In the mirror, my cheeks appeared sunken, and my skin had a waxy pallor.

I took my kiddie meal to the public park on Highrise Trail, the place where the historical marker made that persistent attempt to erase history. There I expected to find a deserted picnic table where the worst-case distraction would be watching some drunken teens struggle to play frisbee golf.

I thought of that marker from time to time because I appreciated how untrue it was, especially now that I'd spent so much time visiting the sick and the dying. Asserting that nothing happened here was either a wry joke or a heedless erasure of history. In even the sleepiest village, countless dramas are acted out every day.

As I pulled the Eggmobile up to the edge of the manicured park lawn, I caught sight of an open-air meeting in progress. This was not the languid scene I'd expected. Beneath the copious awning of the park's centuries-old oak tree, a couple dozen people sat on folding chairs, while the overflow crowd stood. Pacing in front of them as he spoke was a slim young man whose deep voice was made all the more commanding by a wireless public address system.

Walking toward the meeting, I removed my jacket and threw it over my arm. In my button-down shirt and jeans, perhaps I wouldn't look so much like an interloper as I stepped up to take a place at the edge of the standees. These folks weren't dressed in their Sunday best — if they even had other clothes. From the look of the battered campers and pickups surrounding the park, many of them had come in their liveaboards. Others looked disheveled, likely homeless.

I recalled that Lt. Gov. Shackleton had been bragging recently about his new approach to dealing with homelessness in our state. Especially in the cities — not only in KC and St. Louis but also here in our backyard in Springfield — it was becoming much less obvious to see someone sleeping on the street or living in their car. Once the weather had turned mild, typically spring flowers and doorway sleepers would appear at about the same time. But not so much this year.

And yet, here was what looked like a convocation of the downtrodden. At one point, right after Covid and we'd reopened the sanctuary at Evangel Baptist, we put up signs around town announcing that everyone and anyone would be welcome on Sundays. Some stragglers wandered in, but never an eager gathering of this size.

They stared at the strutting fellow in rapt attention as he pronounced, "No doubt you've all heard of the end-times, and the evidence is all around us. Wars and rumors of wars. False prophets. And you can take your pick which of our world leaders will soon be unfrocked to expose the Antichrist!" He muttered dramatically, "It's happening."

He was so worked up he was panting. As he paused to catch his breath, I turned to the man next to me, whose age and demeanor reminded me of Dr. Gropius, and I asked quietly, "Who is this guy?"

He turned to me with an astonished look. "Why, this is Deacon Daniel!" And then, excited to be imparting the news to a prospect, he added, "He is making the way straight for Pastor Obadiah. Just you wait! You'll hear!"

Daniel was scrawny. His complexion was sallow and white. His eyes were sunken and weary beyond his years. A few times when I was pastor of Evangel, I'd visited inmates. I recognized that hungry look, and it wasn't for food.

Daniel had stopped his pacing, faced front, took a deep breath, and confided solemnly, "Many of our dear ones are gone. So many to Covid. So many to spoiled food, starvation, overdoses. And some folks, who knows? Took off for greener pastures?"

A collective groan went through the crowd.

Raising his head and in a louder voice, he told them, "But I submit to you, wonders are taking place!"

Scattered cries of, "Amen!"

He went on, "There is a secret, a most marvelous secret being revealed here today. Now, I'm not going to tell you that the Rapture has happened. No, you haven't been left behind. The secret I will share with you today is that the Rapture is not a single event. Remember they used to say, 'The revolution will not be televised?' It's like that. Remember Jesus said, 'I will come as a thief in the night?' Verily, it's like that."

He took another deep breath, this time perhaps not because he needed it but for dramatic effect, and dropped his voice to say, "What I'm telling you is that the Rapture is not an event — it's a process! Yes, some of your friends have been taken. But, you notice, not only are you still here, but so am I! And I'm here to say, there is hope for us — hope we can still join our dear ones and be borne up to Glory."

He paused again, and the interval was so long that it seemed he wouldn't say more.

"Tell us!" someone shouted. Others stirred and grumbled.

He held up a beckoning hand. "Isn't prayer always the answer? But I submit to you that prayer without a cleanse — beseeching without repentance — will be of no avail. And now I will tell you what you must do, what we all must do to be worthy to gain admission."

Another long pause. No one broke the silence this time. The man had promised.

In a strident tone now, he insisted, "Your cleanse begins with forsaking your worldly goods. Sell your homes, your vehicles, your land. Give over whatever valuables you have left. Accept Pastor Obadiah's open invitation to join us at his farm, identified on its website and literature as the End-Times Retreat Center. There, until that glorious moment you are borne up with him, you will have shelter and plenty of good food. Organic vegetables! You will perform chores, and you will cleanse your body of all the earthly toxins that Big Ag and Big Pharma have pumped into your body since the day you were born!"

He was telling them all they needed was the clothes on their backs. Gropius too seemed to have little else.

I couldn't listen to any more. As he continued to speak, lauding the virtues of life (however short it might prove to be) at the pastor's farm, I strode quickly toward my car, got in, and drove away.

I had no intention of beginning a cleanse, but my stomach was so upset I couldn't eat my sandwich.

9

In my previous visits to the assisted living center, I'd dealt only with nursing staff, never meeting anyone in administration. When I'd gone to see Angus Clapper and then Arthur Redwine, I'd played the reverend card on admission. I'd come to see Clapper to find out what legal advice he'd given to Bob Taggart's Aunt Molly about her will. Redwine had become a dear friend years before he took ill, and then I saw him several times before he passed away.

This time, I was fishing for clues about Hans Gropius, and my interest wasn't in his medical condition. I hadn't made an appointment. I feared that my recent reputation as failed televangelist would precede me, and any advance warning might get me pushed off. Even though the scandals involving the Shining Waters Temple had been widely publicized, there was a chance my status in the community as ordained minister would prevail. My media reputation had been dazzling and brief, but my service as a local pastor should count for something.

Gropius's residency at Knox was guesswork on my part. I'd assumed the Feds would know where the guy was, but Leon hadn't confirmed it. His interest in the matter seemed limited unless he was authorized to open a case, which apparently he wasn't about to do.

So I dropped in on Kathryn Bowers, managing director of John Knox Village, in her private office. It was a comfortable space but modest in size. Its walls were covered in textured fabric, and the one framed picture hanging there showed the obligatory landscape painting of lake country. Ms. Bowers sat primly behind the desk, focused intently on spreadsheet displays that in yesteryear would no doubt have been a fist-high stack of insurance and compliance paperwork.

Her businesslike appearance fit her role. She was middle-aged with naturally graying hair tied back, sharp features, no makeup. She wore a moss-green cardigan over a crisp, white blouse. At her throat, a golden crucifix hung from a delicate, gold chain. Pearl stud earrings. Her aquiline nose made her look slightly predatory.

I might like her if she smiled.

She hadn't looked up as I began to pull back a guest chair. I'd planned to introduce myself as I sat, sliding into place before I could get rebuffed. But when she finally turned from her screen to face me, she smiled stiffly and spoke first.

"Reverend Wycliff, please make yourself comfortable." The way she said it hinted politely at my presumption. No sooner had I sat than she added, "If you're here about Dr. Gropius, understand I can't discuss private patient records."

After I meekly thanked her for seeing me, she explained that she'd taken a call from the St. Clair County Sheriff's Office yesterday afternoon informing her of the accident and the death. On that call, my name had been mentioned as the informant who'd called it in. From that fact alone, Bowers must have assumed I was a friend of the deceased. How she recognized me was an open question I wouldn't press her to answer.

41

I had a ready opening. My inquiry might be quasi-official. I began by asking her, "Have arrangements been made?"

She nodded. These were the details she managed routinely. Without hesitation, she replied, "We have his advance directive on file, and he specified cremation. There's a small reserve balance in his account, so we'll handle it. Perhaps you know there's no next of kin to inform. Was he a member of your congregation?"

"No," I admitted, "I'm no longer pastor of Evangel Baptist, but I'm sure he never attended. In fact, I only met him yesterday morning. He showed up unannounced at my home. I assumed he wanted counseling. He looked like he needed a meal, so I took him to breakfast. I'd intended to get him some clean clothes and find out if he had a place to live. His appearance was disheveled, and I worried he was homeless. We had a spirited chat over our meal, but before I could get much out of him he said he craved a smoke, excused himself to go outside, and that's when he was struck down in the street."

She had no reason at this point to know about the briefing Leon had given me on the doctor's background. It might freak her to know the depth of my curiosity. I wasn't here to give her information, and it would be helpful for me to know what she knew already. She'd stated he had no family, and that was news to me.

Her eyes narrowed as she confided, "He signed himself out of here the day before yesterday. Did he tell you that?"

"No. As I said, we had a spirited chat, but he offered no personal information. He wanted to discuss metaphysics. He was energetic about his beliefs and seemed like something of a conspiracy theorist."

"May I ask what exactly he told you?"

I wondered why she would ask, but it was a hint she knew much more about him than I did. So I answered, "He fretted about the end-times. He said he was a fan of my broadcasts, and perhaps he'd followed some of our panel discussions about the *Book of Reve-*

lation. The topic was a concentration of mine in divinity school, and it was popular with our audiences. I assumed that's why he'd come to see me."

She sighed deeply, pushed back from her desk, and crossed her legs and arms. "The old fellow was a crank, and he's not the only one we have here. Some of our folks are in early stages of dementia, and when it progresses, we must find appropriate placement and care. I wouldn't say he was raving, but he encouraged others who, let's say, tend to be receptive and can easily become agitated. Particularly concerning, he'd heard about the retreat run by this guru, Pastor Obadiah. Perhaps you know about it?"

Wow, connect the dots.

I admitted, "Quite coincidentally, when I was passing through Peculiar this morning, I happened on an open-air rally. This Deacon Daniel must be a disciple. He's recruiting people to drop everything and live there. He has a bizarre message that the Rapture is underway and they'd better get on the bus to the farm or get left behind."

She tensed even more and said, "That story is going through this place like a virus, and some of our people are saying they want to leave."

"Including Gropius? Can they do that?"

"Yes and no. If the client is here under a conservatorship, they can't leave without permission of their guardian. For the others, we have custodial responsibilities, but legally they are free to leave if they've been formally advised of the risks, including an assessment of their medical condition. Quite simply, your friend signed himself out and walked out the door. His absence was not without leave but definitely against advice."

"So when he saw me, do you think he was headed to the farm?"

"I don't know, Reverend. I will say it's all he talked about, so much that he was upsetting some of the others."

"He didn't mention the farm to me. Or its pastor. In fact, he implied he's not a believer. The conspiracy theories he shared with me were all about fakery and hoaxes. I don't think he was buying whatever they're selling. Was he actually encouraging people to move there, to go with him?"

"I can't say. And I must admit I'm getting all of this second-hand from the nursing staff. I haven't said two words to him in the year he's been with us. However, I have my lunch almost every day with them in the dining room, and I open my ears. His preoccupation with the Evangelicals was recent, and he talked about it constantly. For his part, maybe, as you say, he wasn't advocating it. But the others may have heard it differently, especially the ones who don't bring faith with them or don't have family. They become desperate for something to hang onto. When it's close to the end for them, we don't have many atheists here."

I didn't have a calling card to leave her, but I shared my phone number in case she heard anything more about Gropius or his effect on his neighbors, and particularly if any of his relatives showed up.

Before I left, I ventured down to the solarium where I'd played chess with Angus Clapper on his last day of life, also where I'd prayed with Arthur Redwine and he pleaded with me to smuggle him a hunk of his favorite Swiss cheese. I didn't need an escort to make my way around the facility, although I'm not sure how many of the residents recognized me as a clergyman. There apparently weren't any of our congregants living there now.

And here among the nodding heads was Nurse Monica, whose name I knew only from her ID badge. When she flashed that beautiful smile at me, I was tempted to think of myself as single again, even though I was still holding onto the hope that Loretta would want to come back.

"Reverend Wycliff," she cooed, "should I admit it's nice to see you, or are you here about something not so pleasant?"

"I'm pleased you remember me, Monica…"

"Gable was my married name," she said frankly. "I've kept it. So far."

I'd have to learn to flirt again — if I was going to admit it would be evidence of a healthy outlook and not a sin.

"I'm separated," I said quietly, adding, "unhappily. Still with some hope it won't be permanent. Being a minister's wife was obviously the harder job."

She nodded as if to agree we'd set a boundary. "My husband came back a wounded warrior, but he didn't make it through the next three surgeries. My friend Carla's a social worker, and she'd say you and I were trading wounds, which she advises is a normal thing to do but not necessarily the best basis for a new friendship." She drew a deep breath, then asked, "To what do we owe the pleasure?"

"Hans Gropius. I met him an hour and a half before the accident."

She's heard, of course.

"He was a character, sure enough. He could spin a yarn. Kept himself from being bored, and the others loved to hear."

I looked around to make sure there was no one within earshot when I asked, "Did he talk about the End-Times farm? Pastor Obadiah? Was he telling folks to go there?"

"Oh, they all talk about it. Lots of them want to go. Now, understand, complaining about wanting to get out is a regular thing around here, even though you won't find a nicer place or better care. Hans wasn't one of those complainers. He'd get angry and scold them. He was telling them Obadiah is a false prophet."

"He talked to me about the end-times. I think he came to see me because I've studied Bible prophecy. But he was speaking to me about conspiracies, not faith."

She shrugged. "Like I say, he told all kinds of stories."

"Ms. Bowers said he'd checked out of here. Do you think he might have been headed to that farm?"

"If he was going, I'd think it would be out of curiosity, not to live there. We've had some folks leave. If they're going back to a family or into a hospice, we'd know about that. But the others who can, they don't have to say. I will tell you, not one of them has come back."

"Did Dr. Gropius have any close friends here he might have confided in?"

"No, none. He'd go on and on with his stories over dinner, but then he'd go back to his room. Kept to himself. Anytime I'd stop by, he always had a book open."

"Do you know which books? Do you still have his things?"

She walked me over to a bookcase that must serve as the facility's lending library. She pulled out three volumes and handed them to me. *Behold a Pale Horse* by Milton William Cooper, *The Expulsion of the Triumphant Beast* by the medieval monk Giordano Bruno, and the Lamsa translation of the *Holy Bible.* These last two were familiar to me. The other one looked more recent, but I'd never come across it.

The spines of all the books bore catalog labels from the Mid-Continent Public Library System.

"These are library books," I said. "How did he get them?"

"We have a van and driver to take residents on field trips and medical appointments, of course. Most of them want to go shopping or get their hair done. The doctor's go-to was the library on Oldham Parkway. The van would drop him off in the morning on their way into town then pick him up on the return route in time to be back for dinner. He spent most days there."

"Mind if I borrow these?"

She smiled. "Do us a favor and return them? They're probably all past due." She came closer to add, "And if there's a fine, be sure to come on back so we can reimburse you."

10

The role of caring sidekick being temporarily vacant in my life, finding Naomi in the passenger seat as I got back into my car in the parking lot at Knox was a surprise, but hardly illogical — or unwelcome. My reaction at first was one of embarrassment. Monica Gable had come onto me, triggering feelings of arousal I feared had grown hopelessly cold.

I've never regarded the appearances of my deceased fiancé Naomi as visitations by a ghost. As a rationalist, I explained her presence to myself as a manifestation of my own distressed consciousness, evidence of my persistent longing for her. She'd stayed away for more than a year by now, for two obvious reasons. First, at one point she'd vowed to send me help, soon after which not by coincidence her brother, Special Agent Leon Weiss, showed up on my life path as a living, breathing, rain-soaked hitchhiker, and he'd been my helpmate ever since. Then, after Leon played a lead role in the miracle I faked to save Loretta's sister from cruel hands, Naomi's essence had a second reason to stay away when I fell for Loretta and married her.

I worried Naomi would scold me about flirting with my new

best friend Monica. Or about not making enough of an effort to find Loretta or at least inquire about her welfare. I was aware Loretta had hooked back up with Mick Heston, her old boss from the Twin Dragons Casino, and I had more than a hunch he was on the lam from nameless crimes. Some women like bad boys. Maybe they all do when the moon is full. She'd always known how to take care of herself, and it helped me to think she was better off or at least happier.

The heat of the afternoon was beginning to wane in the twilight, but the car interior was sweltering. I rolled down the window, took off my sport coat, and threw it in the back before I slid in behind the wheel. Naomi studied me patiently. She had on a brightly colored floral-print dress I remembered. Of course, I'd attire her as I'd want to see her, appropriate to the weather and the circumstances so as to enhance the reality of her unreal presence.

"A curious mind is the devil's playground," she teased.

"And you know very well I can't deny the existence of evil as a force, but my notion of Satan is as a fundamental aspect of human nature rather than an entity. That is, if you insist on getting technical about metaphysics."

"I don't insist," she protested. "You're the one who sets the stage. And you've stepped into a new drama. Why couldn't you be content to curl up in your trailer and drink yourself to death?"

I took a moment to gaze at her. Loretta was movie-star pretty, but Naomi was endowed with a loveliness radiating from her face, a glow given off by sincerity, clarity, and intelligence.

"This old guy showed up at my door talking nonsense, and I'm worried someone killed him before I could understand the message."

"Not only curiosity but also paranoia. A nasty combination in a man whose faith was never all that strong."

"Are you trying to tell me I'm on a fool's errand? Are you saying the doctor was a wacko? His death was an accident? The universe is empty and meaningless?"

"*Wacko* is a judgment call, the assignment of meaning. So is *accident*. Neither conclusion is inherently meaningless — you're simply fretting that those explanations are not as useful as other meanings you might find if you had more evidence."

She was messing with me. And having fun doing it. I told her, "Dr. Gropius says we're not living in base reality. He says we can't trust anything we see or hear."

She laughed. "Yes, so I'm a character in a video game. It's enough to make a person believe in ghosts." But she looked serious when she added, "But, from a theoretical point of view, living in virtual reality would be a plausible explanation for why I'm here with you now."

"And for the afterlife," I added for her. "I've heard some New Age folks refer to death as 'stepping out of the movie.'"

She challenged me with, "So what are you going to do? If you go looking into this farm situation, you know you'll be turning over a rock. And I don't have to say you won't like what you find."

I hesitated before I decided to ask, "So, does seeing you now mean Loretta won't be coming back?"

She made her bad-smell face, which she knew I didn't find cute, and replied, "Understand, when you ask me a question, you know the answer already."

I came back with, "But hearing you say it may make me believe it more. It's the same with prayer. I am supposed to believe I have whatever I need before I ask, but I need to hear myself say it, and with enough confidence to believe someday I'll see evidence of the answer."

"Then you also know that prayer is useless if you haven't done what you can to manifest the blessing you seek. You're the one with opposable thumbs."

"Are you saying I shouldn't let go and let God?"

"Not unless you've done your homework first."

I was going to ask her what more she could tell me, but switching on the ignition and flipping on the cold air blasted her out of there.

A MOMENT after the engine was purring and the cool air was flowing, my phone winked on. I'd finally remembered to plug it in right before I'd left the car. I wasn't sure how long it had been off.

There was voicemail from the sheriff's office. I sat there with the car idling so I wouldn't stifle in the leftover afternoon heat with the air off. But before I had a chance to retrieve the message, a black-and-white pulled into the parking lot, and, no doubt spotting my distinctive vehicle, drove over and stopped alongside. Quickly climbing out was not Chet but Deputy Della Crandall. She strode over to my driver's side, leaned in, and made that spiraling hand motion to indicate I should open the window.

Flashing an obsequious grin, I complied. She was a large woman, fully aware that on an officer of either sex, her size and musculature would be intimidating. It amused me in the moment that she might not have been Chet's first choice, not because she was black and female but because Griggs had been a slight man and the department would have to stand the expense of new uniforms for her.

She was not happy. "How come you don't return my call?"

I gestured with my phone, which was still plugged in. "Officer, I was about to call you. My phone's been dead."

She scoffed, "You know, guys in your line of work are terrible liars." Then she added with a straight face, "That's a compliment."

I risked asking, "Did you have to follow me way out here across the county line?"

She straightened and huffed, "I'm here same reason as you, but you made it first."

I smiled. "Compassionate visit?"

"You're poking around about Gropius. Now, they might tell you stuff they won't tell me, but the other way around works as well. I don't have time to hear your side. I'm gonna interview anybody in there who will talk. I'll brief the sheriff, and I suggest you do the same."

I nodded. "Got it."

Turning away, she said, "He's having dinner tonight by his lonesome at the Cork 'n Cleaver. The missus got the card game with her lady friends tonight."

I didn't yet know how to read her, so I called after her, "Does that mean he wants to see me?"

"Ask him."

I thanked her perhaps less than audibly and finally pointed the Fiat in the direction of home. The sun was going down, my stomach was empty, and there was an excellent chance the sheriff would be buying my dinner.

11

As agreed, I met up with Otis as he was chowing down on dinner at the local steakhouse. As I eased into the booth, he was polishing off a bowlful of New Orleans-style rue-spiced crawdads, known politely in these parts as "rock lobster," chased down with what I could only guess was his second double bourbon-and-branch.

In front of me on the table was a glass of the same but on the rocks, the ice not yet entirely melted.

Taking a thankful pull on the drink, I asked him, "Are you going to join me in another?"

He scowled into his food as he stabbed a lemon wedge with a fork and twisted it to drizzle juice onto what was left of his appetizer.

"I can get away with two doubles," he confided, "considering my body mass. You won't get me to admit I'm a better driver on a couple of drinks. Not as prone to panic." He finally looked up. "But three? I'd be an enemy to my fellow man — er, humans, that is."

I grinned and gulped again. "Thanks for the drink. I guess we've both had a challenging day."

He grinned back. "Pastor, can you afford to be seen in public sucking down the sauce? I know it's a good man's failing, but we do have our reputations to think of."

"I don't know about you," I said, finishing it off, "but I'm unchurched, defrocked, and if it weren't for the boundless generosity of one Zip Zed letting me housesit a broken-down little trailer rent-free, I'd be homeless. What have I got to lose?"

He shrugged. "Your pride that goeth before your fall?"

"Deputy Crandall surely told you I motored up to Lee's Summit to check on Gropius. I didn't learn much other than that he kept to himself and was an avid reader of books on metaphysics and end-of-the-world conspiracy theories. Pretty much what I expected from the little he'd managed to share with me over breakfast."

"You gonna have the steak, or are you still trying to go vegan?"

"Trying? I admit both Loretta and Cora convinced me that a plant-based diet is healthier and morally preferable. But if I'm a vegetarian these days, it's mostly because whatever comes in cans is cheaper. But maybe tonight I'll go with the fish. After all, Jesus did."

Otis laughed. "As a Bible scholar, I can't match you, Evan. I do know Jesus recruited fishermen, but I don't think it says anywhere he ate what they caught."

"Maybe you want to teach Sunday school? But if we believe Jesus assumed human form so he could suffer in our stead, we'd also have to believe he'd need to feed his body in the same ways we do."

In a low voice he confided, "We may have found that truck."

I felt a chill, suddenly sober. "What about the driver?"

"We've identified a person of interest, but we don't have him yet. This morning, a county EMS crew responded to a reported car fire in a ditch off I-49. Truck is burnt toast, but no occupants at the scene. We got the VIN off the engine block, and it fit the description of your hit-and-run. Registered to one Talker Osceola with an address down by Bolivar."

I'd known the man, but not well. "The family attended our church back when Marcus was pastor. His wife Winona served on the Loving Embrace committee, but then she took ill. Some chronic condition, pretty bad. They have a daughter, Anna. I believe she'd be high school age now."

"Before Crandall caught up with you today, I sent her to the Osceola home. It's a dinky cracker-box on wheels like yours. No one there, padlock on the door. Neighbors gave my deputy the shrug except to say, yes, the guy drove a white pickup, but he doesn't live there. Brings bags of groceries and leaves. We're looking for him. Crandall's a computer wiz like you, tried to find what she could. No employer of record."

"I think he worked as a day laborer. Odd jobs."

"Guys with my job hate the gig economy. All cash, no records. Any ideas?"

Crandall must have started with the obvious, but I had to ask, "Call their phones?"

"Talker's voicemail is full. The wife and kid, also full. The daughter quit school last year, had a job in a store then didn't report for work the day of the accident."

"Winona needed care. Have you checked the hospitals?"

"We got nothing, except the suspicion that the family panicked and took off after the head of the household found himself in serious trouble."

"So what's your ample gut telling you, Chet? Are you thinking this was manslaughter or murder?"

"You said the old guy was trying to warn you. What about?"

"He was curious — maybe even fearful — about whatever is going on over at the End-Times farm. His nurse gave me some books he was reading on prophesies. On the way to John Knox, I happened to pull off in Peculiar. I caught a meeting in the park. This evangelist Deacon Daniel was holding forth in front of an audience. They looked to be nomads, maybe some homeless. Ever hear of Pastor Obadiah?"

"Unfortunately, yes. I could wish that farm of his was located in the next county over. Then it would be somebody else's headache. He's very careful not to have broken any laws — at least none that I know of. But if it's a cult, it's gonna be trouble for law enforcement. Only a matter of time."

"This Daniel was preaching about the end-times, and it seems way beyond coincidental that Gropius was fixated on the same topic. I don't think the doctor was a follower. He told some folks at the home that Obadiah's a fraud."

"Why do you think Gropius came to you?"

"Maybe he wanted me to help him refute the guy. Expose him before he hurts people."

I'd gotten so spun up about news of the truck that I'd ignored the twist in my empty gut. I glanced at the menu. Wild-caught catfish was the only choice. Not my favorite since I ate my weight and then some as a boy, but it would do. They might make it breaded, but they wouldn't pan-fry it in lard like my mother did. They'd use Crisco.

Our waiter was a slight young man who might have been barely old enough to serve drinks. I ordered the fish, a salad, a baked potato topped with margarine, another double bourbon, and a Diet Coke for a chaser.

Chet was already sawing his steak to pieces, which was his habit to do thoroughly before taking the first bite.

As I watched him chew while I sipped a fresh drink and waited for my fish, I hazarded a guess. "Maybe the place to look for Talker Osceola is over at that farm."

The sheriff laid his cutlery back down decisively on either side of his plate, and he was not finished eating. Taking a break in his repast was not his way, but he wanted to make his point without having to chew at the same time.

"Evan, even if I had probable cause to think he was there — which I don't — I couldn't go in there. That's a religious compound. A criminal might not be able to hide out in a church, but to get a warrant I'd need someone to tell me he was there or have some proof they were his employer. And for all I know, they've got weapons! Am I gonna pull up in there all polite and nice in a squad car? And what if I go in with heavy artillery and all they're using is Bibles for their sword drills? How would that play in the press? Freak them out like that, I'd never get back in, even for a good reason."

The waiter brought my food as Chet was finishing his. The young man hadn't brought my drink, and I feared Chet might have stopped him with a frown.

I wanted to dig in, but I took a moment to insist, "Torching the truck makes it look like a hit and run. And if it was vehicular homicide and Obadiah had it out for Gropius, you have to admit that the driver could be hiding out. If Talker isn't headed for Mexico by now, he'll be sheltering in place at End-Times."

Otis leaned back and began to use a toothpick to pry the remnants of steak from his molars. He beamed. "Me, until I've got some solid evidence, I'm going to rely on your compulsive curiosity to nose around for me. Unofficially, as you do."

"So you want me to find out whether Talker is there."

"And who would benefit from the doctor's demise."

I grumbled, "And how am I supposed to do that?" But I knew he'd offer no suggestions.

I got another smirk from Otis as he teased, "Eat up! Nothin' worse than cold fish." As he gulped from a glass of abstemious sweet tea, he asked, "You gonna have dessert? Don't worry I'll force you. I'm ordering for me and I don't want to share."

EVEN THOUGH CHET had finished his dinner before I had started in on mine, he generously delayed ordering his dessert until I was done. I passed on having anything else, although I was tempted to push my luck with him and have some more whiskey.

But it had been a long day, and I excused myself. I left him in the booth staring at a generous slice of apple pie beneath a mound of vanilla ice cream. Was he saying a prayer the cholesterol wouldn't further constrict his heart or the fats and carbs expand his girth? Or was he giving thanks he'd made it through one more day in service to his community for which this indulgence was his blissful but inadequate reward?

I liked and admired him. No doubt he carried worries the rest of us want to know nothing about. Me, it had recently been my role to counsel and console the sick and the dying, but fate and my own ill-advised behavior had granted me a respite. I wasn't retired, just resting on my oars. Or so I told myself.

Agreed, Chet had no probable cause to open an investigation of Obadiah's scheme. The farm was a hundred-acre compound near Taberville, off Route H, the two-lane highway that links Appleton City with El Dorado directly to the south. According to Otis, the place was securely fenced in, and he feared Obadiah employed a security force equipped with licensed semiautomatic firearms. As if those facts weren't enough to discourage even a social visit, the entire property was registered as a place of worship.

As a fellow man of the cloth, presumably I could find an excuse to pay a visit to Obadiah. This was the sheriff's hope anyway. Possibly, Pastor Obadiah might know of my expertise in apocryphal literature. And if there was a link to Gropius, that topic might have been the reason for it.

As much as I wanted to find Talker, I was more worried about Winona. I knew the husband hardly at all. I remembered seeing him at socials, never in the sanctuary. But I had every reason to regard her as one of the faithful. It must have been three years since I'd seen her — before I'd taken over the ministry at Evangel Baptist and before Covid. And if she'd ever been among the throng who attended the ill-fated Shining Waters Temple, I hadn't noticed her. She was a sweet person, diminutive in stature and unassuming. She spoke in a quiet voice and smiled cautiously. She was an easy person to like. Her health was failing even back then, but I never learned why.

Since the Osceola home was padlocked, there was no sense driving over there tonight. And I simply didn't have the energy. I resolved I'd head down there in the morning. Rather than poking around like a skip tracer, maybe if I played the reverend card I could find some helpful and talkative neighbors.

12

I t had been an exhausting day. Cosseted on the narrow cot in my trailer, I fretted about all these things well into the night. At peaks of restlessness, I'd sit up, open my laptop, and search for background on the principal players. (Zip, bless him, continued to pay the bills for all utilities, including Internet access, as essential to me as water.)

I could find nothing more on Gropius. A helpful and perhaps less than scrupulous PR firm could sanitize an online persona, but his background seemed to have been expunged. Competent as I am as a data driller, I didn't know who could do that other than perhaps operatives of the three-letter government agencies. (*Ethical hackers,* they're called, not without irony.)

About Obadiah, whose legal name was Frank Jeremiah Trusdale, I found a wealth of news reports and articles going back four years, but not much before, when he'd adopted the Biblical name of an Old Testament prophet who saw visions. There was no mention of Deacon Daniel. Obadiah's emergence into the public sphere had been sudden and spectacular, as mine had, as a televangelist. With all that publicity, I was surprised I hadn't heard more of him — or met him. His official biographies mentioned his early life not at all, but there was one unedited interview in which he claimed he'd worked as a ranch hand in Wyoming after a boyhood spent in West Texas, son of an oilfield roustabout and a barmaid. Somehow I remembered a celebrity having given those same colorful details recently in an interview.

After two years of burgeoning popularity on the radio, Obadiah went silent, coincident with his founding of the End-Times Retreat Center in Taberville, Missouri. The guy got around. Whatever preaching he did these days must have been to his growing community of followers. At this point, it was obvious he was deliberately staying out of the public eye.

Perhaps I held one fact no one else had discovered. Fred Birchard, the dearest surviving soul I knew, had been close to Winona years ago. He told me he'd been bitterly disappointed when she turned down his marriage proposal and took up with Talker instead.

Birch had served as sexton at Evangel Baptist, then he quit to take a job on the maintenance crew of a veterinary hospital. Then he'd been hired as a janitor at the Myerson Clinic. These days, I'd heard he was back doing regular maintenance at the church. He'd once warned me then that getting involved in the megachurch would be a mistake, and later events had proven him right. He was a quiet man, self-educated and wise, and over the years he'd made more than one suggestion that ended up as the theme of my Sunday sermon.

Winona and Anna weren't in my phone contacts list. It was getting late, past eleven, when a working man would be in bed. I wished I'd thought of it sooner, but I had to try.

"Birch, I'm sorry to trouble you so late. It's kind of urgent."

His voice was groggy. "You in town, Pastor?"

"I drove up to John Knox today to ask about a friend who was in an accident yesterday morning. He didn't make it."

"Sorry to hear. One of our folk?"

"No. Dr. Hans Gropius. Came to me for guidance, I think, but he was struck down before I knew exactly what he wanted." I adopted the pastoral tone I had for breaking bad news when I added, "It was a hit-and-run, and there's some evidence Talker Osceola might have been the driver."

Now he was fully awake. "They find him?"

"No, looks like he took off. But the cops found his truck. Torched. With her husband gone, I'm worried who's taking care of Winona."

He gave out a disconsolate sigh. "Some nights he don't come home. Anna neither. Winona calls me, says he didn't show up last night. She's a shut-in, real sick, and he's supposed to bring her dinner. I can't get him or the girl on the phone. So I go over there with a hot meal for Winona, and nobody home, place locked up tight."

"What's up with Anna?"

"The girl don't live there now. Got a job and a boyfriend. Comes by now and then."

I wanted to think the best of Talker. I remembered him as the powerful, quiet type.

"Has he done this before?"

"Talker, when his buddies go walkabout, she figures they're on a bender, no use tracking him down." He added hesitantly, as if unsure whether he should share it, "And she's not about to go to the cops. He's got a record. Way back, maybe something he didn't even do, but he always warn her he's got to lie low."

I had to let him know, "I've been talking with the sheriff and his deputy about this. They've checked the hospitals and urgent care. What do you think?"

"I'm hoping she's with Anna. Don't know why that girl don't answer."

"What can you tell me about Talker? I hardly knew him. Do you know where he works?"

"This and that. I don't know where. But he's doing something. She says he's off before dawn and home late. Mostly he doesn't stay over. Lord knows where he bunks. If he's told her what he's doing, she's not telling me."

"Do you know about the End-Times farm? Could he be working there?"

"Winona always likes that Pastor Obadiah. Says he's a healer. But Talker tells her not to go there, and Anna says the same. You ask me, that preacher's a no-good. He's the reason she won't take medicine. That said, Talker ain't one to turn down work, but I never heard."

"When was the last time you spoke with him? Has he been upset about anything?"

"Preacher, we're not exactly close. You know she chose him instead of me."

"Yeah, you said."

"He tricked her, you know. She's from a proud native family, and she knew her folks wanted her to marry in their community. No way with a black man. But then she took up with Talker, and he's no more in'un than I am. He's mixed-race and maybe can pass, but Osceola isn't a tribal name. More like some freed slaves took it because they thought it was."

I asked Birch to text me the phone numbers of Talker, Winona, and Anna, along with the home address. I ended the call by promising him I'd do what I could, which seemed lame.

As for Talker Osceola's military record, all I got were dates of enlistment and discharge, which spanned the final years of Afghanistan. He was a corporal in the military police. Serving in the infantry would have its brief moments of sheer terror in fire-fights, but I'd guess that dealing with both unruly soldiers and unpredictable locals on a daily basis could really grind you down.

Birch said that the guy had been wounded, but I couldn't find any evidence of an injury, other than the fact that the date of discharge suggested early termination of his tour of duty.

I remembered Anna from Sunday school, but only to greet her and her mother as worshippers who filed past me leaving the sanctuary at the end of service. All I found on her was a local news item from two years ago that freshman Aiyanna Osceola had won first place in an Appleton City High School science fair for her experiment testing the effects of microwave radiation (in her oven at home) on seedlings. An accompanying photo showed her holding a trophy as she stood in front of her exhibit. Her stoic father, who was fully a head taller, had his arm thrown awkwardly around her shoulders. Yes, here was a giant of a guy who could bash heads. But in the wrinkles at the corners of his eyes, I could see he was not a humorless man.

A quick search showed Aiyanna as an authentic given name for a Kiowa woman. As was Winona, whose family name at birth was Skinner, which could have been an anglicized indigenous name. The Kiowa weren't native to this area, but there had been settlements in Kansas — before a devastating smallpox epidemic. Then the government sent the survivors forcibly to Oklahoma. There are no Indian reservations for any tribe in Missouri.

It was going to be another sleepless night. I worried what Winona would do if Talker had abandoned her. I recalled all the emotions I'd run through after Cora informed me Loretta had gone. Her act was obviously deliberate, and that stung. And the implication was it would be forever. But even falling asleep in that empty farmhouse, as I was trying to do in my leaky trailer now, I knew why. Perhaps it had been obvious to everyone but me. She'd been a cocktail waitress, then I'd abruptly made her a minister's wife and head of household with two teenage children — both of whom were mentally impaired, even if their conditions were more or less under control with medication. Then there was Baby Buzz, Melissa's child (by Luke, we think), which now Luke adores. Without my asking, Loretta had taken on responsibility for the Loving Embrace committee. And also on her own, she'd dressed like the proverbial schoolmarm of a bygone era, as if she were conforming to the stereotype of a church lady. She'd kept a game face all day every day, but it must have worn her down.

Luke and Melissa had moved out before Loretta took off. They were maintaining well, as the healthcare practitioners term it, and that pressure of my concern for them was off, except for infrequent fits of worry when they hadn't called. Luke had found a job in Boulder, Colorado as an assistant librarian, and Melissa was selling her artisanal jewelry. They'd rented a little bungalow, and next year Buzz would be entering preschool.

Even though Loretta might want to cut me off for the sake of her own sanity, she'd hardly be able to forsake her sister. When I'd speak with them, I'd usually call Luke's phone, and if he didn't pick up, I'd call Melissa's. But then if she picked up, she'd hand it politely but quickly to Luke. I was sure she respected me, and I doubt she blamed me for the breakup, but I suspect she kept a lot of news to herself out of loyalty to Loretta.

I couldn't get that picture from the science fair out of my mind. From the look on his stoic face and the hint of a smile, Talker was proud of his daughter.

13

The address of the Osceola home was in a sprawling trailer park north of Bolivar (which locals pronounce "Bolliver"). The park was situated adjacent to Cherokee Homestead Village, a subdivision bordered by the Pomme de Terre River on the north and the city limits of Bolivar on the south. Whatever the place might have been in the past, it wasn't an indigenous settlement today. I knew there were Cherokee over in Oklahoma, but the Ozark region is famous as Osage country. The roads are sparse around there, and it took some GPS navigation to get me over from Highway 83 to the entrance of the property on East 405th Road off Route D.

Right away when I surveyed the route online before setting out that morning, I noted that the distance from Appleton City was greater than I would have expected — more than sixty miles. And it was over in Polk County, outside Sheriff Otis's jurisdiction. He'd therefore only have been concerned with Talker Osceola as a missing person if the man was the driver of the white pickup that killed Gropius. I didn't know whether the Osceolas had been living so far away when they'd attended my church. But folks in these parts did spend a lot of time on the road.

Low-rise brick markers on either side of the road held the housing development entrance signs to the park. The low wall and the signage looked well maintained, unlike the sad condition of the structures inside. Most of them were single-wide trailer homes, varying in length from the cramped size of mine to others as long as a forty-five-foot semitrailer.

None of them looked at all new. Because of the unique residential agreement I have with my landlord Zip Zed, I know something about federal housing regulations and manufactured homes. Quite simply, the FHA will not insure a mortgage on any trailer home built before 1976, and neither will most banks. Therefore, most if not all of the residents here would be renters. Vintage trailers either get demolished to make the pad available for a new unit, or investors like Zip buy them, fix them up minimally, and rent them out dearly. And I know from my experience with banker Stuart Shackleton that these days such high-profit real estate investments tend to be consolidated in mega holding companies, which could be international in scope.

Some banker, trust, or corporate entity must own the whole park. And the rents — provided those get paid sooner or later — would gush one helluva cash flow. Rich guys like to make money while they sleep. During Covid, there was some rent forgiveness, but now that the pandemic clouds were beginning to clear, a common sight along any residential street would be stacks of used furniture, the aftermath of abrupt, wholesale evictions.

And so there were here — couches, mattresses, chests of drawers, dining room tables and chairs, along with suitcases and moving boxes overstuffed with clothes.

The pileup outside the Osceola's trailer was not full-length but perhaps big enough for the family of three. A settee and a mattress. If there had been a microwave and TV, those had already been spirited away. A faded canvas awning with a long gash in it was strung from the entrance door out over a patch of burnt grass and weeds. Two plastic picnic chairs were set in the shade beneath it, a rusted-out barbecue grill alongside.

I thought perhaps the noise of my car pulling up to the house would cause anyone inside to stir, but there seemed to be no activity inside or out, even after I marched up to knock on the door. The intent of the padlock was unmistakable. I stood there for a couple of minutes then knocked again.

As much for the benefit of anyone else who might be listening, I called out, "Winona! It's Pastor Wycliff!" No response.

I didn't see a vehicle. When her husband was away and her daughter didn't call, I'd guess Winona could rideshare with neighbors.

I was intending to walk around to the other side and tap on a window when a voice behind me yelled, "You best not be going in there!"

A middle-aged woman dressed in T-shirt and jeans sidled over. Her shirt was emblazoned with the "Don't Tread on Me" insignia and wasn't ample enough to cover her sagging breasts and belly. Walking seemed difficult for her, and I was guessing a hip needed replacement she couldn't afford. For someone who was in that much pain, it would take considerable effort to be nice.

I came down off the step to meet her. "I'm Evan Wycliff. I was Winona's pastor sometime back. I haven't seen her recently, and I worry about her."

She grimaced, the wrinkles in her dry, freckled skin becoming deep furrows. "You best be fretted," she said. "The woman's poorly."

"Then I should check on her. Do you know anyone who can let me in?"

"No point," she huffed. "The daughter was here night before last, took her away. I'd say hospital, if she can afford it, but they probably can't. If you owe, you can't even get an appointment these days unless you pay up." She shrugged. "There's the emergency room, but then you better be able to show 'em blood."

"Her daughter Anna? Are you a friend of the family?"

She shook her head. "Nope, hardly know many of 'em here. I keep an eye on things for the owners. We get a vacancy, the management wants me to put somebody else in there right quick." I was afraid she wouldn't bother to answer my next question, but then she offered, "Yeah, Anna. Smart kid, maybe got lucky. Has a car, anyway. Gray Honda. Not new."

"Can you tell me anything else? What's wrong with Winona?"

"You'd think it was long Covid, but no. COPD. You could hear her coughing from a ways off. I don't know what you do for that. I guess we fumigate the place."

"What about Anna? Is she still in school?"

"Are you kidding? These folks want nothing to do with medicine for themselves or school for their kids. You can't tell 'em nothing." Then she muttered, as if she knew she shouldn't give out the information, "I heard the kid works over at AllUNeed."

At last, something to go on. "What about the father? Talker. My friend said he hasn't seen him in a few days."

"A *few days?* I haven't caught sight of that bugger in more'n a month. If I had, he'd have got his pink slip from me!"

I took a shot. "Who *does* own this place?"

She growled, "Wouldn't you like to know."

I moved toward my car as I looked back and smiled. "I do appreciate your help. May I know your name?"

She was already striding away but turned around. "You may not, sir. Pastor? I wonder. Years back there was a skip tracer looked a lot like you."

It was pretty obvious she wouldn't stand for me walking around and knocking on doors. I wondered how many of the others were padlocked. No one else was around, and you'd think I'd at least spot a kid on a bike or a skateboard.

I called after her, "You don't have to fumigate for COPD. It can be serious, but it's not contagious."

She wrinkled her nose at me, started to walk off, then shot back, "You the one left the bag of food on the doorstep last night?"

"No, that would have been my friend."

"It was real tasty."

14

I made the short drive over to the AllUNeed Superstore in Bolivar. There I stepped into an alternate universe. In all its immensity, if you can't find it here, you should question your earthly need of it.

Figuring the unofficial approach might work best, right off I asked the greeter whether he'd seen Anna Osceola today. He wasn't surprised by the question, shook his head, and confided, "Sweet girl."

Then I asked him where I could find the manager. He jerked a thumb in the direction of the customer-service counter with an expression that said, "If you gotta."

His badge told the world he was Curt Carper, Assistant Manager. I guessed he was in his early twenties because his face still bore traces of the bad case of acne that must have plagued his teenage years. He was wearing a brightly checkered, no-iron, button-down shirt. His red hair was thinning prematurely, and his practiced smile exposed nicotine-stained teeth. I waited for him to deal courteously with a couple of product returns then stepped up and played the reverend card.

I explained that Anna was a member of my congregation (still true, as far as I knew), and I was concerned she wasn't in school.

He gulped hard, so much that his level of panic outweighed my question. The energy drained out of his face as he recited, "She's part-time, told us she's home-schooled. Unless they fail a background check, we go by what they put on the form. More than that, I don't know, and I couldn't tell you if I did."

"Can you at least tell me what she does here?"

He wasn't sure he was supposed to say more, but at last he said, more relaxed now, "Price compliance. When we get changes, and we get 'em by the boatload, she has to put the new stickers on the shelves or on the products. We got us a hundred-and-fifty-thousand items, give or take. If the price on a sticker doesn't match when the item gets scanned on checkout, the law says we have to give whichever price is lower. Then the inspector from state weights and measures gives me grief, hits us with a fine. It's a headache, believe me, and it's her job to stay ahead of it. Which is why we can't afford to have her off the job."

I threw out, "Sounds like a lot of responsibility for a sixteen-year-old."

The panic returned, and he gulped again. "She was sharp," he snapped. "When she was here, that is."

Maybe he worries I'm from Weights and Measures? Or child welfare?

To calm him, I risked a weak smile and offered, "But if the stickers were your only problem, life would be sweet, wouldn't it?"

His eyes dropped to study his shoes and he muttered, "You got that right." And I was imagining what dramas in his life were worse than dealing with a surprise visit from an authority figure.

"Will you tell her I asked after her?"

He said tersely, "I'm not expecting her back." Then he turned and flashed his smile to beckon the next person in line.

If he had a reason to believe Anna was gone for good, I was sure he wouldn't tell me.

~

ON THE WAY BACK HOME, I dropped in on Zip Zed. For a car dealer, he was about as honest as they come. I wasn't eager to see him, but my motive this time was evidentiary. He had an almost photographic memory for every car and truck and tractor he'd ever sold or serviced. He'd know whether Talker Osceola had ever been his customer.

I hadn't seen Zip since my breakup with Loretta, when he'd generously let me go back to live in one of the trailers he rented to transients and casual laborers. Even though I didn't owe rent and he was paying the utilities, on moving in I'd convinced him to buy me a pint-sized, window-mounted air conditioner. He'd sent his service manager over with a used unit I managed to install myself. The hottest of the sweltering summer months were not yet upon us, but I knew from experience that having to cope with the funky, leaky swamp cooler would compound my miseries. The deal I'd struck with him was I'd pay the extra on the electricity during the hot months. He offered to give me my old job back to help pay the bills. It wasn't a coincidence the old gal at the trailer park had nailed me for a skip tracer.

Predictably, he was in his office at the dealership. In this age of electronic records, it was a mystery why his desk was still piled high with paperwork. It was as if he felt he must visually verify the customer's signature on every loan application, certificate of title, and due bill — but never got around to it.

Thankfully, he'd given up cigars. He chewed gum instead, which was no less unsightly, but he and the room smelled better.

He acted not at all surprised to see me. "Hey, who's living at the Redwine place these days?"

When Arthur Redwine had willed his farmhouse as a parsonage, he'd deeded it to me instead of to the church, and that was where Loretta and I settled after we were married. Luke moved in with us, then we added Melissa and her baby after she completed her treatment at Myerson Clinic for epilepsy and depression, not to mention the trauma of having been abducted and nearly raped by a mob boss (another story).

"Nobody, just now," I replied. Luke and Melissa and Buzz were off on their own, as were our roomers Walter and Leslie. "Too many ghosts for me to be rambling around all those empty rooms by myself." Figuring his question had as much to do with real estate as my personal welfare, I added, "I'll be hanging onto it in case the kids want to move back in."

His two sons were managing well, by all reports. Whiz, who now preferred his given name Wesley, was managing Zip's gas station out on Route P, which they'd appropriately named ZipGas, and his older boy Buzz (born Burton and not the namesake of Melissa's child) was studying veterinary medicine and racking up fraternity-house expenses at UC Davis.

"I told Buzz the vet school at Purdue is as good, maybe better, but the kid thinks the left coast is a chick magnet. I guess nobody told him the campus is in the middle of the state and surfing isn't on the program. His mother wanted him to do med school at U of M, but he figured Columbia was too close to home. Besides — did you know with the insurance headaches and the liability that a lot of vets make more than doctors now?"

I sighed. "At least he won't be an ironworker," I cracked.

"So what brings you to my fine establishment? I can't imagine you've already saved the down for a car, used or otherwise. I guess you're gonna drive the tires off that little Fiat, but if you're wanting to get serious about chasing deadbeats again, you'd better find something that doesn't tell the world who's coming."

"No, I don't want another car, and I'm not ready to go back to work."

"Don't forget I did you a solid with that air conditioner. Good thing you won't be sweating through your shorts this summer. Save your pennies. Might be a good plan to pay me the electric a month in advance so it don't get shut off all of a sudden."

I told him, "It's not like it's a small fortune to you, Zip. You just want me back at work."

"Now that you mention it, yes. Times being what they are, I got a shitload of otherwise fine folks in arrears. I'm not happy about it, my ulcer acts up, and the wife says all I do is complain."

"What do you know about an F-150, white, not at all recent, but I don't know how old. Guy by the name of Talker Osceola, not an Indian by blood but maybe wants folks to think he is."

Zip didn't hesitate. "Kerchief worn as a headband? Chambray shirt, jeans, and boots. Yeah, I remember the guy. Not our vehicle, busted transmission. No way he could manage the factory service rates. So I steered him to a salvage yard and told him if he'd buy the part, I'd drop it in for the cost of the labor. Not easy for him to do himself. You have to pull the engine. Hey, I see a man in need, I take care of him, maybe he gets a few bucks in his pocket one day and comes back for a trade-in. This was back in April. Never saw the guy after that. He didn't know a good deal when it's staring him in the face, so you can bet that clunker is still a clunker."

"You heard about the hit-and-run outside the C'mon yesterday?"

"No way you can miss breaking news in this town. Are you figuring Osceola was the driver?"

"I didn't see it happen, but I watched the truck haul off down the street. For the sake of his family, I'm hoping he sold it after you told him it would cost so much to fix."

"What's your interest in all this?"

"The guy who he — or somebody — killed had come to ask for

74

my help. For what, I don't know. Hans Gropius. He'd been in assisted living at John Knox. Raving about conspiracy theories, the end of the world…"

Zip couldn't help smiling. "Ah, your cuppa tea."

Before I left and after turning down a two-beer lunch at Zip's expense, I asked Zip if he had any service records on Talker's truck. And despite his seeming reliance on paperwork, he punched his computer keyboard, opened his database, and found the quotation for the repair work. Otis already had the license plate and the VIN, but at least my digging had come up with a scrap of information.

15

I had to talk more with Birch. Even though he wasn't one to share freely, he might have the story behind the story. I didn't know Talker at all but somehow hoped he wasn't responsible for the accident — and hadn't deserted his family.

I called Birch, but he didn't pick up. Instead of leaving a message, I decided not to go home but drove directly to the church. I hadn't been back to Evangel Baptist since I'd cleaned out my office. The Board of Deacons had accepted my resignation before I could be dismissed. I hadn't even met the new minister, Olivia Bingham, who had been recommended by retired Pastor Thurston. He'd told me she was a conservative and a literalist, so not likely to be a kindred spirit. I wasn't eager to go back there, and I was hoping, late on a Wednesday evening, that Birch would be the only soul in the place.

And indeed he was. All I had to do was follow the sound to find him with a hammer in his hand knocking out sodden plaster in a restroom where a broken pipe had soaked the wall. He was so intent on his work he hadn't noticed me come through the open door. I didn't want to startle him, so rather than shouting his name,

I rapped on the wall loudly with my knuckles until he turned around.

"Pastor!"

I returned his hug. "How about you call me Evan? I still tell folks I've got the job when I'm poking around asking questions, but you know better."

"You da man." He grinned, making an effort to be good-natured, but there was sadness in his eyes. He might not have slept well either.

"I drove down to Winona's place. Thought I'd talk to neighbors. I confirmed the landlady's thrown them out. And she ate your food."

"You find out where Talker's at?"

"No. Let's sit down and have us a heart-to-heart."

In the past, we'd have settled in the pastor's office, but I told him I wouldn't feel comfortable there. So we slid into a pew in the sanctuary and sat side-by-side. I liked the feeling of it. I should have had more conversations with folks this way.

I told him what I'd learned, most important that Talker might have been the guilty driver.

He said he knew Winona had been ill and that Anna had dropped out of school and taken a job. "Winona's got her stubborn ideas. She won't take any kind of medicine and don't hold with any kind of schooling."

"Why?"

"She takes after that Pastor Obadiah. He says that's how the people in power control you. You listen to him, you're bound for heaven. Says he's the only way, the truth, and the life. You know as well as me he oughtn't to be saying that."

"Is he telling folks he's the savior come back?"

"He won't go that far. He's John the Baptist. Making the way straight, he says. The big show hasn't happened yet."

"How do you know all this?"

77

"Winona tells me. She wouldn't let me visit except to bring stuff. But she'd call me now and then. I wanted to hear her say she made a mistake, but she never did."

"Do you think Obadiah is for real?"

"Like *really* John the Baptist? That's a stretch."

"What I mean is, does he believe what he's preaching, or is it all an act?"

"I saw him on TV a few times. The man sounds sincere, tugs at your heart. You know, folks with no hope, they hang onto anything. He says he's the only one who cares. And they buy it."

"What do you know about the Obadiah place? Do you think she's gone there?"

He stared at me, and there were tears in his eyes. "I sincerely hope not, Preacher. That's some kind of witchcraft going on, but no one will say it."

I asked him what else he knew, but he stiffened. All he would say was, "There's a buzz around the church. People curious. But them that talk about it, they don't know for sure. The people who do know are inside. They're not talking to anybody on the outside, and they're not coming out."

I rested my hand on his shoulder, reflected his sincere stare, and asked him, "Who's telling you all this?"

He began to sob. "I hear talk. They say folks run away," he said then choked before he added, "then they disappear. If Winona's in there, could be nothing anybody can do."

"Birch, I don't want to say this. If Winona is very sick, could be Anna took her to the farm to be healed. I don't think Anna would believe in that, but maybe she'd do it if her mother asked, especially if she was refusing medical help. Next thing, I have to go in there. I'm hoping the sheriff will help me, but let's not count on it. I'm thinking Anna took her mother there and dropped her off. What I'm wondering is whether the girl made it back."

Before I left him, I wanted Birch to tell me he understood that a broken-down preacher had no business interfering in police work. I wondered whether he'd want to go with me to see Obadiah, but I didn't yet have a plan. He stared at me for a long moment, and I hadn't expected what he would say next.

"Pastor, you best beware of that place. Witchcraft, low-level demons, no telling what-all. I didn't ask you to chase after Talker because he's a friend. I want him to do right by Winona and his child. I thank you for how far you got. Don't you fret about this would be my advice."

Something in the way he clenched his jaw told me he wasn't done with this. We'd arrived at a fork, and he was taking the other path.

I phoned Chet as soon as I was back in the car. He needed to know about the connection between the Osceolas and Obadiah. This time I got him on his cell.

He must have been off duty because he sounded annoyed. "You know, just because a guy leaves his wife saying he needs a pack of smokes doesn't mean I need to go checking all the convenience stores."

"That's a terrible analogy, Chet."

He raised his voice, which was not a habit with him. "What probable cause do I have to pull a raid on Obadiah's farm? Because you've got some hunch?"

"So you still do nothing?"

"Do I have to remind you about that time you and the Feds shot up Shackleton's pretty boat? That was kidnapping, child endangerment, and a high-profile wanted criminal. Maybe we're not so lucky and folks get hurt this time?" He cleared his throat, tried to settle down, and continued calmly, "Maybe I shouldn't have hinted for you to go nosing around. Hey, get some rest."

"When you're dead, they say rest in peace. You know me. If there's an afterlife, no way I'll be resting. Every dog needs a job."

That brought a smile. "My job is tough enough. I don't have to warn you being an angel has to be hard work." His voice dropped when he said, "Evan, don't go barging in there. If folks moved there, unless someone says different, they went under their own power. And if there are kids, I have to assume their parents took them. Stay out of it."

16

Birch was telling me to give up on all of it, but I knew he was as worried as ever about Winona. Chet's advice to stay out of it was like telling a kid to ignore the sound of the ice-cream truck. And he knows I don't quit. But I had to get a meal and some sleep first.

So I headed over to the C'mon Inn. I had some bucks from Leon's stash. Even if I hadn't, I knew Cora would let me eat on the cuff. But no need to waste a coupon.

I was pleased she was working behind the counter. As I took a place there, she quipped, "Happy to see you didn't bring anybody with you this time."

She was already pouring me coffee, and I grinned as I asked her. "Are you saying I'm bad luck?"

Cora leaned into me and cooed, "You wouldn't be if you'd let me straighten you out."

"What happened to Clint?"

She winked. "I'm not asking for a replacement. More like a supplement."

She's a shameless tease. I know she's not serious. Or let's hope she's not.

Ignoring the remark, I ordered biscuits and gravy. Rather than give me a lecture about salad, she stepped along the counter to refill the next guest's cup. His was a new face to me. He was dressed like an insurance man, maybe a claims adjuster. Pressed slacks, crisp shirt, polished shoes. Neat, close-cropped beard. Sunburned face. Not a fisherman. Maybe a golfer.

I turned to ask him, "On your way somewhere, brother?"

He took a sip from his coffee as he stared straight ahead. "And who wants to know?"

"I used to be pastor around here, and they haven't run me out of town yet."

That brought a chuckle. "What did you do? Steal from the collection plate?"

"They say I burned down a church but cleaned out the safe first."

Now he turned. "Reverend Evan Wycliff! I used to see you on TV. You looked better then."

I gulped some more of mine and sighed, "Back then, poverty and saintliness went together, and wealth was the sinner's reward. Now seems like it's the other way around."

"You must've made a buck or two out of all that. Did you really do all they say you did?"

"If you mean the fire and the theft, I did not. And there's no proof that I did. So I suppose that's why I'm still on the loose."

"What about all that faith healer stuff?"

"Are you kidding?"

He stuck out his hand. "Harry Ardmore."

As I clasped it firmly, I said, "I don't know you, but I feel I know the name."

Referring to the Springfield paper, he said, "I write for the

News-Leader." Then he emphasized, flashing a grin, "On the crime beat."

I hoped he was kidding when I reacted, "You're not here for me, are you?"

"Nah," he said. "I figured you'd be long gone by now. No offense, but you're no longer a thing — as a person of interest, that is."

"Oh? Who is?"

He lowered his voice to say, "Pastor Obadiah. This crank is making friends fast in Jeff City. I'll trust you to keep your mouth shut. I'm gonna break the story."

17

This new happy accident of meeting the reporter called for a drink. Probably more than one. We adjourned to the sheriff's favorite booth at the Cork 'n Cleaver, but fortunately for the sake of this clandestine meeting we didn't find him there.

Ardmore's summer drink was gin and tonic, another indication he was a golfer and not a fisherman. I was intending to let him buy, if it came to that, but even if I got stuck with the bill I could justify it to Leon as a project expense, even though he's had to remind me several times the government won't reimburse for liquor. Maybe I could get the reporter to order a plus-sized bowl of shrimp and I'd say we had dinner. Would such fraud under the circumstances be a necessary evil? I wished I didn't fret about such questions.

I told him what I knew about Gropius, the accident (withholding the suspected driver's identity), Deacon Daniel's evangelizing the homeless, and the rumors that folks had been disappearing inside Obadiah's compound. I stopped short of telling him I'd urged Sheriff Otis to go in there looking for the Osceolas.

Ardmore summarized what he knew so far. "The guy's got bank

accounts all over the place. Besides generous contributions to the television ministry when he had the show, he's got considerable assets. The way I figure it — and I don't have proof yet, mind you — people have to sign a contract — including strict nondisclosure — to go live at the farm. But first he tells them they have to renounce their possessions. If they have them, they sign the deeds to their houses and their farms over to him. They clean out their bank accounts, sell their vehicles, and give him the cash. Of course, some of those transactions are public records, but the paper trail isn't easy to follow. The evidence I have is circumstantial at this point. No one is talking to me."

"Fraud on that scale must have attracted a lot of attention."

"Oh, it's got attention. But no one's been able to prove coercion. So the contracts would probably hold up in court. How many charities want you to donate your used vehicle? Or your land or your boat? His church is a licensed nonprofit. The corporate records are filed quarterly with the state, all clean as you please. Even minutes of their board meetings, which you can bet are either sanitized in the extreme or total fiction."

I remembered that Arthur Redwine, when he lived as a hermit and survived on bread and cheese, would write big checks to the Daughters of Calvary.

I asked the reporter, "What's this about his connection to politicians?"

"That's where it begins to look like not only major fraud but also big-time corruption. He's throwing money behind candidates — most of them extremists."

"Which ones? How extreme?"

"Know-nothing up-and-comers who make Stuart Shackleton look like a moderate." He paused to take a drink, but it was also for dramatic effect. "I take it you know him?"

I told him I knew Shackleton as an unscrupulous investment banker and real estate developer who operated in the gray areas of the law. He'd tried to take my late friend Bob Taggart's family farm away from his estate. He owned the Myerson Clinic, a for-profit treatment center. He'd developed the Twin Dragons Resort and Casino, and in that venture he'd been a close associate of the international mobster Dmitri Churpov. Shackleton had funded not only my media career but also the founding of the Shining Waters Temple, which, far from being a philanthropic project, turned out to be part of a larger design to make the local area a tourist destination like Branson.

And after my career demise because of the rumors surrounding my associations with him, Shackleton had wanted me to come on board as his speechwriter when he ran for state office. I'd declined, but in the short time since, with no political track record, suddenly he'd been appointed lieutenant governor when the fellow the voters had elected died of heart failure. I don't know why I also felt the need to tell the reporter, "Oh, and a matter I hope is wholly unrelated, I took as my ward Shackleton's son Luke, who was diagnosed and treated for schizophrenia and is now married to Melissa Benton, my estranged wife's sister."

He was amused. "Look me up when you want to write your memoir. You've got some stories." His inevitable question to me followed. "What ever made you get in bed with that guy?"

"He was indicted for the murder of Father Coyle, who some claim was involved in trafficking minors with Churpov. The case couldn't be proved, and Shackleton's accusers might have thought it a righteous act if he had done it. After he was cleared, he claimed to have been born again. I baptized him. I was never sure of his sincerity, but church leadership advised me it wasn't for me to question. Then he helped me reach a wider audience and build a big church. I kept telling myself it was all for the greater good. At the same time, my wife was gravely ill, and he paid for her care. Even now, his son is dear to me, in ways perhaps Stuart could never understand. I happen to think the boy's affliction has given him spiritual gifts, but his doctors think I'm nuts if I mention it."

Ardmore thought a moment, then asked, "Did you agree with his politics? Do you now? I didn't know a lot of this, but it sounds like you're a colleague, if not what you'd call friends."

"I think Shackleton is wrong all kinds of ways. As a human being, I don't think he has a moral center. He's an opportunist, and it would be a fair accusation to say at times I've gone along with him — for reasons I thought were justified at the time."

The alcohol was having a pronounced effect on me by now, and this session felt like a long-overdue confession. So I decided to share, "Harry, the faithful have accused me of being an agnostic. And I'd be the first to admit, there are days I have my doubts. Whether other ministers are being completely honest, I can't say. But I will tell you that I don't believe in Satan. I don't believe in devils, familiar spirits, or witchcraft. I can't deny the evil that's inherent in human nature. And it's not always malicious. Sometimes it's just plain ignorant. And that's how I'd explain Stuart Shackleton. He's capable of evil acts, but a lot of the time he can't see what's wrong with simply acting out of self-interest."

"All very interesting," Ardmore said as he tossed a couple of large bills on the table, along with his business card. He got up and was about to leave when he asked, "Do you think Shackleton has anything to do with Obadiah?"

"No idea. But I think someone is warning the sheriff to stay away from that farm."

He mused, "There's one more reason the authorities might not be eager to go after Trusdale."

"More important than money?"

"It's not evidence of corruption, rather the public servant's usual habit of looking the other way in the face of trouble. No doubt some of the folks who move into the farm may have assets they're willing to surrender. Some legit retirement homes at least want a lien on your stuff. But you told me that guy Daniel was pitching homeless types. Well, homelessness is on the decline these days, and maybe no one wants to ask why somebody might be rounding them up."

He left me sitting there with a finger of bourbon left in my glass and no ice. I couldn't tell him I didn't believe in ghosts because I'd be at a loss to explain Naomi's occasional visitations.

18

The most pressing question was whether Pastor Obadiah was a sincere, committed evangelist, a man who'd dedicated his life to preaching the gospel, providing counsel, and offering earthly and spiritual help to anyone who asked. The news that he might be giving sizable contributions to politicians was troubling but not necessarily damning. Wanting to influence public policy could imply concern for the welfare of his flock and the survival of his nonprofit business.

I knew from firsthand experience that simply achieving widespread media exposure can create enemies. Questioning the legitimacy of another clergyman could be misguided. Granted, theological differences abound, but without evidence no minister should be alleging that a priest or an imam or a guru is a charlatan.

Obadiah could be housing and feeding and healing the indigent and the sick in there. He could be offering hope to people who have lost it. He could be building a loving community that, in its self-sufficiency, is answerable only to itself. Students of history know that, despite innocent intentions, the Walden Ponds of this world have all failed eventually.

But in the aftermaths of the Peoples Temple and the Branch Davidians at Waco, even if these settlements were begun with righteous intent, the motivations of their leaders now seem megalomaniacal, if not consciously evil.

In the past, when I have been troubled by personal or doctrinal questions, I have always consulted my mentor, Reverend Marcus Thurston, my predecessor as pastor of Evangel Baptist. When he retired, he insisted I step in for him, which was a daunting and sobering step for a guest preacher. At the time, he'd offered to move out of the modest parsonage in town — or at least pay rent — but the Board of Deacons insisted the place was his for life. I didn't want to trouble him now because he was off on a rare vacation. All during his tenure, his occasional days off were picnics in the park as church-sponsored outings, and he rarely traveled any distance. But now he'd taken the opportunity to visit relatives in Jamaica, finally seeing the ancestral homestead where he'd never been.

The appropriate choice of guidance for me should have been to request a meeting with Reverend Bingham. We'd not met. Whether or not she knew anything about Pastor Obadiah, I was pretty sure her views wouldn't square with mine. If she was as conservative as Marcus had implied she was, I expected she would hardly approve of a tired progressive who made it no secret he drank and was no longer living with his wife.

Even though I'd assiduously avoided stopping by the church until that time I met Birch there, it was freakish that I hadn't yet encountered Bingham. On recruiting her, the deacons had promised her housing, but there was nothing in town available to rent, and the church coffers couldn't stand a new mortgage. So without informing me (no reason he should've), Zip Zed, still a member but not particularly active, made her the same deal he'd given me.

She now occupied the nicer, newer, larger trailer on the lot adjacent to mine and paid no rent. The previous tenant there had been a nurse who was transferred here to work in the hospital's Covid ICU. She'd stuck it out for two years then went back to KC. I hadn't taken the initiative to meet her either. No doubt my reluctance had something to do with the fact that the tenant before her had been the pretty cocktail waitress I'd married.

Knocking on that particular door has had its consequences.

So that was another reason I had avoided dropping by to welcome the new preacher to the neighborhood. Perhaps I worried I'd find her attractive.

I knew she drove a black Chevy Volt, which was one of the few EVs in town. I didn't have her phone number, and seeing the car parked outside the trailer I summoned courage and ventured over. The car was plugged in to a long orange extension cord that led inside through a window. Since Zip was making me pay for extra electricity, I wondered whether he'd foot the bills for charging her car.

She responded right away to my knock, and I could tell from her raised eyebrow that I needn't have introduced myself. Nevertheless, she beckoned me in and offered a chair with padded cushions embroidered in an old design that matched her deliberately country décor, centering on a dining set with turned-oak legs.

The sweet aroma of pastry baking in her compact oven filled the room, which was nearly twice the size of mine. Despite the oven's heat, the place was downright chilly. No doubt the cooling was cranked way up. She wore a flowered apron over jeans and a lumberjack plaid shirt. The shirt was so blousy it was impossible to imagine the figure it hid. She was round-faced with wide hips and a pouch under her chin. Her light brown hair was beginning to gray, drawn back in a bun. Perhaps she was not yet forty. I guessed her history would be interesting, but I wasn't about to ask.

"So nice we finally meet," she said.

Not even her definition of nice *would agree with mine.*

Busying herself at the stove, she offered tea, which I accepted.

The water in her kettle had already boiled, and she promptly handed me a mug with the teabag tag dangling from it. The tea was some kind of aromatic mint, and she wasn't offering milk or sweetener. I'd bet there was no Folgers in the house.

Holding her own cup, she eased herself into a chair at the table. Her stiffness made me think she'd sustained some injury to her back. A chronic bad back would be one thing we had in common.

She surprised me by asking bluntly, "Do you have a dog?"

"I did," I told her. "Murphy died last April. Late enough in the season to smell some spring flowers, I hope."

She offered, "Oh, I'm sorry," which sounded sincere but automatic. "You see, I'd been told you had a dog. A big, black one. And it's not as though I dislike dogs. I wondered because I never heard any barking from over your way. But you see, I'm a birder, and dogs, particularly if they are allowed to run loose in a yard, they scare the birds away. All except the crows, of course, and they can be as annoying. I do love to wake to the sound of songbirds. I'd go on field trips when I can, but for now I'm limited to what I can see with binoculars from my porch."

"I know we have sparrows and finches. That's a guess. I'm sure you could identify them more accurately."

She didn't comment but asked, "Are you planning on getting another dog?"

"No," I replied, sipped my tea, and waited cautiously for her to speak next.

"I'd offer you fresh brownies, but I'm baking them for Loving Embrace. I understand your wife did a fine job with that group."

"She did," I muttered. "She's a fine woman, threw herself into every task she took on."

"You weren't abusive, were you?"

The baldness of the question was appalling, but I simply said, "No. She decided she preferred a different life."

"Will you remarry?"

92

Wow. Whatever she's thinking comes right out of her mouth.

I wrinkled my nose and shook my head. Sipped some more.

She pressed on with, "And I assume you don't want your old job back."

I gave her another nonverbal no, this time emphatically, and tried to manage a smile.

"You got a reason for stopping by." It was a statement, not a question.

"I wondered what you knew of Pastor Obadiah and his End-Times farm."

"Oh my stars," she sighed. "That man's a puzzle, sure enough."

She told me she knew him by reputation, not personally. But because of her own background, she knew more of his early career than his recent followers would. Olivia told me she grew up in a farm town in Iowa, the daughter of a Pentecostal minister and a parochial schoolteacher. Her parents had wanted her older brother Tad to enter the ministry, but he enlisted in the Army and died pointlessly in an antidetonation exercise on a military base before he got shipped out. Then she took up the challenge of pleasing her parents and enrolled in divinity school in Florida. During her undergraduate work there, she found herself drawn more to the teachings of Frank J. Trusdale, who was not affiliated with the college.

"He was a charmer," she said sheepishly. "Probably still is. I was a schoolgirl, and you could say I had a crush. And the fact that he was a man of God... Well, I was looking for a hero to worship."

She told me she and some of her classmates attended his rallies in Orlando, which at the time were growing in popularity with Christian youth groups. His messages emphasized the increasingly rapid and bewildering pace of social change, along with an alarming decline in moral values. He claimed that world affairs were spiraling into the Last Days and insisted that, within their lifetimes, the Day of Judgment would be a real event.

Never mind that Judgment Day was predicted to occur after the thousand-year Tribulation. I won't engage her about what she believes. She's already implied she doesn't respect him anymore, so perhaps she also rejects his teachings.

"He was all about the healing and the laying on of hands," she said.

I was familiar with the way we'd performed the rite at Evangel Baptist. In a special ceremony, elders would file past a new deacon as each placed a hand on the person's head and conferred a blessing. Most of us regarded it as symbolic but meaningful, hardly supernatural but conveying solemnity to the vows of ordination. But Olivia said Trusdale claimed his touch could heal people. That was when she began to lose faith in him, perhaps because some of the demonstrative practices of Pentecostal worship had driven her away. Her father's congregation back home didn't handle poisonous snakes, but she knew some congregations did as part of their worship service to show faith in God's protection. Nevertheless, the snakes sometimes bit and victims succumbed, which the congregation probably thought proved a lack of faith rather than a failure of doctrine.

She'd been taking dainty sips from her tea all along. Now she drank the dregs and blew out a disgusted breath. "I lost faith in Trusdale completely after I witnessed how he handled what should have been an inconsequential event at one of his rallies. I was telling my friends they should go, but I realized I'd seen only white folks there. Now, the school's admissions were open, and our class was mixed, even though most back then were whites from southern states. You see, I had this friend, a cute guy from Baltimore, Wesley Lewis, African-American. We didn't have a thing going, not yet anyway. He was my study partner, and I hoped we could be more. I invited him to a rally, and I was pleased when Trusdale sought us out after the benediction."

Olivia had started to wriggle in her chair. I could see she wasn't sure she should be sharing all this, but now that she'd started she plowed ahead. "He downright gushed about welcoming Wes to the service. Pumped his hand, slapped him on the back. He laid it on thick. Sincerely wished more people of color could hear his message."

I can guess where this is going. She obviously had the hots for Wes.

She went on, "Okay, well, on our way back to the dorm, Wes tells me, by singling him out, Trusdale made him so uncomfortable he never wanted to go back."

"Killing with kindness," I suggested.

She nodded vigorously. "He came across as a sweet, sincere man. And to this day, I believe he still thinks he can heal. But they threw him out of Florida for practicing medicine without a license. He came here and changed his name to Obadiah. Mind you, he's still the charmer, I've heard. He doesn't come out and preach racial purity, but I bet there's not many people of color among his followers."

I won't say anything. If I let her speak, maybe she'll blurt out what she's wanted to say all along.

She continued, "Odd thing is, Trusdale's not white. Maybe he's not black either. He never said, as if nobody should care. And they shouldn't of course." After a long and pregnant pause, she said, "I kept waiting for Wes to propose. Now I think I should have sucked it up and asked him."

I asked her, "Have you been in touch with Trusdale recently?"

"Oh, no, not since that time in Florida. I could say I understand why people flock to him, but I really don't."

As I got up to leave, she added pleasantly without prompting, "I'd marry a gay couple, you know."

I smiled back, not wanting to engage today in such a fraught topic. I did ask, "Anybody ask you?"

She shrugged. "Not so far."

Recent news out of the Southern Baptist Convention was that a conservative faction was trying to expel female ministers — and the churches that dared defend them.

I wonder how much longer she'll have a job. Marcus seems to be respected by the leadership, but how much longer will he be around to take her side?

Now that I knew about Obadiah's past and his real name, from then on he was two people in my imagination. Frank Trusdale was a man with a history, however sanitized. Like some creation of a Hollywood publicist, Pastor Obadiah was a stage name, a brand to be sold to the public.

I'd gone in there expecting not to like Olivia. Shame on me.

19

Rev. Evan Wycliff suspected Talker was working at the compound, but he still had no solid evidence of the man's whereabouts or how he might have been employed.

At End-Times, Ida was the one to fire and hire. She didn't dislike people, but she'd never trusted Talker. She was simply wary of everyone on the planet but her brother. Her inner life was not panicked. As Frank had seen in her trance-like bouts ever since they were little, she had faith in herself. Where her cleverness came from was a mystery to him. She observed closely, continually on the lookout for threats.

After only a short acquaintance with anyone, she could predict their next move. She easily saw through phoniness and deceit. Because she understood their motivations, she could advise Frank how to manipulate them to counter any opposition.

Especially as his ministry and reputation began to grow beyond small congregations, she learned to adopt a saintly demeanor. Most of the time, her face bore a serene expression, permitting only the briefest smiles of approval. She spoke in calm, low tones. From childhood, she'd learned that putting on a pouting or angry face could get her slapped.

"This Talker Osceola is not to be trusted, you know," she told Frank. "He leers at me, and when I give him instructions, he doesn't acknowledge them."

The pastor looked unconcerned. "My dear, if I rebuked every man who gave you an appraising glance, I'd be tempted to murder half the population. Come to think of it, I'd have to include the women, as well, considering those who are attracted carnally and the others who would be furious with jealousy."

"He's hard to read. He's not a believer. He came here with the construction crew, but now that the work on the sanctuary is finished, I've kept him on because whether it's electrical or plumbing or whatever, he can fix it. And he doesn't complain."

Trusdale had his nose in a book and looked up only long enough to say, "He's all about cash. He has a sick wife. If he's so useful, I'm surprised he's not jacking his rate."

"He keeps to himself. He was here at dawn and stayed late. He was useful for errands with his truck, especially going for the old man. But the doctor was a chatterbox. And I worry Talker heard too much of our plans."

His attention still in his book, Trusdale muttered, "From what I can tell, the fellow wouldn't understand any of it, and if he did, he wouldn't care. Pay him with folding money, and I think he will do whatever you tell him to do and ask no questions."

"The strong, silent types are the worst. You have to test them to see how they will react."

"If Talker gets out of line or even makes you suspicious, don't fire him. Have Daniel straighten him out. Now that his wife and daughter are here and he has no truck, he should stay here as well. Just keep them apart."

Ida had set up a small, separate housing unit inside where her personally accountable crew could stay round the clock. Philip Hart had been recruited from among the residents. He'd turned out not be a believer, but he was venal, cooperative, and didn't shirk even the most unpleasant assignments. Supervised by Deacon Daniel, both Talker and Philip bunked with the crew.

Besides cash, the crew had one other inflexible requirement — hot meals with ample portions of meat.

20

Considering Olivia's having known Trusdale, I'd wondered whether I might be able to leverage that relationship into access to the farm and an appointment with the mysterious evangelist. But she had no more idea than I did what went on inside the End-Times compound. She'd admitted she used to catch Obadiah's broadcasts from time to time — listening out of a kind of morbid fascination for as long as she could stand it. I'd told her I'd listened to him as well, but I'd never had the stomach to endure an entire episode.

I had shared with her what I'd seen and heard in Peculiar, along with the guess that he was relying on emissaries like Deacon Daniel now.

I assumed she'd heard about the accident, but I'd stopped short of telling her Talker Osceola's possible involvement. It wasn't that I didn't trust her. I thought Winona and Anna had stopped attending before Olivia came on. I wanted to ask whether they were still members, but since she was dealing with our members on a daily basis, I didn't want to start rumors.

Now I realized that the End-Times farm was the last place Olivia would want to go.

THE SHERIFF HAD WARNED me not to go to the farm, which, if he was hinting I should, meant he wouldn't want to know if I did. And I wasn't about to tell Leon I was going in. He might want me to wait until we had an official reason to involve the bureau.

The one precaution I took was to change vehicles. The Easter Egg was much too distinctive. They'd see me coming, and anyone in the compound who knew me by reputation would remember I was there. So I drove over to Zed Motors, asked the service department for an oil change, and took a loaner — a used, metallic-blue Toyota I'd helped grab on the last repo. (I usually try to try a workout before we take a car, but I hadn't shed any tears over that guy. He held a decent job, but he had expensive habits. Not only was he stiffing the dealership on his car payments, but he'd also never come through with his child support.)

The route to the farm east of Taberville seemed straightforward enough, but the nav map didn't show that the last half mile of it was a deeply rutted dirt road. I drove cautiously over it, not wanting flying gravel to ding the borrowed car's paint or, worse, break an axle.

I was reminded of a conversation I'd had with old Redwine when I'd complained that the road up to his house was in a sad state of disrepair. He said the lack of maintenance was deliberate. It provided security because it would prevent intruders from making a fast getaway.

The road ended at the entry gate, which was the only visible access point in a perimeter bounded by an eight-foot-high chain-link fence topped with razor wire. Prominent signs attached to the fence warned it was electrified.

There was no signage to indicate I'd arrived at the End-Times Retreat Center.

No guard stood at the gate, and I couldn't see anyone inside. There was a squawk box atop a pole four feet above the ground about a car length in front of the gate. I pressed a red button, and the intercom speaker responded, "Welcome. State your name and your business."

I answered, "Preacher Evan Wycliff. Here to request Pastor Obadiah's guidance on a doctrinal question."

Seeking his wisdom. Appealing to his vanity. It's hardly a lie, not even a half-truth. I'm betting he won't refuse to see me. Whether I intend to follow his advice is another matter.

As the automated gate swung open, the voice came back, "Drive toward the house, and park in the holding area. Leave your vehicle unlocked with the trunk open."

The gate closed behind me as I followed instructions. A stately old clapboard house towered two hundred yards ahead, behind it a cluster of industrial-looking, steel buildings, and behind that a dense stand of trees. Inside the fence, the road was paved and smooth. A big arrow on a sign up ahead indicated a right turn into a parking lot with an adjacent guard shack constructed of aluminum and glass. As I pulled onto the concrete pad, I could see two uniformed men inside standing in front of a wall of video monitors. As I stopped and popped the trunk, one of them came forward with a long wand, which he used to scan the underside of the car. Then the other stepped to the rear of the car to peer into the trunk and finished his inspection by opening the doors on the passenger side of the sedan.

Both of the guards were white males, trim and fit with military bearing in their strides. Neither smiled nor frowned nor spoke as they checked me out.

Finally, the fellow who'd opened the door ordered curtly, "Take the path up to the house, and you'll be greeted before you get there." Then he added, unexpectedly, "Peace and blessings."

As I got out, I muttered, "Thank you, sir." It was the same reflexive response I'd have used to address a peace officer on a traffic stop.

As I walked away from them, I left the car door open, but I was glad they didn't ask for the key. And I still had my phone. Of course, I didn't know what to expect, but I hoped they wouldn't try to detain me. It occurred to me I should have notified someone I'd be going here.

The path to the house was lined with wildflowers and surrounded by a lush, manicured lawn. Sprinklers had come on in one section. About an acre was carefully maintained this way, including picnic tables and a small outdoor meeting space with a podium and mounted loudspeakers.

At the side of the house, a half-dozen children were running about and giggling on a playground as three women dressed in light-blue robes watched them.

As I strolled up the path, a tall woman dressed in an identical robe emerged from the house and approached. We met halfway between the parking lot and the house. What looked like a gracious gesture of welcome might have been a routine tactic for vetting guests before they got too close.

She was gorgeous with long, straight raven hair. No makeup, no jewelry. She reminded me of a young Cher.

Her voice was soft, but her tone lacked emotion when she said, "Reverend Wycliff, how good of you to come. I'm Ida, Pastor's assistant. I understand you request an audience."

"I'd be grateful for some time with him, if that's possible. I apologize for the short notice, but it was unavoidable."

Her face betrayed no concern. She simply asked, "Is the matter confidential?"

"Yes," I said, hoping I didn't need to invent an excuse to explain why. Finding the Osceolas was certainly urgent, but I wasn't ready to tell her why I'd come.

She turned and took my side as we walked toward the house and she asked, "Will you be joining us for the midday meal?"

"That's very kind. I'd be pleased."

She explained, "Pastor won't be available until later. Meanwhile, you can sup with us. You've not visited us before." She was the gatekeeper, and it was a statement. She would know.

"No, but I admit I've been curious."

"We hope you'll be impressed. We are so fortunate."

THE REFECTORY WAS A LARGE, converted dining room in the old house. It all seemed recently renovated, its rooms full of new furniture in colonial style, the plain upholstery fabric in the same powder blue of Ida's robe.

About thirty people of all ages were seated at two long cafeteria tables covered with blue tablecloths and rustic crockery place settings. Water glasses were full, but there was no food on the plates yet.

The others at the table looked happy and expectant. But they weren't talking among themselves. As Ida showed me to my chair at the table, she said softly, "We take our repast in silence."

There go my chances for informative chit-chat.

As I sat, faces beamed at me. I didn't think I was recognized. None of them looked familiar to me. They were all dressed in street clothes, and even the children seemed freshly scrubbed. But those faces seemed gaunt. No fat cheeks, particularly on the adults.

Four young women in those distinctive robes filed in carrying big, steaming bowls. A large pot was set beside Ida, who took her place at the head of the table where I sat. The others bowed their heads as she said grace briefly. On her other side was a stack of dinner plates. She ladled vegetable stew onto each plate, which was then passed down the table until everyone was served. The other bowls coming in from the kitchen were heaped with mashed potatoes, yams, rice, and bread. The other servers spaced them out on the tables with long spoons so that the diners could help themselves family-style.

It was an ample lunch. The vegetable stew was hearty and good. The room was warm in the summer heat, windows opened to catch a breeze. It might have more appropriately been a day for salad, beans, and hot dogs, but this crew minded not at all. The stew pot was cleared after all the plates had portions, so it was evident there would be no seconds. The diners cleaned their plates quickly and with enthusiasm, sopped what was left with bread, then passed the bowls to help themselves to generous portions of the starchy stuff.

Slices of watermelon were presented for dessert and quickly consumed.

Ida then instructed them to return to their rooms for a brief rest before the commencement of Bible class in this same room at 1 pm.

As they got up and filed out, still without a word, they flashed smiles in my direction. Even considering their silence, from their body language during the meal I sensed they were as new to this experience as I was. Serving themselves after the main course had taken some coordination. Children who seemed to need help were shushed promptly by their parents.

That left me and Ida alone in the room, and she asked, "Reverend, did you have enough to eat?"

"Oh, yes. Delicious. Thank you." I'd have felt overfed if I'd helped myself to potatoes, but I didn't mind sopping with the bread. It seemed the thing to do, all around. I risked asking, "Are these all the residents you have at the farm?"

As she got up, she replied, "Not even close. We have a school, workshops, and recreational facilities. But those are closed to outsiders. I hope you understand. We run the farm as a retreat from the cares and stresses of the world, and seeing visitors can create needless anxiety. The people who joined us here today are new arrivals. This is their first day. Their study session will be an orientation." As I rose to follow her, she said, "Pastor will see you now. He has commitments this afternoon and will address the orientation class later, but he will take time to hear you out."

IDA SHOWED me into Trusdale's study and left me there in a comfortable guest chair. The room was handsomely appointed with walnut paneling, plush carpet, and a suite of executive furniture to match the colonial décor of the house. It was as if an interior decorator had been retained to do the whole place in a single project as the final phase of the building's renovation.

Newly laid wall-to-wall carpet has a distinctive odor. So does fresh paint.

He didn't keep me waiting more than a few minutes.

The man I saw met my expectations not at all.

Somehow in my imagination I'd pictured a tall man with movie-star looks, a cracker with a veneer of intelligence and charm, the stereotype of a cunning TV evangelist who professed the need for a private jet and a mission to build hospitals to serve the poor.

This guy was downright diminutive — so thin he looked scrawny as if he were on an extended fast himself. His face was narrow, eyes piercing beneath a bushy, furrowed brow. The smile he flashed me was broad and toothy.

His complexion was neither light nor dark, and I could see what Olivia meant by his being neither white nor black — a man for all seasons, a brother of all races. His straight hair, combed straight back, was raven-dark.

His wire-rimmed glasses gave him an academic air, the devoted student of scripture.

Perhaps most striking, he was dressed in an electric-blue silk suit, dazzling white shirt, and string tie fastened with a dollar-sized blue stone.

He strode in confidently, broadcasting that smile, closing the double doors behind him.

He was a head shorter than me.

He offered his hand, and as I rose to take it, his grip was not firm. As we shook, he patted my forearm with his other hand. If I hadn't loosened my grasp, I feared he'd have pulled me into a hug.

"Reverend Wycliff," he said, "I know your work, and I commend you for enduring your trials." His voice was thin, almost tentative. I wondered how, with his small stature and his meek tone, he could command a crowd.

He was hinting he knew me by reputation. I was appalled that I didn't know of him, hadn't paid closer attention to his broadcasts. "Some things went the wrong way. Lessons learned," I said dismissively. I didn't want to be recapping my bad decisions or explaining my compulsive habits of inquiry. "Call me Evan, please. Shall I address you as Obadiah, Frank?"

His smile faltered for a second, and he beckoned me to sit back down as he took his regal place behind the enormous desk, which, unlike the rest of the furnishings, looked like a museum piece, a throne for a railroad magnate during the Gilded Age.

Seated in his enormous chair, he looked like a child king who needed a regent.

"What brings you to our ministry?" he asked politely.

"Thanks for the generous lunch, by the way. Your new guests ate eagerly."

He leaned back in his high-backed leather desk chair, smiling behind clasped, prayerful, bony hands. "They settle in quickly. This is such a haven, you see. I apologize, our time today must be short. What is your concern?"

"I caught some of your Deacon Daniel's message at the park in

Peculiar. He told them the end-times are imminent, and I wonder about your interpretation of prophecy. You're probably not aware that the *Book of Revelation* as reflected in Dante's *Divine Comedy* was the subject of my thesis in divinity school."

He chuckled, "You may have studied it as literature, as inspirational metaphor. To me and my people, it's a roadmap. I'll not reveal it to you."

He either believes this fervently or he's a salesman who intends for it to be true, even if he knows it isn't.

I hadn't studied the text enough to argue with any interpretations of his, but I had my own speech to deliver. "I think it's risky to try to be precise about any of it. You're making a very specific promise. Scripture says none of us will know when. I worry that some of my neighbors — perhaps dear friends from Evangel Baptist — will follow you blindly. And eventually regret their decisions to join you."

"I'm making no promises of my own. I preach the promises in the book. Are you saying you doubt the Word as it's been given to us?"

"You know, Frank, I visited Patmos and the cave high on the hill where they say John the Divine had visions and dictated them to a scribe. By the way, scholars don't know which one of many prophets by the name of John wrote the book. And that tourist attraction might or might not have been the actual cave. But even in the summertime, the mountain on that wind-swept island would be a forbidding place to hide out.

"So here's this mystery-man John, fleeing from the soldiers of Emperor Domitian, shivering in this damp cave, huddling against violent sea storms, his meager food sneaked to him by local partisans, and driven to vivid, hallucinatory fantasies by his terrors and suffering — if not magic mushrooms, which we know the ancients used in their temples. He probably thought the emperor then was the Antichrist. The book is so different in character from the rest of scripture. It wasn't part of the holy canon for centuries, and some sects still don't recognize it."

His jaw tensed as he recited, "Different in character? You haven't read your Bible closely. *Revelations* fulfills prophesies embedded in Isaiah 18 and 19, Ezekiel 38 and 39, Daniel, Joel, Zechariah 14, First Thessalonians 4 and 5, Matthew 24, Mark 13, and Luke 17 and 21."

I countered with, "Without looking them up, I'd say these prophesies could apply equally well to the Roman Empire or the Soviet Union or any other oppressive regime in history. At least the 16th-century sage Nostradamus came close to nailing Hitler as the future despot he named *Hister.*"

I sighed. I hadn't intended to debate him, simply open my ears, but his arrogance was annoying. "All you're telling me is that this John — who probably wasn't the man by that name who wrote the gospel — was a careful student of scripture. Those other teachings, however conflicting or confusing or obscure, no doubt informed his fantasies. It would be easy to fulfill prophesy when you're the one writing the story."

Now he was amused again, asking, "Do you know Pascal's Wager?"

This guy is full of surprises!

"So, you do know something of metaphysics. Yes, Blaise Pascal wrote a logical exercise to establish that reason can't prove or disprove the existence of God and the promise of eternal life. He poses it as a game we have no choice in playing but a bet we must make by choice. Even if chances are slim that God actually exists, we gain everything by believing. If there is no God, yet we believe, we have nothing to lose. It's used in modern decision theory by high-stakes gamblers and investment bankers. The pro athletes express it differently: *You are certain to miss a hundred percent of the shots you don't take.*"

"Then might we apply the same logic to the truth of *Revelations?*"

I wonder whether his game is chess or poker.

I admitted, "We could, and many believers do. But if believing the end-times might be tomorrow makes people sign over all their earthly property and move to this farm, they have a lot to lose if you've got it wrong."

He stood, and his gesture was polite but firm as he reopened the door. I moved past him, and he rested a hand on my shoulder, asking confidentially, "Would you say those happy people you had lunch with are losers?"

Dodging the questions, I said pleasantly, "I suppose I have a lot to learn about your ministry. Could we continue our discussion another time?"

He smiled, and his hand moved to pat me on the back, giving an insistent non-answer, "If you're willing to make the bet, I'll count you among the survivors." He added, making it seem an offhanded suggestion, "Perhaps one day you'll honor us by attending service."

I wanted to press him on it, but his hand at my back was urging me out, giving me the impression his invitation was not sincere.

As I left the room and he closed himself in, I was met right away by Ida, who approached with hands folded dutifully in front of her. She escorted me out, and I was about to step down off the porch and onto the path back to the parking lot when I turned to ask her, "Oh, I just remembered. I promised to help Talker Osceola get his truck repaired. May I have a moment with him?"

Ida flinched even more than Obadiah had when I called him Frank. Her reply was stiff. "We go only by first names here, and Talker is not known to me. I'll have to ask Pastor about him."

I winced. "Ah, it's kind of sensitive, you see. Talker promised his truck to you guys. He told them it's in good condition, but it's not. The transmission needs some expensive work. The car dealer in town is a friend and a member of my congregation, so I told Talker I'd get him a deal. Then he could get it fixed on the sly before he turns it over. He wants everybody to know he's a straight-shooter and doesn't want to be caught in a fib."

"I don't deal with these kinds of things."

"Ida, please tell me. Is Talker here? I'm really worried that if he goes back on his word to Frank there will be consequences."

I thought it was a subtle ploy. If Talker had ever worked here, I was sure she'd know. But she might not know whether he'd been involved in the accident or about the suspicious fact that the truck had been deliberately destroyed. By using Obadiah's real name, I was implying I knew about his past and his character. After all, he'd let me in, and I assumed she couldn't know what we'd discussed. And by mentioning consequences for Talker, I was playing my hunch that the pastor had a mean streak — which she'd know all too well.

I handed her my old business card from Evangel Baptist, which showed my mobile as well as the office phone.

She stared at the card as if she could read an answer there. Then she said, "We don't keep things from Pastor, but if Talker made him a promise, we should help him honor it."

"So he is here, isn't he?"

She said stiffly, "People here have no need of their cars."

She spun around, walked back into the house, and I returned unescorted to my borrowed car.

AFTER I WAS BACK to my car, I was tempted to phone Otis right away, but I didn't want those guys in the guard shack to see that I was eager to make a call. I drove away calmly, and they seemed to pay me no notice.

I was hoping on my visit to the farm I'd see Talker or at least spot his truck parked on the property. Or run across Winona and Anna. But the whole experience was designed for me to see only wide-eyed new recruits, none of whom knew any more than I did about what was about to happen to them. Ida had made the place seem like a blissful summer camp, but at best it looked to me more like a minimum-security prison.

I was suspicious that Ida didn't offer to take me on a tour and doubly concerned about the other residents in those dormitory buildings where they were isolated from outsiders.

My story to her about the truck repair was meant to prod her, but I wasn't sure how to read her reaction. I guessed she knew the truck had been destroyed and that Talker was now on the farm.

I had what I thought I needed — probable cause, a clue as to Talker's whereabouts — for Sheriff Otis.

I expected I would phone as soon as I was back on the paved road and I could pull over. But the signal strength out here was nil. Ironic that Trusdale's encampment would be a dead zone. If his wards smuggled a phone in, they wouldn't be able to call out.

I had one more card to play before I left the area. A half-mile down the dirt road on the crest of a hill where I could still see the entrance to the farm, I pulled the blue sedan over to the side of the road, got out, and raised the hood. I'd lingered about ten minutes pretending to fret over the engine compartment when a school bus lumbered down the road. As it passed me, I could see it was full of expectant parents and children — about the same number I'd seen at lunch. I didn't get a good look at the driver, but I saw he wore a headband.

The bus was unmarked, the name of the school having been painted over. In some states, I knew the law says a bus that is not being used for a licensed school must be painted some other color than the distinctive yellow-orange. This one was light blue.

Scarcely a few minutes after I saw the bus pull into the farm, here came an ATV speeding toward me. As it got close, I recognized the guys from the guard shack.

Both hopped out, approaching with officious strides. Each wore a sidearm, and I could see an assault rifle strapped to the window at the back of the cab. They were both fit, with military bearing, wearing aviator-style, mirrored glasses that obscured their facial features and expressions. Their uniforms, which had no insignia or name tags, were blue.

The taller one spoke in an even-tempered tone. "Reverend Wycliff, do you need help?" Not exactly calling me a liar, he gestured toward the open hood. "You made it out of the parking lot okay."

I lowered the hood and closed it, careful not to seem disrespectful by slamming it down. I moved toward the car door as I explained, "I got an indicator on the dash, worried it might be overheating. But I checked the hoses and the levels. It's cooled off enough by now that I guess I can make it back to get it checked."

If I'd been able to see the man's eyes behind those lenses, I'd bet they became slits. "Service station? Where?"

I was getting in as I fetched an image from memory and answered, "I saw a gas station over on the highway."

The man who'd spoken took a moment as if he were going to challenge me. "No mechanic there," he muttered.

But his partner offered, "There's a full-service place on the way to Taberville. I don't recall the name."

"Thanks," I said, closed the door, started the engine, and drove off, leaving them on the spot, staring after this suspicious character who'd shown up unannounced and might not be allowed back.

21

From the farm, I drove west, heading toward a preserve shown on GPS as the Taberville Prairie Conservation Area. The name implied it might be a good place to get a breath of fresh air and a sigh of relief for having gotten away clean from End-Times.

I wonder whether that high-tech dynamic duo can track me this far.

Despite the cold officiousness of those guards, I hadn't expected the friendly reception I'd received. Instead of hostile resistance, I'd hit a seemingly impenetrable soft wall. Trusdale was indeed a master manipulator, but the question was his own sincerity. If he were sure of his beliefs and not foisting them on his followers as a con, could he be more dangerous? The enthusiasm of those newbies at lunch was unnerving. Because of their gaunt faces and even the grayish pallor of some, I'd guess these were borderline indigent folks for whom food insecurity rather than crises of faith was their urgent need.

They'd been lured there on the promise of food, which they'd received — at least on day one. Since I hadn't been able to interview anyone who was on the inside, the nagging concern was, besides signing over their worldly assets, what would be expected of them now? As inmates in the prison system were said to be doing, were they busy as subcontracted sweat-shop labor? Or was it Bible study and prayer around the clock? Were parents caring for their children, or were the young ones segregated as on a kibbutz for indoctrination?

Or was the place a sustaining retreat for the careworn from the world, no more threatening or taxing than a summer camp?

I had some familiarity with apocalyptic church congregations, but most of it was based on articles I'd read. Despite their highly varied beliefs, predictions, and timelines, one thing they all had in common was that, if they were busy, it was in preparing, not building. They might be furiously stockpiling, but only for the short-term needs of the living. There might be future generations, but those unfortunates would be the "left behind," the unsaved whose fate would be to keep perpetuating themselves throughout the Tribulation.

A sign advised that the state-protected park was dedicated to the preservation of the prairie chicken. There was cell data service here, and I found a longer description online about protecting the endangered American burying beetle, which inters dead birds and rats and then feeds on the decomposing carcasses. These bugs are nature's literal undertakers. Living birds would, in turn, eat the carnivorous insects. Here, at least, was a cycle of life everlasting but not eternal. Both astrophysicists and Pastor Obadiah were predicting that earthly existence would have an end, even though there was a difference of millions of years in the predictions.

The vista from horizon to horizon was a grassy plain studded with wildflowers of red, yellow, and white — the Indian Paintbrush Meadow. On this weekday, mine was the only car in the lot, and I was looking forward to a stroll on a hiking trail through the damp greenery.

But I had to call the sheriff first. I reached him on his mobile. Perhaps he was running errands at the supermarket, because the background noise on his end made conversation difficult. Nevertheless, it would have been a short call anyway. He claimed that my strong hunch about Talker Osceola being on the farm based on Ida's reaction was a suggestive tip but hardly actionable evidence. He wanted a photo of the man himself. He was unimpressed that I'd seen the bus driver wearing a headband.

I knew he was reluctant to send anyone in there, so I suggested he at least put a surveillance vehicle near the entrance. He replied curtly he couldn't justify it and ended the call before I could ask whether his reasons were lack of budget or excessive fear of legal overreach.

I walked for a few minutes, but the abundance of flora also made the park a habitat for bees. Their buzzing, blending with whispers of the afternoon breeze across the prairie, should have been comforting, but it did nothing to calm the incessant buzzing in my brain. I jumped back in the car and headed for home. Before I set out, I left voicemail for Leon. Maybe he'd know what to do.

By early evening, I was home in my little hotbox with the air cranked way up against the humidity, and Leon still hadn't returned my call. I'd stopped off at a 7-Eleven on the way back and made a meal of a prepared sandwich and a Diet Coke. I'd put myself on a budget to make Leon's loan last. I'd return the nondescript car to the dealership in the morning, whereupon I planned to give in and hit him up for an advance. I could offer to do some data drilling for him, help him bore through the stack of past-due invoices on his desk. He wasn't even diligent about sending out collection letters.

I worried that some of these same folks who were in arrears could be targets for recruitment by Trusdale. Maybe I'd shared lunch at the farm with some of Zed's debtors. They'd be relying on Pastor Obadiah's promises, but if and when those promises weren't met, there would likely be no second chances.

I admit I was in a funk, discouraged I'd achieved so little. I'd expected Chet would be willing to do more based on my tip, but I didn't have the pressures of his job to contend with. He was acutely aware that whatever he did must eventually stand up in court. Watching smiling bad guys get away with it has to be more than a heartbreak for him.

What use am I now — to anyone? If I'm honest, I know only one prayer: Right here and right now, the power and the presence of God is. *I know that's not grammatical, but in what's left of my belief system, the power and the presence are one and inseparable.*

Data drilling and analysis are something I still do well. It was still early in the evening. I could stretch out and listen to the blues until I got sleepy, but I needed to undertake some task to redeem my opinion of myself.

So I opened my laptop, took out a yellow pad and a nearly dried-out BIC, and thought about the demographics of Trusdale's flock. Besides wanting to know what happened to folks who lived on the farm, an important question was how many of them he'd taken in.

The smells in Trusdale's office, combined with the newness of the décor, made me think he hadn't been in the place long, at least not long after it was redecorated. As happens with new-car smell, it can take a month or two before the synthetic materials in carpeting and foam cushions fully outgas and the odors dissipate. I remembered that Obadiah's broadcasts had stopped about six months ago. If his compound had existed before then, I think I'd have heard of it. If he'd been bringing in daily busloads of twenty or thirty for months, he could have a sizable population in there.

Working for Zip gave me access to consumer and government metadata stored in a wide variety of data warehouses, some available only to businesses by subscription. If folks were signing over their property, I could compare vehicle sales volumes, including cars and truck and vans and campers and mobile homes, in the surrounding area to averages in the wider region, even in neighboring states. Likewise sales of real property, reflected in recordation of title transfers of farms and houses. I could check rent arrearages, residence evictions, and possible decline in public school enrollment. As well, while admissions to the farm might be voluntary, any spike in the number of missing persons reports in the county would be suspicious.

I worked into the wee hours of the morning. The results became so intriguing I had no desire to sleep.

Over the last six months in St. Clair County, I had a rough estimate of the number of disappeared persons that deviated from the norm.

About five hundred.

22

I'd intended to catch at least seven hours' sleep, but only four hours after I'd gone to bed at two, here was Leon on my doorstep wanting to buy breakfast. Sometimes I think he only drops by because he's hooked on Cora's banana-walnut pancakes. Also perhaps because unannounced is the only way he can deal with the likes of me off-the-record.

I poured coffee for us, dressed quickly, and he drove me in his staff car to the C'mon. On the way, I summarized my visit to the End-Times farm, the presumed happiness of its new recruits, the surprisingly specific apocalyptic predictions of Frank J. Trusdale, and my SWAG (scientific-wild-ass-guess) that there could be as many as five hundred people living at the farm. I told him I had reasons to believe Talker Osceola was there, perhaps also his wife and daughter, but even though there was a warrant out for Talker, the sheriff was not about to go in there based on my hunch.

We were already seated in a booth with steaming mugs in front of us when I got around to asking him, "So how are you keeping busy?"

"One word," he said with a straight face. "Fentanyl."

"I thought you stuck to booze, smokes, and guns."

"Reassigned. Manpower shortages — excuse me, staff-hour limitations."

Cora waltzed back over, asked simply, "Pancakes?" We both nodded gratefully, and she breezed away.

Leon went on, "Cartels don't need to grow anything anymore or deal with anyone who does. Big Pharma's got the opioids, and the cannabis operations are or will be domestic, legal, and regulated. The shadow-market folks used to worry about black helicopters surveilling their crops. Not anymore. Fentanyl is one hundred-percent synthetic. The raw materials come in barrels of chemicals, shipped to Mexico from China into the port at Sinaloa, then by truck to factories only a few miles away. Finished product is a pill or inhaler — high-dose, small, and lightweight. Smuggling is a lot easier because sniffer dogs will miss it, and we can't inspect everything. We can't even profile the person because the poor kids they used as mules have been replaced by business travelers and airline crew."

"So what's the approach?"

He shrugged with a wan smile. "We're all data drillers now. It's also getting more challenging because a section of the Patriot Act that allowed us to comb through phone records has expired. We've still got FISA, but we're supposed to ask mother-may-I from a judge every time we want something. And like your sheriff buddy — the court can get hung up on a strict definition of probable cause, so we can't go to them on a hunch."

He's going to tell me the FBI won't go in there either.

"Leon, the skewed statistics tell me there could be hundreds of people inside the gates of the Obadiah farm, and whatever they're doing, they're anything but free to come and go."

He mused, "You can say what you want about injustices in the good ole US of A, but our cops can't make thousands of folks disappear like armies have done elsewhere. During the Cold War, more than a hundred thousand went missing in Central and South America. How much did we do as fellow Americans to stop that? From everything you've told me, this preacher knows how to operate within the law. If someone wants to sell everything they've got and check into his religious retreat, generations of presumably sane people have willingly checked themselves into convents and ashrams. If you're worried they're being duped, you'll need hard evidence at least one of them has been seriously harmed."

"I changed my opinion of our new minister. She ran into Trusdale years ago when she was in divinity school. Her evaluation of his character is short and sweet. She says he's a skunk."

"Okay, are you guessing he's a white nationalist? You discussed end-times prophesy with him. I take it you're an authority on the subject. Are his views all that extreme — considering what Evangelicals are preaching on any given Sunday?"

"He makes the case for urgency and immediacy. Jesus said, 'Take up your cross and follow me.' He meant deny yourself and your selfish ambitions. But — sell what you need to survive from day to day when you have next to nothing? Trusdale is preaching a very specific timeline. By his reckoning, it could all come down tomorrow. You can bet his followers won't be marking their calendars to test his claims. They'll take whatever he tells them as gospel."

"You said some reporter told you the people who want to be admitted have to sign contracts. Do you think you could get hold of one of those documents? As a legal transaction, the people signing over their assets should get some guarantee in return. A straight-up donation might have no strings. If you have the name of an individual, along with the terms of the contract, you could make some headway if you could prove Trusdale didn't deliver — or misrepresented. That's the only way I know to nail a cult leader for fraud."

Leon made me realize I should double back on Harry Ardmore with my presumptive evidence about how many people Trusdale has defrauded — or abused. After we'd each polished off two plates of flapjacks, I phoned the reporter while we were still sitting in the booth. I got him on the second ring, and I kept my voice low.

"Harry, I went out the farm, pastor-to-pastor, but I came back with nothing. I saw a couple dozen new recruits there, happy campers. But I didn't get a tour. When I came back, I was analyzing statistics on property sales and population, and I came up with an estimate there are several hundred people in this county who have effectively disappeared. You said they have to sign contracts. Did you ever get a look at one?"

He sounded mournful. "I want to get that from people who considered going but never went. They were told they had to sign, had to fork over their stuff. But that scared them off. They never saw the documents or the details. Hey, if I had specifics, I'd have run with the story already. If you get 'em I'd better be first on your list."

"Can you give me names? Of those intenders who didn't go?"

He drew a long breath. "I haven't found anyone yet who's been in and then come out."

I thanked him and promised to share any new developments that hadn't been shared with me in confidence.

My business has its ethics, as well, if you have to be that way!

I told Leon, "He's guessing as much as we are. He got second-hand information from intenders who didn't make the deal and opted out. No documents."

The C'mon Inn retained some of its rustic charm by providing guests with checkered-cloth napkins. Leon wiped his mouth with his and pressed his palms on the table, preparing to struggle to his feet despite the leaden repast in a tummy that was edging over his belt.

"Where are we going?" I asked him.

"I'm dropping you wherever you want to go, then I'm off

chasing bad guys. I got the check while you were flapping your gums with the yellow journalist."

"And that's all the help you can give me?"

"For now, yes." He got to his feet and straightened his tie, which was striped in red, white, and blue. He still looked every bit the G-man. Flashing smiles in Cora's direction, as soon as we were on the curb, he confided, "Two possible lines of inquiry. First, the property deed to the farm. Maybe a paper trail starts there. Second, those folks going in, these days they all have phones, probably even most of the kids. Of course he'd have to take those away. But what does he do with them? Toss 'em in the Osage River? Okay, maybe. But he's got expenses, and if he's grabbed that many, it's a sizable chunk of dough. So I'd guess he sells them in bulk, must have a deal with a broker or a fence."

"Wouldn't he make sure to nuke them first? The data might be more revealing than a paper trail."

"Sure, if he were careful, maybe he'd have the new recruit do the reset with a staff member watching before they handed the phone over. But that's giving them another chance to refuse to go along. It'd be a lot simpler to just make the folks toss their phones into a bag, like taking up a collection. Simon says, and when one of them does, probably a parent, they all follow. Then he relies on the dealer to do the erasures because otherwise the device can't be sold as refurbished."

Leon was indeed my guardian angel, which makes me sure some must be Jewish.

I asked him to drop me at Evangel Baptist. I needed to pay a call on the church secretary.

I WAS GOING to sweet-talk Lynn Olinger, who'd also worked for me back when, but Olivia was already busily working in the pastor's office, so I didn't risk going around her. I stuck my head in and told the pastor I'd been to the farm, met Trusdale, and come away with no evidence he was hurting anyone.

Then I asked, "Any church records for the Osceola family? I haven't been able to get in touch."

She sniffed. "We don't keep those kinds of records, Evan. Maybe we should, but then I'm not sure I could give them to you if we did."

"What about field trips? For any of the kids, don't we need a permission form for them to go? Those aren't personal profiles. More like need-to-know, and I bet the permission language says something about sharing the information as appropriate to ensure the personal safety of the participant. Well, the whole family is missing. They may be in danger."

Olivia invited the secretary in and explained what I needed, sparing the reasons why I should have it. As I expected, Lynn was all smiles to see me. She never did understand why I'd had to resign.

It took some digging through musty banker's boxes, but we found a folder of release forms for an outing two years ago, including parental contact information for Anna Osceola, her own phone number (which matched the one Birch gave me), and her date of birth.

Checking phone repair services, the closest to the farm was a FonesFixtFast store in Taberville.

Before I could make that trip, I had to return the Toyota sedan to Zed and reclaim the Egg from the service department. When I did, service manager Max Alumbaugh wasn't at all surprised I'd left the Fiat with him overnight for a routine oil change. Perhaps he assumed I was off on a repo mission for Zip. Nor did he push back when I asked him to put the charges on my house account. I didn't even know I had one.

23

The guy behind the counter was dressed all in black, his hoodie worn open to expose the message on his T-shirt, "Kenny has left the building." His head was shaved bald, and a footlong, black goatee dangled from his chin. Colorful tats on his hands probably extended elsewhere on his body. I had new respect for Curt Carper, who at least cared how he looked to customers.

Behind Kenny, shelves of electronic gear reminded me of Walter Engstrom's basement when he was a boy and into amateur radio. Walter was my favorite local geek, who besides being a wiz at all things electronic had been my stepson Luke's math tutor, his close friend, and for a time our handyman around the house.

This was no commercial display of phone accessories in neatly carded blister packs. Here were routers, cables, amplifiers, music keyboards, and an audio editing control panel. Cables dangled everywhere like tangled vines in a garden courtyard. He was obviously a geek who hoarded gear of all kinds, and I wondered whether Walter knew him.

My excuse to Kenny was as close to the truth as I could manage. I told him, "A young member of our church signed up for a field trip over at the End-Times Retreat Center, and she thinks she left her phone there. I called them, and they were nice enough, but they told me their lost-and-found stuff comes over here. I have her phone number." And I handed him my business card from the church with Anna's number written on it where he couldn't fail to see my reverend credentials.

My bet was, even if this guy was doing crooked deals with Trusdale, he wouldn't want to admit as much to anyone, much less a clergyman, whatever his beliefs.

His expression was dour, not about to give anything away. As he started to tap on his keyboard, he couldn't resist telling me, "We erase 'em, so the numbers don't matter. But some folks paste a sticker on the back, you know, 'If found, return to...' Now, crazy thing is, most of them use an address label they already got. And besides the home address, it's got the number of that phone on it! How lame! So if I find your phone, like, am I gonna call the number that rings it? Stupid. I log the information though. You know, law enforcement could ask. I mean, it could be reported stolen, but how am I to know?"

"All you can do," I agreed.

He chuckled, his faith in the lameness of human beings confirmed. "Aha! Here it is!" He walked over to a bin, rummaged through the contents, and returned to the counter with a smartphone. It bore not only a label with Anna's contact information on the back but also a sticker with the image of an open Bible superimposed on a glowing cross.

A look of concern crossed his face. Before I could walk out with it, he advised, "That model used, it's two hundred bucks."

I had no advance as yet from Zip. Leon's stash was dwindling, and I didn't want to fork over that much. I reached into my pocket, came out with two twenties, placed them on the counter, and said, "How about I don't tell anyone you're selling stolen property you get from Trusdale?"

As I walked out, he called after me, "You won't get shit if you don't have the unlock code!"

I was betting he wouldn't alert Trusdale's staff. If the pastor found out what he'd done, the consequences might be more painful than simply losing a client.

PERHAPS ONE DAY the police would be able to confiscate a carload of phones from the repair guy, but as of now he'd want to presume they had been surrendered voluntarily. I disliked lying to him. Sooner or later, I might be compelled to turn him in.

He was right. Without the unlock code, I wouldn't be able to retrieve data. And too many false tries and the thing would go hopelessly dead. But I had Anna's date of birth. The unlock code could have as many as six digits. She'd need to use them all, which meant preceding a single-digit day or month with a zero. But when I tried as soon as I got back in my car, entering month, day, and year that way didn't work. She might omit the zeros and add initials. But realizing she'd been sharp at science and math and also computer savvy, she'd know of foreign and scientific date formats. So trying again with preceding zeros, I entered two-digit year, month, and day.

The phone winked on then winked off.

It wouldn't power back on. The battery had given up all it had left for this brief glimpse. But in that flash, the lock screen showed a selfie.

My stomach turned. It wasn't Anna, but I knew the face. The little I knew suggested all kinds of worrisome complications.

In my imagination, I could hear the support tech's snarky voice, "Are you sure it's plugged in?" I didn't have a charger cord for this model, so I took it to Walter Engstrom's repair shop. He was supporting his new bride Leslie by operating walk-in service in town for whatever device, mechanical or electrical, might need fixing. There was no sign on the door because he didn't have a business license yet, and I prayed that when he did he wouldn't be fencing lost phones for the likes of Trusdale. But such I supposed were the risks of that business.

After I told him what happened (but not who owned the phone), Walt plugged it in, and while we waited for it to accumulate a charge, we chatted about his new life at home. I'd intended for him and Leslie to live rent-free as house sitters at the Redwine farmhouse, but they'd preferred to be off on their own. I asked him whether they'd heard from Luke and Melissa, and his news was more recent than mine. He said they'd settled, at least temporarily, on the outskirts of Boulder. That squared with what I knew. At least they hadn't taken off in some new direction. Walt confided that Luke told him Melissa had an episode in the grocery store, fell down writhing and then vomited on herself. He wasn't sure he was supposed to tell but assured me I was not to panic because it was weeks ago and she was fine now. I blamed myself for a case of parental benign neglect and resolved to call Luke sometime soon.

After several minutes on the charger, the phone still wouldn't power on. Walt said, "I fear this device is fried, sir."

"Anything you can do?"

He smiled. He had his own brand of magic. "I've got a few hacks, some could be destructive. But you'll have to leave it with me."

"Let's risk it."

I called the sheriff's office and let Deputy Crandall know that I'd found Anna's phone, and it strongly suggested she and her mother were living at the Obadiah farm. As I expected, the answer was suggestive but far from evidence of child endangerment.

I'd made the call only because discovery of the phone needed to be documented. Perhaps the sheriff would take action on it if I could get to Anna's messages.

But I had a strong suspicion who might have received them.

24

"I don't do that," Talker said flatly as Deacon Daniel pushed the handle of a shovel on him.

"Don't tell me you got a bad back," the man snarled. "You do everything else around here."

"I drive. I walk the fence. I fix what's broke. Not this."

The guy with the headband was tall and broad-shouldered. He stood a head above Daniel, who was even more slight of build than Trusdale was. Standing at the little man's side was Philip Hart, whose swarthy body also looked built for hard labor. Hart had already grabbed his shovel and was waiting for instructions.

Daniel's voice was annoying and sharp-edged. "Listen, you two. We got to put all these in the ground, and you know there's more to come. If we can't handle it, I gotta hire crew from the outside. That means more eyes to see, more mouths to talk. We're all of us in up to our necks already. There's gonna be a cash bonus for every grave we get dug. Think of it this way — how many ways do you want to split?"

Philip spoke up, keeping his voice down, even though they stood in the middle of a field that was empty — except for a dozen corpses wrapped in sheets and laid out on the ground. "Ida told us in the beginning these ones would be doing it to themselves. They're supposed to help each other get it done in time for whatever they think is coming."

Daniel turned on him. "I guess she didn't reckon you can't expect a weakling to dig a ditch. And as for giving up the ghost, maybe we got to expect some won't go all the way without help."

That stunned both of the big men. When they'd hired on, they must have assumed if there was any killing to be done, these folks would be doing it to each other.

DANIEL FOUND Ida in the crew quarters. She was folding laundry with the other women, issuing a steady stream of instructions about all aspects of housekeeping as she worked alongside them. He knew that the precision of Ida's orders wasn't just because she was picky or bossy, which was certainly true. It was all about discipline, getting them to follow her every word, no matter how trivial. Everyone, including himself, knew she spoke for Obadiah. These women were able adults, kept healthy with modest meals so they could remain helpful. All of the laundry at the farm was done by hand. They needed to keep a lot of people busy serving the people whose strength was ebbing by the day.

He grasped Ida's arm gently and led her into an empty corridor. He knew she wouldn't object. She discouraged him from speaking at all in front of the others. He resented the implication he was so rash he might blurt out some secret.

There were few windows, the building being of quickly constructed prefab metal. The light in all the rooms was garish and cold, and the temperature wasn't regulated. The place looked like a prison, and he would know. But it was better run. It still amazed him that the otherwise healthy inmates who weren't dying to get in were coming here to die.

"Pretty soon we won't have enough diggers," he told Ida quietly. "I need big guys with strong backs and endurance. I know you don't want to hire from the outside."

She was unconcerned. She always spoke as if she and Obadiah had already discussed plans for every eventuality. "Walk the dorms," she said. "Have a reason for everything you do. Some kind of inspection. Spot your candidates, then take them aside one by one. Tell them, if they do this job, they'll get hot meals — with meat." Not only was Daniel worried about ditches for more corpses, but he also wanted to get ahead of the need before winter and the ground froze.

And she was right. As the cold weather came on, few would crave a bowl of greens when it was bitterly cold outside.

He nodded in agreement, then confided, "So far, I've got a dozen stiffs stacked in a shed. All of those went without help. And none of them are children, except that stillbirth. But how do we deal with the ones who panic as they reach the end?"

"When you did time, you learned quickly which ones to be afraid of. Just make sure those guys you recruit are capable." Then she added harshly, "As you proved yourself to be."

He didn't want to be reminded. She'd always be able to hold it over him. "Talker wouldn't do it, then or now. Good thing for us I was riding with him that day. The old man wanted to brag about what he'd done, but he refused to go along with the plan. He'd started calling us a concentration camp."

"But now they want Talker for it. How about using him on the crew? Will he go along?"

"I don't think so. This guy Philip Hart did time with me, and he's a hollowed-out man. He'll live for his next meal, but his health's not too good. Talker is stubborn, and he refuses to dig, let alone be an enforcer."

She surprised him when she said, "Don't make him dig. Put him on the perimeter at night. His type won't mind the lonely work. Now that we have Winona and Anna, we've got leverage, but he won't be saving money anymore for his wife's cure. He won't be useful forever, especially after the woman expires. I haven't yet figured out how to deal with the daughter. She's sharp. I haven't yet found out what she wants so much she'll do anything to get it."

"So, if her father gets out of line, what do I do?"

"Since you torched his truck, we'll give him Anna's car, swap plates with a junker. He can run errands into Bolivar. If he thinks he's free to come and go, he will continue to believe we trust him."

"I don't understand. He could just drive off!"

"Sooner or later, he will. Then some helpful citizen will tell the sheriff they've spotted him."

"But when they pick him up, he knows too much!"

"Not if you get to him first."

25

It had been two weeks since the doctor's tragic demise. I needed a break to recharge my own batteries, and I wanted to make sure I was careful before I took the next step. I still craved Marcus Thurston's wise counsel, and hoping he'd returned from his vacation I drove over to the parsonage.

Over the years, he'd grown accustomed to my surprise visits. He even told me he rather liked seeing me show up unannounced. Other than tending to his rose garden, which he did diligently and masterfully, I had no idea how he spent his time.

Thurston was a man whose face exuded calm at the worst of times, and today he seemed downright mellow. When I remarked he looked rested, his reply was, "You look terrible."

There being no liquor in his house, we settled down in his parlor with our usual cups of steaming Folgers instant, mine extra strength, black, and with a shameless double dose of sugar.

I declined to give him a recap of my recent partial recovery from misfortunes. I told him about Gropius and Talker Osceola, along with my suspicions that Winona and Anna might be in danger. I also told him I'd had a sit-down with Olivia Bingham and developed a cautious fondness for her. That brought us to the topic he might know something about, Pastor Obadiah.

"I knew of him," Marcus said. "Never met him. To me, he was always fringe. I knew he operated a retreat, and I believe some of our folks went over to him. At one point, he claimed affiliation with the Baptists, but if he did, he was 'defellowshipped' when leadership learned he was all about the end-times. It's not like we can't preach it, but it's kind of a red flag. Folks these days seem to think even unwanted attention is better than being ignored, but there's also guilt by association. He smelled all kinds of wrong."

"Have you ever had reason to believe people who check into the farm never check out?"

"I never knew enough about it, and frankly I didn't want to know. From time to time, folks leave our flock for all kinds of reasons, particularly during Covid when you were pastor. I'm not saying it was any fault of yours, and I don't know whether anyone follows up with them. I hope they're over with the Methodists having nice picnics."

"I want the sheriff to go in there, but he refuses unless I can show him blood."

"I'm sorry to hear about Talker. He's another one I hardly knew, but as you know, Winona and Anna were with us for a while, and I believe Winona was a help to Loretta."

"Olivia knew Trusdale, years back. She told me she'd followed him for a time when she was in school in Florida. *Skunk* was the word she used."

He mused, "For her sake, I hope she didn't have a crush on him."

Whoa. I hadn't thought of that angle.

"No, on a black boyfriend who Trusdale tried to discourage from attending. That's what soured her trust in him."

He frowned. "Do you think Anna has gone missing?"

"Yes. Anna and her mother, probably right after the accident. I learned that Winona's sick with chronic lung disease. My guess is Anna took Winona to End-Times hoping Trusdale would heal her. Given that Anna is or was a science geek, I'd say Winona wanted the treatment and Anna went along with it. My fear is they were detained. I recovered Anna's phone, and if I could get it to turn on, I might get some answers. But it's dead, and I left it with Walter hoping he could fix it."

Marcus drew a deep breath, then confided, "I'm not sure what to tell you about Anna."

Until now, I'd had no clue Marcus knew her other than as a face in the congregation. I asked cautiously, "I didn't know she'd been active. Have you seen her recently?"

"It was three weeks back, before I left for Kingston. She wouldn't go to Olivia. I don't know why. She phoned to request a counseling session, which we had here. Now, you and I don't have secrets, and a meeting with me is not exactly a confessional, but counseling girls at that age, any of us would have to be careful of how it looks. The kids are calling it a post-truth world, and I expect they fib more than we ever did for all kinds of reasons. They seem to have no notions of privacy, but I sensed Anna wanted things kept confidential, and I have to respect that."

"What are you trying to tell me? I have a hunch she was involved with someone — an adult — but, as with all these things, if we go making assumptions without proof, we could bring harm to folks who've done nothing wrong."

That's as diplomatic as I can be about this. I want to tell him everything I suspect, but if I'm wrong, there will be no taking it back.

He hesitated, then said, "I'll put it this way. Yes, she was worried about her mother's health, but that's a chronic thing, not a crisis, or wasn't yet. She did say that she was worried Winona has refused to take her meds. No, the reason she came to me you might say is typical but in her case concerning. She was fretting about this boyfriend, someone she met at work…"

I finished it so he didn't have to. "And he's married, he says unhappily, and she wants to know whether she can trust him. *Trust* is their code word for sex. And because she's underage, she worries if she does trust him, he'll be in trouble if they get caught."

Thurston pursed his lips as if he wanted to smile but wouldn't let himself. "Why do you come to me, Evan? You know my coffee's terrible, but I treasure our friendship and your company. People in this town seem to think you have all the answers. And a lot of the time, I think you do, simply because in that swirling mind of yours, you'll fret for days about a question, however small, everyone else has forgotten."

"Are you saying I'm right? Is that what she told you?"

He sighed again. "As I say, your instincts are uncanny. What are you going to do?"

"I think I know who it is, but I'm far from sure."

"Please don't tell me the name, but do whatever you feel you must do."

26

I told myself I'd have to stop living on convenience-store snack food, and breakfasting on pancakes was only marginally more nutritious. I felt I hardly had the time, but I dropped into the C'mon and had Cora whip up a carryout bag for me — a freshly made tuna sandwich on whole-grain bread with lettuce and tomato, carrot and celery sticks, an apple, and a chocolate-chip cookie. I was back in grade school, and the contents of my paper sack were comfort food of a bygone age.

Handing me the bag, as if she and Marcus were linked telepathically, she offered, "You look terrible."

Eating nervously as I drove, I directed the Easter Egg back to Bolivar.

~

THIS TIME, Curt Carper was sure I was a cop. His body didn't know whether to freeze or tremble. His gulps were so frequent I was afraid he would choke.

"Curtis, we need to have a word outside. *Now.*"

In his job, I'm sure there were times he had to force his voice to sound commanding. He failed to do that now. "I…I can't leave the counter. We're short staff."

I leaned into his face and growled, "Do what you have to do or I make a call and you'll be in cuffs."

On our way out the back, he pulled the greeter I'd spoken with aside and muttered an order. We emerged from the exit door to stand by the dumpsters.

Isn't this always where the cops confront the perps in a crime movie?

I began with, "I recovered Anna's phone. Besides seeing your handsome face on the lock screen, it was interesting reading."

As far as I knew, the phone was still lying dead on a table in Walt's shop.

His voice quavered, "Are you a cop?"

"I work with the authorities from time to time." That was the truth. Impersonating an officer is a crime, but it's fair to say I'm a private investigator without portfolio.

"We haven't done it," he insisted, "if that's what you want to know."

I wanted the whole story, but I doubted he'd give it, and I had more urgent concerns. "When she quit, where did she go?"

"She was going to take her mother to that preacher's place over to Taberville. She wanted me to go with her, but it's impossible. I told her it was a lame idea, but she said she was just going take her and come back. She wanted me there as a witness in case she had to sign something."

"So did she make it back?"

His eyes narrowed as suspicion clouded his face and he stopped shaking. "You don't have her phone," he grumbled. "You'd know if you did."

"What would I know?"

"Listen," he said and he began to sound downright cocky, "if you're not a cop, I don't owe you any explanations. I warned her those folks are crazy up there. No, I don't know whether she's back. If you did have the phone, you'd know the last texts I had from her were, 'puke in a bag,' 'vomit up demons,' and 'no food.' Don't you think I'm worried about her?"

I leaned into his face again, saying, "Curt, my boy, I'm going to believe — because I sincerely want to believe — that you haven't raped a minor. And I'm not going to worry, for now, that you don't have the required paperwork for Anna's employment. But you're telling me she's in serious trouble, and if you want me on your side, you're going to come with me now and help me find her."

He choked, "I have responsibilities."

"Yes, son. You sure do."

HE DID hand me his phone so I could see the message thread. Perhaps having grown wary after our first meeting at the store, he'd deleted all her earlier messages.

Yes, she was starving, and she didn't think she was ever getting out of there.

When I'd impulsively enlisted Carper's aid, I'd had no action plan, which pros like Otis and Leon would have thought foolish. But here was one of the few people in the world, perhaps the only one, who wanted to find Anna as much as I did. That determined motivation was our only edge.

As I drove, he busied himself with sending text messages, presumably to cover his ass for leaving his job so abruptly. I hadn't learned enough about him to know whether he also needed to leave excuses for his wife. I don't know why I knew he had one. Marcus hadn't disputed my guess, but he hadn't confirmed it either.

He broke the ice with, "Where did you get such an ugly car?"

That was when I knew we might be less than enemies. "One type of investigation I do is track down folks who've skipped on their auto loans. The dealer lets me use this little Fiat because he's never managed to sell it." I didn't offer how much I loved this car and all it had come to stand for.

Now that Trusdale had met me, the color and make of my car wouldn't matter. It was entirely possible I wouldn't be allowed back under any circumstances. But I'd gamble that his ego still wanted to score. How many people, especially clergymen, dared challenge him in debate these days — and on his favorite topic?

I asked Curt, "What was Anna's relationship with her father?"

"She told me he wasn't around much, and it had been that way for years. She knew he'd see her mother every now and then, mostly when she wasn't there. Once she had work, she got her own place. She figured he gave Winona some money. They got government checks, but not enough even for that crappy trailer she lives in. Me, I never met either of them. Anna was sure they wouldn't approve."

"A fair assumption. Are you in love with her?"

"What am I supposed to say?"

"I don't know. Whatever pops into that empty head of yours."

"Yeah," he sighed. "Believe me, I wish I wasn't."

"Forgive me, but it's only big words come to mind. Forbearance, restraint, prudence, judgment, morality. Should I go on?"

"My mother was her age when she had me. She said it was a mistake. How would that make you feel? But I figured if she could've done otherwise, she would've. Nowadays, she'd pop a pill and it would be done. No sin, no Curtis."

I'm not about to speculate with him that his soul might have chosen another body. I'm not sure about that one myself.

I'd drafted Curt for this mission on impulse. I hoped Trusdale would let me back in, if only out of curiosity. Most of our discussion had centered on theology, so perhaps he considered me a hopeless intellectual. Their seeing the Eggmobile coming this time might not seem a threat.

My intention was to gain an audience with the preacher then

introduce Curt as someone who cared sincerely about Anna's welfare.

The pastor's vanity may prove his undoing.

Before we arrived at the farm, my only coaching to Curt was, "I'm going to talk our way into seeing Trusdale. Don't say anything to him until I introduce you. Then say whatever pops into your head."

"I don't understand."

"That's the plan."

27

My distinctive vehicle proved once again to be a stellar calling card at End-Times. Maybe the guards ran my plates on seeing it, or Trusdale's staff had researched my reputation after my first visit. Everyone in Appleton City knows my car.

As before, Ida escorted us into the house and directly into Trusdale's office. I introduced Curt to her only by his first name, remarking he was a friend who'd told me he greatly admired Pastor Obadiah. A sparkle in the young man's eye on seeing her betrayed his healthy appetites. She was undoubtedly aware but remained impassive.

An exception to the routine this time was that Ida promptly relieved us of our phones. I remembered the service was dead here, but so much for recording anything.

Trusdale waltzed in, dressed exactly as he had been before, as was Ida. He didn't extend a hand and sat regally in his chair. Exuding pleasantness, he asked me, "Reverend, who have you brought me?"

I replied, "This is my friend Curtis. He's a deeply troubled man.

He admires you, I know. We've come because he's had a recurring dream. He's worried it's a vision, a revelation. He came to me for guidance. He is sure his vision is a sign, but he has no idea what it means or what he is expected to do about it."

Trusdale nodded. "Visions can be powerful messages, of course."

Curt wasn't sure whether this was his cue, but I held up a cautioning hand before I let him speak, explaining, "In his dream, he sees his girlfriend, the love of his life. She's gone missing, and he doesn't know how to reach her. The vision is, he sees her on her knees in prayer as she vomits into a paper sack. She's starving, and he watches in horror as her body shrivels until it's a bag of bones."

Trusdale now glared at Curt, and I turned my gaze on him as well. This was his moment, and his voice quavered, "She tells me there's no food."

The pastor nodded, and here came the characteristic gesture of pressing the fingertips of prayerful hands to his lips. "And you find this vision disturbing?"

"Yes," Curt insisted, "I worry she's trying to tell me she's in trouble."

Trusdale looked up with an expression of calm reassurance. "My son, on the contrary, this vision is a gift of hope. May I know the name of this sweetheart of yours?"

"Anna. Anna Osceola. She's the one who told me about you, about your ministry."

Trusdale stiffened slightly. "Ah."

Trusdale knows the name!

Then he said, "The message is that Anna has undertaken a cleanse. She is purging demons from her body. Fasting cleanses the soul."

I asked, "Is the message literal or symbolic?"

Trusdale replied sternly, "Our rituals are known to the elect." And he wouldn't say more.

What did I expect? He needs to tell us she's not starving herself to death.

Curt asked urgently, "Is she here?"

Trusdale's hesitation perhaps was meant to convey his respect for the confidentiality of his wards. He said finally, "As I believe Ida may have told you, we go only by first names here. I believe I know the young woman you speak of. Let's do this. I ask you to wait while I inquire whether the girl wishes to see you. If she's willing, I will show her in, and she can put your fears at rest. But I must ask you to respect her decisions, whatever they may be. You are not to challenge her. I must believe in your sincerity — as I know Reverend Wycliff does — which is why I trust you have not come to lead her astray."

I affirmed, "It would be a blessing to Curtis, Pastor, to know she is content in her commitment."

Trusdale pounded his desk once then stood up and walked out.

No sooner had he left than Curt demanded, "I thought you said we'd come to get her out!"

"He's not about to let her go. And you can bet she will tell us she is safe."

"Then what's the plan?"

"We're making it up as we go along."

We waited for about ten minutes. Curt tried to sit still but occasionally wriggled nervously in his chair. I wondered whether he was still suspicious I'd turn him in for molesting a minor. But my guess was that if he thought he'd abused her he wouldn't be going along with this.

When the office door opened again, Trusdale entered with Anna on his arm. She was wearing one of those blue robes, this one perhaps two sizes too big for her because she had to lift the hem as she walked. She was stooped. The slippers on her feet shuffled along the carpet. He pulled up a guest chair for her, which he positioned, not alongside ours, but beside the desk, facing us. She was on his side, after all.

The girl was slight of build like her mother, which made it difficult to know if she'd grown frail. She had her father's straight, jet-black hair and dark eyes with an intense gaze. She smiled faintly at us as she sat, a look of recognition passing between her and Curt. I wondered whether she remembered me.

As Trusdale took his seat, he advised, "Understand, a cleanse may seem to weaken the body, but it strengthens the soul. Anna has been making great progress here." He gestured to her. "Please tell them, Aiyanna."

He's using her indigenous name as if it's a term of endearment. How well does he know her?

She said, "Don't worry about me, Curtis. Pastor Obadiah is doing God's work. All of us here are blessed."

I said, "Anna, I'm Reverend Wycliff. I used to be pastor of Evangel Baptist."

"I know," she said simply.

"Did you bring your mother here to be healed?"

Anna looked over to her pastor for approval, he nodded, and she stated, "Yes, she's here."

"And your father?"

She was studying him again, and the slightest smirk must have signaled her. "No, I haven't seen him. They tell me he's left us."

I asked her, "Do you know where Talker has gone? His friend Birch is worried about him."

Her look tells me she knows her father and Birch are not close friends.

Trusdale was obviously uncomfortable with this line of questioning. She shook her head. "My dad didn't want us to come. He wanted to take Mama to the doctor, but she refused to go. She wanted to come here, and I'm helping her."

There was resentment in Curt's voice as he asked her, "So are

146

you ever coming back? You told me we have to break up, Anna. No reason. That hurt. You quit your job, makes no sense. You don't look sorry."

Her eyes watered as she told him, "This isn't the place for you, Curtis. Stay away. People here are on a chosen path, and it's not yours. We're not meant to be together. I see that now."

Curt swallowed hard. He could think of nothing more to say.

Anna was about to say more, but Trusdale interrupted her. "Anna, thank you for sharing your faith with us. That's enough. This must be tiring for you." He crossed over to help her up and showed her the door, where Ida met her and led her away. She didn't look back.

Trusdale remained standing by the open door as he addressed me tersely, "Wycliff, we don't do this. We needn't justify ourselves to anyone. Our people renounce the world to come here, and they remain committed. Please tell anyone who asks." Then to the young man he said, "Curtis, it's obvious Anna knows you well enough to say you don't belong here. I will pray for you, as I know she will. One day, in the fullness of time, you may be ready. We would welcome you then."

He waved us out the door, and Ida escorted us back to my car, where she returned our phones, adding softly to me so Curt couldn't hear, "Pastor invites you to return this evening at seven. Without your friend. You may attend service, and we're sure many of your questions will be answered."

One of those questions would be whether Talker is still around. But I simply smiled and nodded, stunned that after witnessing Anna's situation they'd have the nerve to welcome me back.

I drove Curt back to his car in the lot at the superstore. He sulked the whole way. Eventually, he asked me, "Are they holding her there? She wasn't into that stuff before."

"My guess is she took Winona to the farm intending to sign her in but not necessarily to stay herself. I was betting Pastor Obadiah would let us see her to prove he's not abusing anybody. But seeing Anna proves that those messages you got were for real. She's being forced to puke. He's calling it a fast, but they're starving her."

"But she insists she wants to stay!"

"We didn't ask to see Winona. She's too sick, and I'm sure they'd refuse. Our visit couldn't seem like a confrontation. Curt, all I can do here is guess. Trusdale could get Anna to say anything if he threatened her mother — whether or not Anna believes he has healing powers, which I suspect she doesn't. Winona has refused medical treatment, which is also consistent with Trusdale's teachings. Talker Osceola is a mystery man. From Ida's hints, he may have worked on the farm. But he might not still be there."

"So what was the point? It's unbearable seeing her like that. Can't the police get her?"

"Until now, the authorities haven't been interested. It's a religious facility, and presumably the followers are there voluntarily — even if they're harming themselves." We pulled up to his car, and Curt was about to get out. "I know you have to get home. Maybe Anna's right. She might not have been telling the truth about wanting to stay, but I'd say she was serious about not wanting you to go in after her. She worries you could get trapped. I'm sure she cares about you more than you think."

"You took me away from my job for this? Okay, I know she's alive. Maybe she cares about me, maybe not. But what's the plan? Didn't we make it worse for her by going in there?"

"Sheriff Otis told me if I can bring him proof, he'll do something. If you go with me tomorrow to his office, we can both swear out affidavits about what we saw today. That's evidence from credible witnesses. We've also got those messages on your phone."

I wasn't about to tell Curt I'd be going back to the farm tonight. My guess was Trusdale's ego would make him think he could turn me into an ally. At the least he'd be showing off his bag of tricks to a colleague.

I could have driven Curt directly over to see Deputy Crandall. I debated whether to force him, in effect, to go on the record about all we'd witnessed. But I knew he had responsibilities. He'd willingly given me his cooperation today, and I wanted to be fair.

Another reason to hold off was that by morning, if I survived the night, I might have more information about what's really going on at End-Times.

I gave Curt my business card and promised to call him the next day.

I worried leaving him then might be a mistake, but I'd asked a lot of him today. He had a lot to lose, more to think about.

Besides, before I could take Curtis to see the sheriff I was eager to see Pastor Obadiah's magic show firsthand.

28

Ida glowered at Frank and demanded, "What are we going to do about this girl?"

Trusdale replied, "Which girl?" as if he didn't know.

"The new little hottie who's asking all the questions. The one you're lusting after."

He was offended, beyond annoyed. "I'm as celibate as you are, and you know it."

It angered her that he could be so dismissive, especially when she felt she knew she could read every thought before it crossed his mind. "We may be righteous, but you're impotent, and I'm simply disgusted."

"Keep your voice down!" he snapped, although he'd had his office door carefully soundproofed.

Ida insisted, "Anna Osceola is not a believer, and she's underage — so there's no informed consent. She's precocious and shows signs of being difficult. She'd expected to leave, but now she's staying and pretending to be cooperative. I think it's because she's waiting to see what we do or don't do for her mother."

"Winona is weak and visibly ill. We can use it to set an example. We'll shoot her up with a dose of adrenalin before the healing ceremony, and the change will be remarkable. Later, when she expires on her own, her fasting will be an inspiration for the others."

"And how do you expect Anna to react? You won't be convincing her."

"The girl will participate in the healing. She won't refuse for her mother's sake. That's why she brought her here, isn't it? Then afterward, when she sees her mother go downhill, we may have to take steps."

"We said we'd never have to go there."

"We adapt to survive, my dear." Then he cautioned, "We'll have to keep Talker away from both of them, of course."

"He never knew they were here. He drove off in that car. I told you, but you were in one of your moods."

Trusdale was dumbfounded. "He's *gone?* What if he does something stupid?"

"He knew why Daniel had to torch his truck, but he wasn't happy about it. We let him have Anna's car because it was his anyway, and that shut him up. He came and went by the back gate. He was restricted to the crew barracks and the building with the nonbelievers. He wouldn't let go of what happened to Gropius, worried he'd go to jail."

"So what's to keep him from going to the authorities?"

"Who's going to defend him — or back up his story? That guy wants to get as far away from here as possible. His kind will end up taking some no-account job in a slaughterhouse, and then he'll drink himself to death."

"Send Daniel after him."

She nodded. "As you wish." Then she reminded him, "You had me tell Reverend Wycliff he could attend service tonight."

"Oh, yes. The congregation is to be Faithful and Repentants only. We do Winona, give the preacher a show he won't forget. You know how to coach Anna. How about Winona? Will she be ready?"

"That poor woman doesn't know what day it is."

29

From the outside, the End-Times sanctuary building looked like a warehouse or an airplane hangar. It was all corrugated steel, shiny and glinting in the moonlight. As Ida escorted me, the jubilant song of the choir and thunderous organ music could be heard from a distance. Inside, by contrast, the décor was elaborate and elegant. The walls were draped in bold tapestries, and the elevated proscenium stage was ringed with scrolled gilt appointments. A cross at center stage in the narthex was two stories high.

Contrasting with the richness of the expansive room was its austere seating, row upon row of varnished wooden benches. I guessed the capacity was several hundred, and every row was filled with excited worshippers. Before we'd entered, Ida had asked me to take off my suit coat and tie, which I carried over my arm. Now I saw the reason. The men had all been issued clean, white long-sleeved dress shirts. The women wore simple white shifts that came down below their knees. I realized there were no children.

Dazzling theatrical lighting, which flickered and played over not only the stage but also the audience, made the throng of faithful gyrating to the music seem like a single organism.

Anna wasn't with us. Ida found us a place in the audience center front, which was occupied, but on seeing her in her distinctive blue robe, congregants wriggled and scooted along the bench to create enough space for us to sit.

The choir was likewise dressed in long, flowing blue robes. There must have been fifty of them and, like the attendees, consisted of men and women of mixed races. I didn't recognize the music. It wasn't a traditional hymn.

We praise the Maker.
We hail the creation.
But more glory than this
Awaits us, the chosen!

The message was simple, repeated with myriad variations and counterpoints. I flashed on the memory of my grade-school teacher demanding I write some punitive phrase a thousand times.

I saw no organist or choirmaster. Instead, from my vantage point I could see an enormous digital control board in the wings. And seated there wearing a headset and orchestrating it all was the tech wiz proprietor of FonesFixtFast, Kenny.

The singing reached crescendo and concluded with an *Amen,* repeated for emphasis.

The enormous cross was suspended directly above the choir, the singers standing on risers. Then the group parted in the middle, moving to either side, as if to make way in the center.

Just then, the cross burst into flames!

The flames jetted out, the effect explosive and brief, then quickly extinguished. The lingering image of a smoking cross and the strong scent of burnt cedar were as chilling as the fire had been searing — I could feel the heat on my face.

Before the aftereffect had subsided, at the foot of the cross and from beneath the stage floor, Pastor Obadiah was raised up in a silky robe of midnight blue and gold, speckled with sequins that reflected the intense spotlight like a field of stars. He stood with outstretched arms bestowing his blessing on the multitude.

The worshippers had been obviously disciplined. There was no shouting, no applause. Some couldn't help emitting amazed moans and ahs.

Obadiah stepped forward and began to speak in low, resonant tones. His amplified voice, no doubt accentuated with reverb by the tech at the board, echoed through the hall from an array of giant loudspeakers.

Whether by then I was in a trance or simply bewildered, I couldn't report his message verbatim, but I was surprised by its conventionality. He repeated the end-times prophesies from the *Book of Revelation*, emphasizing that the Savior's appearance and deliverance could happen at any time. Tomorrow, tonight, in the next breath.

What I didn't hear — and perhaps omitted for my benefit — was any instruction as to what these worshippers were expected to do at the farm. There was no railing against the evils of medication. No admonitions about fasting or starvation. No orders to work or even to pray.

Moreover, there was nothing in Obadiah's preaching that could be considered political or disruptive. There were no calls to action.

Fasting wasn't mentioned. Healing was to be the order of the day.

At the conclusion of his sermon, Obadiah folded his hands in front of him and bowed his head. That was the cue for the choir to stand and sing "Shall We Gather at the River?" I knew that one. But in Trusdale's plan, the river was Styx, not Jordan.

The congregants were not invited to sing. They were enthralled. To me, their passivity was remarkable.

Throughout the song, Pastor Obadiah remained standing center-stage, head bowed. On the last chorus, from the wings came Anna, now dressed in a blue robe identical to Ida's, struggling to stand tall and pushing a wheelchair, in which Winona sat, clothed all in white. A green oxygen bottle was affixed to the back of the chair, a clear plastic tube feeding the gas to a nose clip on Winona.

On their entrance, a blazing follow-spotlight hit Winona, and the effect was blinding. She winced, closing her eyes shut in the glare.

The look on Anna's face was blank. I feared she'd been drugged.

As the chair drew close to Obadiah, he reached out to take Winona's hand. He announced, "Our sister, Winona, has suffered much. A crushing, debilitating disease has been her cross to bear. Her every breath is a struggle for life! It is time for her to lay her burden down." Then to her, he asked, "My sister, do you wish to be healed?"

She croaked, her voice cracking from congestion, "Yes."

"Do you believe you can be healed?"

"Yes, Pastor."

"Do you renounce Satan and all his works?"

"I do."

"Will you from now and ever afterward trust and obey?"

"Yes, I will!"

Notable to me, Obadiah didn't conduct this as a rite of salvation. Either he knew Winona had been baptized already or he feared he might blaspheme, as if fake healing wasn't enough.

Keeping hold of her right hand with his left, Obadiah rested his right hand on her head.

"It is done!" he shouted, leading to the most spectacular special effect I'd ever seen take place. I'd resolved to be an objective observer here, fully aware that Obadiah might resort to tricks of illusion. But this was so sudden, so real. Bass tremolo echoed through the hall, penetrating every chest, momentarily halting each breath. Billows of steam jetted from the floor.

The simultaneous vision must've been some kind of golden holography. The pastor and his penitent were bathed in a glowing cocoon of light and sparks. No sooner had this miracle manifested than the cross burst into flames again.

Grasping both of Winona's hands firmly, he stood her up slowly from the chair.

What happened next seemed like a vivid hallucination. But I'd been given no drug, and I can't imagine how it was induced. A pair of translucent lions appeared, one on either side of Obadiah. The beasts stood in unison, rested their forepaws on the preacher's shoulders, reared their heads, and roared!

The vision couldn't have been mine alone because the crowd reacted to the sight and gasped collectively as the kingly animals bestowed their blessing.

Then in an instant, the magical beings were gone, but unreal effects persisted. As Winona stood proudly before her healer, both still surrounded by golden light, electric bolts shot into her from the pastor's hands. Her body convulsed as ripples of current appeared to flow through it. She ripped the oxygen tube from her face and beamed at the exultant Obadiah.

The dazzling, supernatural effects faded, and the flames on the cross were extinguished, once again leaving the crucifix smoking ominously.

As soon as the smoke appeared, all light in the hall was doused, bathing us in total darkness. Colorful afterimages of the scene throbbed in my eyeballs. A physical curtain dropped quickly to obscure the stage. Then soft floodlights above the exit doors winked on, which the congregants took as their signal to quietly get up and leave.

As we filed out, soft organ music played another tune I didn't recognize — except to know it was a lullaby.

~

As we walked out, Ida saw the tears glistening on my face. She no doubt assumed I'd been transported by the experience. I wasn't about to tell her why I was moved. I gave her a smile and let her speak first as I donned my coat.

"He has the gift," she pronounced.

No doubt of that! The most talented revival preacher I'd ever met had sold encyclopedias door-to-door, and working as a car salesman would be a more useful credential than a degree in theology. But this?

I fought the strong temptation to ask, *How did he do that?* Stunned as I was, I needed her to believe that I believed an experience that was beyond belief. I said, "I hope the Reverend won't think me rude. I'd like to go home now." She hadn't made a move to detain me, but I wanted to get off the property because I still feared I might be entrapped.

She smiled back. "Of course." Simple as that. She added, "Pastor is understandably exhausted. If you have questions or concerns, it will be best to schedule an audience for another day."

She didn't escort me back to my car, perhaps because she regarded me as an insider now. Letting me think I was free to go could give me the impression others could leave if they chose. She turned and moved away, joining a group of worshippers who must've been headed toward the dormitories. She merged with them, took hold of hands on either side of her, and walked into the night. The compound was not well lit, except for narrow pathways, one leading back to the main house and the other to a group of outbuildings, also constructed of corrugated steel, a hundred yards in the distance.

A flock of white shirts moving in the moonlight might be a flock of seabirds — or a convocation of ghosts — one more reason for them to believe they are living in a miracle.

I knew why the emotion had welled up in me. The sanctuary

reminded me of my Shining Waters Temple. And the healing ceremony had been eerily similar to a milestone event in that other church that had changed my life, for better and then for worse. My wife Loretta had been recovering from brain damage she'd suffered in an auto accident. Her doctors had told me she might never recover from the coma. I'd spent hours at her bedside, praying and watching her breathe on a ventilator. I sang to her quietly. I even wore an unlaundered sweatshirt in the faint hope she could at least sense my presence by my body odor.

She'd not only awakened eventually, but from that moment her rehabilitation had been rapid, culminating in that Sunday morning when, on the dais at Shining Waters and in front of a broadcast television audience, she'd stood up from her wheelchair and walked over to join me at the pulpit. Until that moment, I hadn't seen her walk since the day of the accident. Her standing hadn't been rehearsed. I had no idea she wanted to surprise me, much less create a media sensation.

My joy was countered by unintended consequences. Suddenly, I had a reputation as a faith healer. I refuted the rumor in my sermons and in public announcements. The voicemail greeting on our church phone and an auto-response to email had to carry my assurance that I believe in the power of prayer but that the power was not mine.

It occurred to me that Obadiah knew details of my past and had tailored the experience tonight for my attention, to trigger my reaction. He'd also know what provocative messages to leave out of his sermon, lest I return home with evidence of his fostering abuse.

Anna might have been punking Curt with those messages from her phone, but I doubted it. Even now, I wondered how much she'd bought into Trusdale's scheme, whatever it was.

All along, I'd wanted to think the best of Pastor Obadiah. If indeed his wards had come to no harm, and his Christian message was sincere, how was he to be faulted? I disagreed with his interpretation of scripture, but he wouldn't be the first evangelist to engage in sensational showmanship to achieve a sincere result. His faith healing might be unethical in my view, but I doubted anything I'd seen tonight was illegal.

There was nothing in tonight's experience that I could use to convince the sheriff to take action. I still had no clues as to Talker's whereabouts. And although I'd hoped Anna had been prevented from leaving, her part in the ceremony suggested she was now a willing participant, at least for now, in whatever cure Obadiah would claim to have worked.

I couldn't prove anyone was being harmed. On the contrary, I'd witnessed new arrivals being fed when I had lunch there, and the attendees in the sanctuary tonight were subdued in their demeanor but looked otherwise healthy.

I came away with the impression that Kenny could do a lot more than fix phones. He may have been the one to design the multimedia effects, supply the equipment, and rig the hall.

But that golden cocoon wasn't merely rockstar show-tour special effects. Enveloped in light, Winona's body had rippled and undulated in ways no physical form could.

And those lions! The scene was an icon come to life. Through the ages, rampant lions on crests had conveyed divine power on kings through history — earthly kings. Angels with wings might seem unworldly, but those beasts crowned rulers.

I was reminded of Gropius telling me I could no longer believe anything I saw.

30

Lemuel Grady was an old hermit who lived in a shanty on land that bordered the Obadiah farm. What he encountered one morning affected everything that happened next. Lemuel was a squatter whose earthly wealth was tied up in a small herd of goats. During the night, a windstorm had knocked his improvised residence over, and come daybreak he resolved to seek a new location. He owned a pup tent, but he'd preferred the only slightly more spacious confines of the wooden shanty, which had once served as a farmer's toolshed.

With the tent and his one pot fastened to his backpack, Lemuel unhitched his goats and proceeded to explore the surrounding countryside.

The storm had also uprooted a long-dead oak tree, which was so rotten it was ready to topple over. In its descent, it smashed a section of the electrified fence surrounding Trusdale's compound. The farm crew had shut off the electricity to prevent fires, but they'd not yet ventured out to repair the fence. Lemuel and his goats marched right through.

He ventured into a grove of trees, so thick it might be regarded as a small forest, which he remarked to himself could be a lovely, shaded place to make his new home.

Chasing an errant goat who'd strayed from the rest, Lemuel came upon a disturbing sight. From a distance, he thought he saw a man who was leaning against a tree, perhaps napping in the morning sun. On coming closer, he realized it was a frail man, even older than himself. He'd been lashed to the tree with a rope.

And on being approached, the bound man heard the sound, his head bobbed up, and he snorted. The man was apparently too weak to speak and could only whimper piteously.

Lemuel took his tin cup from his belt, ran after his straying female goat, milked her, and returned to the fellow with a generous offering of warm milk.

The fellow gulped it down, drew a breath, and after a few more heaves exclaimed, "God help us!"

And scanning the horizon, the goatherd could see a dozen other people of all ages, dressed in tatters, milling about, appearing dazed from starvation.

As Lemuel freed the old man from his bonds, the fellow began to sob, taking in sorrowful gasps. He couldn't manage to say more, but he pointed at the ground not ten feet from where he was standing.

Lemuel squinted in the shade at a human hand protruding from the freshly dug earth.

The hand was small. A child's. It was bony, the flesh having been desiccated and then picked over by scavenging creatures. A delicate forefinger pointed skyward. Lemuel doubled over and threw up the goat milk he'd had for his own breakfast.

With the fellow's arm slung over his shoulder for support, Lemuel marched the fellow to the nearest road, which was about a half-mile off. They stood there until they could flag down a passing truck. They hitched a ride to a gas station, where Lemuel asked the attendant to make a call for the benefit of his ailing friend.

Deputy Crandall picked up.

31

Harry Ardmore had the story before I did, though I didn't know how. On getting the news when the reporter phoned me, I tried to call Curt but got a recording that the number was no longer in service. I tried the main number for the AllUNeed superstore and was informed by a young female voice (not Anna's) that Curtis Carper no longer worked there.

When I pressed on by asking about Anna Osceola, the name must have already been erased from their system. More information could not be provided, per company policy.

So much for fairness. Assuming the best in people might be a worthy attitude for a minister, but not for an investigator.

That morning, squad cars pulled into the End-Times compound, preceded by an armored van carrying a SWAT team from the Missouri State Police. Ambulances were dispatched soon afterward. They were not met with resistance, armed or otherwise.

The other people who'd been bound and some who were dazed and wandering about were seen by paramedics then loaded into ambulances. The police had cordoned off the main entrance, but the perimeter of the compound was so extensive that some staff and residents took the opportunity to flee. Buildings were searched, and no weapons were found other than the few in the guard shack. The SWAT team was sent home.

The coroner's team arrived and exhumed the baby's corpse. They found the body of a woman, presumably its mother, in the same shallow grave.

Frank Trusdale and his staff offered no resistance and no explanations. He, Ida, the security guys from the guard shack, and a dozen other people, who seemed to be staff rather than residents, were taken into custody. Talker Osceola was not among them, and neither was the fellow who called himself Deacon Daniel.

Searches of the dormitory buildings turned up more than a hundred people, all of them passive, not apparently sick, and none who demanded to be rescued. The size of this group would account for the people I saw in the sanctuary. None would respond to questions or offer information. The authorities must have decided the well-being and security of the residents couldn't be assured if they were allowed to stay. So buses were brought in to transport them to a local school gymnasium, which was rapidly set up as a shelter, as would have been done to house local residents who were fleeing wildfires or storms. Those emergency operations included both professional and volunteer caregivers, along with beds, packaged meals, and triage.

Two-dozen people were liberated from the farm's infirmary, including Anna and Winona. Far from having been miraculously healed, the mother was judged to be so ill she was transported in an ambulance to the Myerson Clinic, which maintains a state-subsidized ER. The sick people who'd been wandering around in the forest were also taken to Myerson for triage before placement in protective custody.

If Obadiah had claimed to heal any of these, including Winona, their isolation in the clinic could have prevented the others from learning they were sick as ever. When those sick ones were taken into custody, questions about the presence of medical staff at the farm were met with shrugs, and no one could be identified as a caregiver. They were cooperative about being led away, but despite their weakened condition, they were also refusing to eat, and none of them, some too weak to answer but others defiant, were reluctant to respond to questions about what had happened there.

So, many had fled, many who seemed healthy were bussed away to a shelter, and a smaller number of sick ones were taken into protective custody to receive medical attention. Crucial questions remained. *How many are there in the ground? And who put them there?*

Not having a vehicle but having been assessed by paramedics on the scene not to be ill or incapacitated, Anna was asked where she preferred to be taken, and she asked for me.

32

Ardmore broke the story just before noon on the day of the discovery, and it was on news media worldwide by midafternoon. Because the forensics team was only beginning to dig, the bodies of the child and its mother — and the condition of the unfortunate wanderers in the woods — were the only findings included in news reports.

Those facts were sensational enough for breaking news. But then like a hail of locusts, the misinformation and gossip rained down on our little community. The most sensational of these alleged that a religious cult had buried a baby they'd sacrificed in a Satanic ritual, resurrecting a persistent conspiracy theory that dates back at least as far as the Roman Empire. Other, more topical speculations for the present day held that the End-Times Retreat Center, using religious conservatism only as a cover story, was an underground abortion clinic.

Another story alleged that the farm was a secret internment camp run by communists, operated as a model for widespread persecutions to come by the censorship-industrial complex, culminating in the eventual imprisonment of freedom-loving dissidents.

Frank J. Trusdale's infamous past was also dug up, and accusations of being a charlatan and con man were inevitable conclusions of those stories, probably true, even though on scant evidence as yet. Based on my brief experience with him, I still wondered whether he might actually believe he was John the Baptist — and whether he thought faith healing was among his divine gifts.

Feature stories on evening news reports — along with posts on alternative-press websites — surveyed the history of scandals about cult-personality televangelists. Unaccountably, my short history with the Shining Waters ministry didn't make it into the list of usual suspects. Admittedly, I was a little fish in that big pond, a minnow among whales. I never bought a private jet for myself, nor did I try to justify why God's messenger would need one.

More than one opinion piece urged increased oversight of religious orders by the government, including registration beyond the usual applications for nonprofit status. Others took the view that fusing church and state would bring on a better world in which such flagrant abuses by outliers would be impossible.

By the next morning, prominent church leaders were pushing back: "Don't blame Christians — fundamentalists especially — just because some of us are so zealous we're driven to excesses. All the sensational speculation is fake news (true enough)." Authorities no doubt wished there was nothing more to see here. According to the favorable opinions, most God-fearing people were responsible citizens, even though during the last two generations they'd been forced to take firm stands on political issues.

Of course, Trusdale lawyered up right away. So far, he, Ida, and the others were persons of interest, being asked questions in depositions. But whatever the questions or answers might have been, the authorities made no announcements and conducted no press briefings. News coverage speculated endlessly about the identity of the baby and its mother, the circumstances of their deaths, and the urgent question of whether other people were in jeopardy and more bodies would be found.

Most surprising to me — and potentially disturbing — was the stand taken by state Lt. Gov. Stuart Shackleton, who was quick to rise to Trusdale's defense, which would become a recurring political theme in connection with the controversy. Shackleton's innocent-until-proven-guilty message about the pastor was wise enough, but he followed it in the next breath with the notion that secular authorities had no right to place any limitations whatever on religious practices and free speech.

The irony of a conservative politician arguing fervently for separation of church and state seemed lost on everyone but me.

33

My first duty was to the Osceola family, which was how I'd wandered into this veil of tears. My unofficial assignment was to find Talker, but so far I'd failed. Winona seemed beyond my help, except in my prayers. Perhaps I could give Anna the support no one else would.

The morning of the discoveries at the farm — after the cops had taken over the scene but before it was breaking news — I had Anna under my wing, and I took her where we could get comfort food, attended by the angel Coralie. As I sat across from Anna in a booth at the C'mon, I watched her struggle to spoon chicken soup past her nervous lips. I flashed on the factoid I'd read that the soup's main healing property was its high salt content, not the chicken grease. But no one ever beamed thankfully at Mother over a bowl of steaming brine.

The cops had wanted Anna processed through social services, but I played the reverend card. I pray it will keep on working. I'll try to get her whatever help she needs.

Anna had remained sullen and quiet, which was not the behavior

I expected from such a bright teenager. I resisted the impulse to cross-examine her. I wanted her to speak first, when she was ready, if she ever would be. She finished the soup, childishly sucking down the noodles on the bottom by tipping up the bowl to her lips then licking it gratefully. As she ate and relaxation showed in her face, I tried not to stare. I went through three mugs of doubly fortified coffee. It was dawning on me that these past few days had been an emotional strain on me as well, although nothing like what she'd experienced. But as I sipped, I cataloged muscle aches all over, the most aggravating being the chronic pain in my back, which had flared up from sitting during those long car trips. I resolved that on my next trips I would pull the car over from time to time, get out, and stretch.

But I give myself a lot of advice I don't take.

She finally asked, "Can we go see Mother?"

You see? The miracle of chicken soup. In the next generation, vegans can make miso the standard.

"Sure, Anna. You know they've got her over at Myerson, and she's in good hands."

"They have to get her to take her meds. The doctor gave her three different ones for the lung congestion. But Pastor told her medicine is poison. She wouldn't take them. Before we left home, I bought her an oxygen concentrator. She used that. I guess no one turns down their next breath. They took it away but gave her oxygen for the ceremony. She still believes him, even though she got worse after he worked his miracle."

Trusdale wouldn't be alone in preaching against medicine. That wouldn't be a crime unless Winona had asked to take her prescribed medication and he'd withheld it.

I asked quickly, "So until you found out his healing didn't work on your mother, did you think he was a fake?"

She smirked. "What do you think?"

"I don't believe in supernatural miracles, but I have to admit the vision of your mother's healing was like nothing I ever saw or imagined. Do you know how it's done?"

Her smirk became a frown. "Look, the first thing you lose there is curiosity. People who ask questions, people who complain, people who won't believe — they disappear."

"Where? How?"

"If I'd asked, would I be here to tell you?"

I'd been worried she'd bought into Trusdale's ministry. A hopeful clue was her interest in science, but the clippings I'd seen were from two years ago. Then, when I'd see her push that wheelchair across the stage, I feared she'd been won over.

I phrased my question as a statement. "You took her there hoping he could help her…"

"No!" she insisted. "I took her to the farm to get her out of that stinking shack and because it's the only place she would go. Yes, she was sure he could heal her, which is crap, of course. Could her faith do it even if he can't? You tell me. My plan was I'd take her there and leave. Then I'd come back in a couple of weeks, and if she showed no improvement, I'd pull her out of there. Then maybe she'd let me take her to the doctor. Or the hospital."

"But then they didn't let you go. Either of you."

She muttered, "Yes, the place is a prison, but it's fear that keeps you in there."

"How do they do that? Abuse? Torture?"

She shook her head defiantly.

I have so many questions, but if I pester her, she might shut down.

Perhaps neither of us knew much about what went on in the deeper circles of that hell. I asked, "How many do you think were in there?" I'd seen the people in the worship service — but were there others? I'd guess there could have been a lot more.

She answered frankly, "I really don't know. You see, there are levels in the place. The new people get fed. But after you start fasting, they put you in another building, and the new folks don't see you or what goes on."

"Are you saying some fasted until they starved to death?"

"I really don't know."

I was aware from what Ardmore had told me that an investigation was underway at the compound. I worried about what we might know by sundown. I'd been ready to believe that Pastor Obadiah's program was what it appeared to be on my first visit — a restorative retreat, a haven offering hope for the disadvantaged.

She's saying the disobedient ones "disappear." What I'd hope would be misguided sincerity must be deliberate evil. To what end? To rob folks of their phones and used cars? I still don't understand. But now investigators besides me are asking questions. Perhaps all I can still hope to do is help the Osceolas.

I asked cautiously, "What happened to your dad? Was he trying to help your mother? Was he working at the farm?"

She gave me a wan smile, which might have been broader if she hadn't been so weak. "Talker? I never knew any man who said so little. He was all about money. He'd take any job. They said he was at the farm, yeah. I don't know what he did." She looked down as she spat out, "I never saw him."

"Why didn't he offer to take your mom to Obadiah?"

"He doesn't believe any of that. He wanted her to take her meds. When she refused, he'd be furious. He wouldn't yell, wouldn't hit her, just drive off in his truck."

So, if Talker's working for Trusdale, he's not among the faithful. There has to be a deal, and it's certain to involve money. Most likely money then threats. Having Winona and Anna there would give Trusdale leverage — that is, if Talker cared at all about his family.

"Anna, everyone needs to know, who gave the orders in there?"

She sniffled and I handed her a paper napkin. "Ida, Daniel. Any of those women in blue robes. I didn't get their names. They'd speak to you quietly, like it was a secret, like this was something you were supposed to know. It was creepy."

Talker wasn't giving orders. That was something. "It sounds like your dad isn't a believer."

"I didn't tell him I was going to take Mom there. I took her because she wanted to go. I was sure he wouldn't allow it."

"When you took Winona, did you know he was working there?"

"The first day we were there, I saw his truck. I asked Ida about it, and she gave me attitude. She has that look like she might hit you, but she never does. At least, I didn't see her hurt anyone."

"Where is he now?"

"No idea. You ask a lot of questions. What's it to you?"

"I expect you know your father may have been involved in a traffic accident. I saw it. A man died."

She didn't react to the news, demanding instead, "They took my phone and my car. They got to give 'em back."

I assured her, "I'll ask the sheriff what can be done."

I asked her if she wanted more to eat, and she said not now. I'd take her to Myerson as promised. Before we got up to leave, I had to ask, "When we saw you there, it was a big risk for the pastor. How did he keep you from saying more?"

"He said if I didn't behave, my Mom would suffer."

I'd reached a dead end, but I had to ask, "How about Curtis? Can he help you now?"

She grinned. "The guy's a coward, but I'm glad they didn't try to keep him there."

Maybe she doesn't know he took off. Now's not the time to tell her.

34

Sheriff Chester Otis disliked going in front of the cameras. They say the TV image adds weight. He felt that his girth and bulk added authority to in-person confrontations, but he feared pictures made him look oafish, and closeups emphasized his double chin and broad nose. He was happiest sitting at his desk or behind the wheel of his Crown Vic Interceptor. Today, as the news crew was about to signal he was on the air, he tugged at his belt buckle to center it, straightened his tie, and quickly mopped the sweat from his forehead with his sleeve.

When the tiny red lights of the cameras winked on, he reported concisely, and toward the end of his speech he struggled to keep emotion out of his voice.

He told the world what had transpired at the End-Times Retreat Center that morning. People who needed medical care were in protective custody in treatment facilities. Some said they'd been fasting as they prepared to meet Jesus. Those who still refused to eat would not be force-fed, but they would be given as much medical assistance as they requested and the law allowed.

No cache of weapons had been found on the compound, as

law-enforcement had feared. Nevertheless, an FBI team had joined the investigation.

Inspection of the property by the forensics team had discovered patches of disturbed earth that appeared to be multiple mass graves. Bodies were beginning to be exhumed, and a temporary mortuary facility had been set up on the property.

Some corpses were in advanced states of decomposition. DNA testing would be undertaken to identify those individuals. The coroner's office had created a website where relatives of missing persons could register to provide their own tissue samples for matching, as well as to be notified of results, which would take time for laboratory analysis.

DNA might spare the trauma of having to inspect the remains of loved ones, especially since positive identification on viewing fragmentary remains might be impossible, as well as traumatic for the loved ones.

Preliminary findings indicated the bodies had been interred without personal artifacts, most without clothing. There were no items of jewelry, watches, or wallets that might help to identify the owners.

Finally, before ending the briefing, Otis cleared his throat to say, "The deceased appear to include men, women...and children. Autopsies are being conducted. The medical examiner has yet to advise on causes of death."

Once again, he gave a web address, superimposed in text at the bottom of the screen. Perhaps unnecessarily, he concluded by saying no further details could be released at this time.

TV NEWS SERVICES and Internet video feeds showed scenes of crews in hazmat suits digging to exhume bodies. Either the cameras weren't allowed closer or the footage was edited for sensitivity. No corpses — only body bags — appeared in the shots.

Trusdale's defense team was led by Bertram Harrison, the same attorney who had defended Stuart Shackleton in the Father Coyle murder case. Harrison stood in front of cameras to say, "For two years now, Pastor Obadiah has provided the End-Times Retreat Center as a haven for the disadvantaged and the oppressed. People of all ages and walks of life have gone there voluntarily, drawn to his message of hope and redemption. Yes, there was fasting and prayer and Bible study. People who requested food and medical attention received it. No one has ever been coerced to do anything. Furthermore, about the recovery of deceased persons — sadly, a female resident died in childbirth and the infant soon afterward. If there was any misdemeanor here, it was failure to obtain a permit for human burial. As for Obadiah, if he is guilty of anything, it's preaching the gospel with passion and conviction to anyone who will listen."

Responding to the obvious questions about mass graves, Harrison insisted, "We have no comment at this time other than to assert that everything that transpired at End-Times was voluntary. There was no coercion, no abuse."

The attorney wouldn't say more. Moments after the conference, social media posts were claiming that news of mass graves was a hoax. The scenes of exhumation were faked.

As I SAT in the diner with Anna, I caught the news on my phone with audio feed to my earbuds. As shocking details emerged, I tried to keep a reassuring look on my face for her sake.

For now, I decided to keep the news to myself. I could report what I'd learned to the authorities, beginning with the sheriff. But the digging, exhumations, and forensic examinations were underway. The coroner's teams would need no assistance from me. As of now, I could only offer suspicions. I hadn't witnessed any crime. Anna would need to be deposed by the investigators, but I took it on myself to make sure she gained physical, if not emotional, strength first.

When I'd picked Anna up from the farm, I met Deputy Crandall. They let Anna leave with me because she'd requested it and also because I played the reverend card as a legitimate caregiver. The officer cautioned me that Anna would have to come in for questioning the next day. And if she showed signs of trauma, she would have to be remanded into protective custody. I didn't want that for her.

Anna had said she wanted to see her mother. While we sat in the diner, she used my phone to call the nurse's station at Myerson. They informed her that Winona was on a respirator, having been placed in a drug-induced coma. Brief visitations were permitted, but the patient would not be aware.

As for me, I didn't want to be the one to take the girl to Myerson. At one time, I'd undergone what I thought was unnecessary treatment there. The hospital administration in those days was downright crooked, and I'd been taken there against my will and sedated to keep me quiet about my dogged attempts to expose a crime. After that distressing episode, I met my ward Luke, who was under treatment in the mental health wing because he said he heard voices.

Then Loretta was a patient there for months after an auto accident. Her coma had been long-lasting, and the prognosis had not been hopeful. That she recovered — completely, regaining glowing health — was a miracle.

So Myerson was not a happy place for me, even though prayers were answered and healing had taken place there. When I was pastor of Evangel during Covid, I went there routinely on compassionate visitations, including that time Stuart Shackleton's wife Ann had a near-death experience and then awoke suddenly minutes after she'd flatlined from a heart attack.

I explained to Anna, "You know, a drug-induced coma is likely to be controllable. The doctors put you under to give your body a deep and profound rest. Then they bring you out of it chemically, after your vital signs have improved. It's rather like putting you under and then bringing you back with anesthesia for surgery."

Anna needed a change of clothes and a place to stay. I called Reverend Bingham, explained the situation, and asked her to help. She was full of questions about the news reports, but I explained I couldn't talk. She'd known Anna briefly about a year ago, before the girl had left the congregation. So one might say Olivia was her pastor. I recalled that, when the woman who would become my wife lived in the trailer Olivia calls home now, for a time Loretta's sister Melissa stayed with her. I was hoping Anna could bunk there, at least until we could sort things out for her. The main worry was Winona's health and the state of her family.

Anna's reaction to staying with Olivia was blank. She said only, "I need my phone."

35

Walter's shop was within walking distance, and I figured the stroll would be good for her. I had her take my arm in case she faltered. All she had on were a T-shirt, shorts, and flip-flops, and I worried she might slip in those sandals. She didn't exude strength yet, but she was improving.

Walt had done his magic with the phone. When he handed it to her courteously, she grabbed it and immediately gave it a series of taps.

I asked, "Are you letting Curtis know you're okay?"

She snapped back at me as she tapped, "No, I'm deleting all his messages."

I wish she hadn't done that!

I shouldn't have taken her directly to Walt's for the phone. Because I had the password, I could have gone there on the sly and examined it first. Notions of privacy be damned. But I'd been exhausted.

Before we left the shop, I asked Walt, trying to make it sound offhand, "Say, do you happen to know the guy who runs FonesFixt-Fast over in Taberville?"

"Sure. Kenny Pulaski — an alternative thinker, if he thinks at all. Why'd you want to take your business there?"

Anna had already stomped out of the store and was on her phone outside when I confided to Walt, "He's the one who had Anna's phone. I'll need you to help me put him out of business."

On my friend's startled expression, I hurried out.

Seeing me, she quickly ended the call. I actually hoped she'd called Curtis. Maybe he'd texted her his new number. She needed a friend.

By now, it was early evening. I drove Anna over to Olivia's and dropped her off. I stayed in the car, and when I saw the front door open, I waved and drove off. Bingham might think me rude, but I couldn't deal with her questions now. No doubt she'd quiz Anna, but I hoped she'd be kind and let the girl sleep.

I drove back to my trailer, took a bit more than the recommended dose of a combo painkiller-and-sleeping-aid, and flopped onto my cot.

Especially for someone who grappled with spiritual matters on a daily basis, the question of why bad things happen to good people was recurring and persistent. But here were essentially good people who'd marched into that farm voluntarily and apparently made deliberate decisions to bring evil treatment on themselves.

And on their children!

How could atrocities be committed without coercion? On my meeting Trusdale, he'd seemed charming, no doubt overbearing, but hardly crazed.

If only Talker could be found!

I SLEPT through to daybreak the next day. I was beset by lucid dreams, which woke me multiple times, then moments later I couldn't remember any of it. I prayed for guidance, and I expected Leon Weiss, wise brother of my departed love Naomi, to be the living soul sent to give it.

36

The morning after the discoveries at the farm, even before my eyes were fully open and I'd had my first cup of coffee, I exchanged brief messages with Leon. He'd always advised these were to be brief, lacking in investigative or personal details:

Headed this way?

At this moment. We could wish for a different reason

Crave your help

To this, he offered no reply. Like a soldier down on the battle-field, I'd have to try to calm my breathing and wait.

I also wanted to find out from the sheriff if he'd made any progress tracking down Anna's father. Perhaps Chet would tell me if there was also a warrant for Deacon Daniel and whether the investigators had gotten anything out of Ida.

My call to the sheriff's personal phone got a recording that the mailbox was full. Hardly a surprise. He'd wish it stayed that way. When I called his office, Deputy Crandall was far from friendly. Also no surprise. She'd be new to this level of stress — unless she had a fraught personal history. I needed to get to know her better.

But now that it was an official investigation, she wouldn't be giving out information that wasn't contained in the department's press releases.

In our brief conversation, I asked whether they'd questioned the preacher known as Deacon Daniel if they were holding him or would be going after him if they weren't. She wouldn't confirm or deny. She thanked me for my help and promised to make a note of it.

Anna would need her car back. I asked the deputy whether any vehicles from the farm had been impounded. I could only describe it as a gray Honda hatchback. I was advised it wasn't a match for any of the vehicles impounded from the farm. Crandall told me Anna should file an auto theft report, but the girl couldn't remember the plate number. She did know the car was registered in her father's name.

As with the phones, Trusdale would need to spin those cars for cash, but when I searched auto broker databases and new registrations, I couldn't find any transactions that matched.

37

The used-car angle was frustrating. Zip told me he wasn't aware of unusual volume in the market, which in any case was glutted with defaults and repos due to Covid. He remarked that, for older cars, the catalytic converters might be worth more as spare parts than the car itself. And a junkyard — rather, an auto recycling center — might not be too diligent about transfer paperwork. He reminded me that, if I had the plate or the VIN from Anna's car, I should be able to run the traces myself.

I asked him for a loaner for Anna, and he teased me with sincerity that I was overdrawn at his favor bank.

Then there was the question of real estate property transfers.

My go-to person for all such matters was Jeremy Bailey, the attorney in Butler who was handling Bob Taggart's estate. I was executor of the bitterly disputed will, and the case was still pending in court. Even though Jeremy's fees were guaranteed from the probate escrow account, my own pro bono credit line with him was also seriously overdrawn.

He'd heard the news reports of the early discoveries at End-

Times. "I hope you're not involved with this guy," he said when I got him on the phone.

I told him, believing it was mostly truthful, "One of the affected families, including at least two of the victims, are members of our church. There's a teenage daughter, Anna, whose health may not be in jeopardy, but her mother is seriously ill. They've put her in Myerson. The sheriff released the girl to me at her request, and I prevailed on our new Pastor Bingham to see to her care. I expect Anna will be a material witness to whatever went on there. But she was such a new resident at the farm that she might not have been aware of the full extent of any crimes."

"Does she need my help? Or did you call for advice on improving your golf score?"

Bailey was a workaholic with one vice. When he finally retired, if he ever did, his lovely wife Marcella, who worked as his assistant in the office, would not be any happier. Despite his devotion to her, she'd finally be a full-time golf widow.

I told him, "Before they discovered those bodies, I went in there and met with Pastor Obadiah, who is one Frank Jeremiah Trusdale, a faith healer who tells his followers to fast but maybe starve to their deaths. He's saying the Second Coming will be any day. The authorities are holding him, but this is reminding me why I kept digging into the reasons for Bob Taggart's suicide. Seems to me driving someone to end it all is as sinful as murder."

"Yes, Evan. But the law isn't written that way. And what little I know about this situation tells me, even if Jesus doesn't show up tomorrow, we're in for a perfect storm in the courts. How is this preacher liable if he tells people to jump off bridges but doesn't push them? What if he's not even on the scene when they expire? If he's got deep pockets and can mount a sophisticated defense, whatever charges they bring against him could take years to litigate. And even then, he might skate."

"Before any of this, I'd urged Chet Otis to go in there. He

refused. Private property and hands off religion. But I also got the notion his superiors didn't want him nosing around in there. It was general knowledge Obadiah's foundation was making political contributions. Big ones."

My friend mused, "Covering his ass, no doubt, for a day like today. Thinks he's clever. If he shames those guys, they'll bite back."

"There's a rumor he made his followers divest themselves of their assets and donate the proceeds. Many of those people probably don't have much, maybe a used vehicle. But if any of them had houses or land, shouldn't there be a record?"

"Of course. There will be a title transfer. Those are public records. Haven't you looked?"

"Yes, whatever I could find online. But you need parcel numbers and such. I couldn't find a way to search for recent transactions in a general area."

"The recordation of the deed might lag by a month or two — overworked bureaucracy, you know. In my limited experience, if you need quick answers, someone has to go to the clerk's office and paw through the paper files."

I scoffed. "I'm working another angle. We don't have much time. They can't hold Trusdale forever if they can't charge him with something."

Jeremy agreed, "If he's cunning, it will all have been deniable and hands-off. Nonprofit corporations with only law offices for addresses and blind trusts."

"Following the paper trail — isn't that your second-favorite sport?"

He was not amused but didn't refuse to help.

38

Gropius, Talker, Daniel, and Trusdale were connected by secrets and lies, I was sure. I had a mental picture of their network but no idea where to look for the connections. Officially, I had no responsibilities. My role had always been the guy who cared when no one else did, who nosed around when no one else dared. Now that investigators were on the case, perhaps I should stand aside, retiring from an assignment I'd never been given. Oh, the moral obligations persisted. I'd never gotten back to Birch, and I was ashamed I had no news to give him.

Anna was with Olivia now and for the time being might not need her car. She could easily walk over and borrow mine, but I feared its distinctive appearance might make her a target if anyone intended to follow me. When the young woman felt better, she'd need to either go back to her job or finish school. I didn't know, but I expected that Curtis Carper was long gone by now. Anna probably cared enough about him not to press charges for harassment or statutory rape, but he might not know her well enough to be sure of that. I wondered what reason he'd give his wife why he had to quit his job and they needed to move.

Why hasn't she asked about her car? She seemed worried enough about it before.

~

I NERVOUSLY AWAITED the sound of Leon's car pulling up outside my trailer. But when you were under this much stress and facing terrors — known and unknown — waiting was agony.

Harkening back to the notion of the fallen warrior, I was frozen by the fear I'd been a coward. It might have been bold to throw Curtis in front of Trusdale. I'd concocted that useful lie about the young man's having visions of Anna's suffering, thinking I might fool the charlatan as I had Churpov when I convinced the gangster he'd crossed Satan and would suffer hellfire. Trusdale had taken the dare and produced Anna, cocksure that she'd lie for him, but then, having summoned her, I'd had no plan. I'd hoped she'd blurt out some evidence. Trusdale was gambling she would continue to cooperate.

Could I have whisked her away? No chance. Did my stunt endanger her further? Almost surely.

I wanted to retire to my cot with Jack Daniels, but I couldn't scrape up enough cash to buy a bottle.

Who will buy my next meal? Zip or Leon. Or Cora. No worries. I'm ashamed to pray for it. Mere mortals will provide, and I'm still ashamed.

After all my fretting, it was only midday, and I was still on my cot with no plan. Knowing full well I couldn't opt out of the solution to my problems, as I closed my eyes, I prayed my world would heal itself as I slept.

She's not a dream, not a vision. Here's Naomi again.

"You're a mess," she said flatly. "The last time you were this desperate, I sent my brother. Now it's like he's your patron saint. Don't expect miracles from him. He's as human as you are. You just don't know him well enough to doubt him."

I propped myself up in the bed.

"Aren't you going to take my side? Isn't love still possible in the dimension you're floating around in?"

"More than ever," she insisted, "but you're the one who preaches God's work should surely be our own. You know, that sermon about our hands belonging to the Holy Spirit? You've given it more than once, and I know you believed it at the time."

"Naomi, my dear, my endless love, and you know I care for Loretta no less, but both of you are out of reach, out of touch, and I'm human enough to miss the comforts of the flesh. Who cares, now that there's an evil army marshaling on the horizon, whether I'm in the fight? If tomorrow Trusdale should die in jail, what in the scheme of things would change? I know there are larger forces at work. Maybe they are unstoppable. History is unfolding again, and soon there will be some other worldwide sickness we must endure. Will it take a generation or more to put it right? Or are things never right and peacetime is simply an era of mass denial?"

"What do you think?"

"Oh, you're a shrink now?"

"There are facts. And there are suppositions. Is discovering evil some revelation? The question for you, as it is every day you draw breath, is how should *you* act? What must *you* do? Not because you are powerful, but because you serve."

I took a long, deep breath. I was no longer sleepy. At this point, if I'd had that bottle, I'd have downed a double shot, waited to feel the flush in my face, and then had another.

I confessed in my timid voice, "You know, there are times I doubt the soul exists. Apart from the psychophysical self, that is. From the earliest dawning of consciousness as a toddler, we ask ourselves, *Who am I?* And we ask it over and over, every day of our little lives. The soul, the identity, the essence of the person, isn't it simply the sum total of the answers we give ourselves?

"It's not a constant. It changes every day, sometimes every moment. I'm good at softball. I suck at math. I want sex. I eat the wrong things. I sing in the shower. I never have enough money. I crave the whole bag of sour-cream-and-onion potato chips. When I die, when I'm presumably where you are — if you exist anywhere but in my perishable brain — the organism that thinks I am, along with its opinions and its behaviors will no longer exist. Will I see you in heaven? The *you* and the *I* are defined here — what if there's no *us* there — or no *there* there?"

"Oh my, you're so clever," she sniffed. "Are you done?"

"No. I have all kinds of new opinions about myself. I never wanted to be pastor of Evangel. I took the job because Marcus wanted to retire and asked me. It was Covid. I was needed. I did more counseling and visitations during that time than he ever had to do, bless him. I let my vanity get the best of me by undertaking the Shining Waters ministry, and I got sucked right into shame and scandal. I tried to be a husband to Loretta and make a family with two disturbed kids we sheltered, and all that fell apart, leaving a pile of useless good intentions. I expect there are many people in this town — members of our church among them — who think I must be an embittered man. Every dog needs a job, but this time I'm chasing a beast that could eat me for a snack."

"Is that who you are? An embittered man? And is that what you want to do? Bark and bark and bark at the vicious predators until you're exhausted?"

"No," I said. I could deny it all, but I had nothing to affirm.

She sighed as if summoning a fresh reserve of patience. "Evan, you can doubt your faith all day long, but it's one of the few teachings that offer hope. That's why it endures. You know you will die. You may even think you deserve to die. But from that place, in that dark night of the soul, you ask, and it is done. You're never alone, never helpless."

In the space of a breath, she was gone, and I heard the sweet sound of tires on gravel.

39

Leon asked, "Thin skin, Evan? Strong stomach?"

"What do you mean?"

"When you were pastor of Evangel during Covid, you must've seen a lot."

He might think those experiences of visiting the sick and officiating at funerals were grim, but they weren't.

"No, I never had to identify a corpse — except the time I found Bob Taggart shot dead in that cornfield. Yeah, I retched, but it was before breakfast. And except for the bloodstain on his shirt, he looked like he was sleeping. Then there was that time I tried to visit Ann Shackleton and got there presumably too late after her heart attack — only to find out she'd miraculously recovered! I officiated at funerals, but the ceremony was only open-casket if the under-taker could make them presentable — pancake makeup, of course, and if they wore eyeglasses, that helps."

Leon was driving, and we were on our way to End-Times. He handed me a "Consultant Contractor" badge, advising, "You look, you listen, and you say as little as possible."

"What if someone asks me?"

"You say, 'It'll be in my report,' and you walk away."

"Can you tell me what the nature of your assignment is? I'm glad to have you on the job, but are you still with the Feds? What's their interest here?"

Is he FBI or ATF or some other three-letter agency? He won't say.

We were pulling past the guard shack at the farm. Leon had flashed his badge at the gate. He said only, "We'll recap what I can share with you on our way out."

WITH THE EXCEPTION of sleepless nights watching my wife Loretta lost in a coma in the ICU, what came next had been the worst experience of my life. As Leon seemed to think, my visiting the sick and the dying during Covid should've made me less squeamish. But in all those situations, my mission was to offer hope, even if I didn't feel it myself on that particular day. The mission was the message, the essence of faith's practical purpose, not to edify the spirit but simply to sustain the mortal being from one day to the next.

Here, I could find no hope and could see no point. A small army of gravediggers in hazmat suits flailed at the ground with shovels — busily but gingerly, lest their blades not sever the limbs of the corpses and thereby disrupt the chain of evidence. Defiling the dead might be a concern, but the agents of decay were busy reclaiming the Earth's molecules.

Leon gave me a handkerchief soaked with essential oil to put over my nose and mouth. It did little to stifle the stench but offered a slight distraction to the senses. I had to walk away, bend down, and retch twice, as I'd done on seeing Bob. Most of the deceased (dare I call them victims?) had been wrapped in sheets and so were not recognizable even as human. The sight of so many half-length and even shorter parcels triggered horrific thoughts and shudders.

Leon told me, from the evidence so far, none had been interred for longer than a few months, but already the advanced decomposition would make bodies difficult or impossible for their relatives to identify. DNA matching might spare the necessity of viewing but would take time in each case.

Working in teams of twos and threes to support the burden, a crew would lift a corpse onto a wheeled cart then promptly jostle it to slip a heavyweight body bag over. A large tent set up on the edge of the site served as a makeshift morgue, and after inspection and recordkeeping, the remains would be loaded into a refrigerated semitrailer truck, one of three parked around the perimeter.

The care and the slowness of the process made the scene look ceremonial. My mind flashed on my preoccupation with *The Divine Comedy* when I was in seminary. Despite the ugliness Dante pretended to have witnessed, I never got the sense that his reactions were visceral. These were my neighbors — perhaps even some from my congregation — being wrenched from the earth. I had always believed that the body — whether thrown in the ground, meticulously preserved, or burnt to an ash — is a useless husk. Resurrection of the body — if indeed the result is in any way physical — must work on less perishable stuff. Otherwise, too many of our deserving forebears would stand no chance of an afterlife.

Leon told me two-dozen bodies had been disinterred so far. The crew had been working for only three days, and the extent of the field of mass graves was as yet unknown.

We'd been observing the activity for about ten minutes, which seemed like hours. We had both seen enough, although what Leon expected us to discover was unclear to me. I admit I had been curious and certainly worried, but those emotions now seemed like childish naivety.

As we strode away briskly and got upwind, Leon let his makeshift mask fall to say, "It's a fresh crew this morning. These guys are National Guard. Ops thought they'd save budget by rounding up day workers each morning — you know, the ones who wait outside the building supply store? But after only one day onsite, not only won't they come back, they've passed the word to their buddies no one should do it at any price. And it's not just the nastiness of it all. Also, they share the superstition that disturbing someone's eternal rest will jeopardize their own. Or invite angry ghosts into this life."

I shook my head. "I couldn't begin to imagine this."

He turned decisively in my direction. "Having you here as a consultant is no joke. This investigation has to go in all directions — and it's bound to be a clusterfuck of local, state, and federal. But you'd be the expert on some of the most urgent questions. Why did they do it? Oh, we get what he preached, what he told them. But why so many and why now? Did they lay down their lives willingly with their eyes wide shut? Did he make them do it or are there killers on his staff? Or did the suicidal ones first kill any who hesitated?"

"Causes of death might not be all one thing. I'd bet some bought the message and some didn't. But Trusdale couldn't risk letting any get away. So that means either murder or assisted suicide, probably both."

"Are there members of your church who would submit to this willingly?"

"I didn't know the Osceolas, but from what Anna told me, her mother wanted to come here to be healed. Obadiah had a reputation. But if some came here for that, they might not have expected they'd be committing to stay. Or to die."

"Leon said, "I never understood Evangelicals. Now, not at all. I always figured they were as political as anything, and at least those motivations could be understandable. But this... This is off the charts."

"I didn't recognize any of them when I sat down with those new folks at lunch. And then there was that crowd in Peculiar, the poor folk that character Deacon Daniel was trying to recruit. If I was to profile them, I might generalize and say homeless and hungry. I'd guess many of them expected their worries could be over. Then maybe work detail, like they'd be expected to do in a shelter."

"So don't you think they were buying the end-times story?"

"I had two meetings with Trusdale, then they let me attend an evening service. At no time did I hear him preach starvation. I get he was careful what he said around me. Some of his followers must've bought into the end-times story, but what effect did they have on any who didn't? Trusdale had a scheme here, a structure, and I'd say once you cleared admissions here, you were effectively in prison, whether you knew it or not. You know, Pastor Bingham told me she'd attended Trusdale's rallies when she was a theology student. But even as impressionable as she was, it didn't take her long to see through him. No doubt he's upped his game since then, refined his techniques. My main question — even after I've talked with him — is what he believes in his own heart. As a faith healer, he's a fake. But if he doesn't believe his own message, what's he doing here? Something on this scale is a helluva risk. How much money could he hope to rake in?" I finally asked Leon, "You haven't told me what you're doing here. You gave me some hints, but how can I help? You're still a G-man, right?"

"I'm still on that side of things, Evan. We were actually expecting we'd find an outbuilding full of weapons. That'd give us something to charge him with right away. Otherwise, unless the medical examiner says some of these folks were murdered, there might not be sufficient grounds for any jurisdiction to hold him."

"We could understand him better if he had earthly ambitions. Money and power."

"The disturbing part is what we *didn't* find, or haven't so far. Obviously, those folks in the ground were never meant to join some militia. That small security staff might be armed, but they aren't potential combatants. So far, the employees from outside all say they thought this place was some kind of rest home. If Trusdale insists all he did was preach, if he never laid a hand on anyone or so much as ordered goons to do them in, I worry he won't be held accountable. Isn't he a terrorist?"

Leon shook his head. "Domestic terrorism law is still practically nonexistent. And who did he threaten?"

"The punishment might not be nearly enough, but maybe they can charge him with fraud. He took everything those people had. Most of them were poor, but maybe some had serious assets. I've got a guy looking into property transfers."

40

Leon disappeared again like a wild animal slipping back into the jungle. He wouldn't tell me where he would be staying or whether he was staying at all. If the investigation found no illegal firearms, I had to assume he'd be quietly reassigned somewhere else, in which case he might be powerless to help me further, at least officially. I still had the distress code we used for texting, which he'd cautioned me to use sparingly.

I did manage to hit him up for some cash before he dropped me at my place and sped off in his unremarkable, unmarked staff car.

Now that I had cash, I could eat, but the crucial question was whether I'd be tempted to drink. If I sat alone in my trailer, I could nurse the hope that Leon would reappear soon, a lesser god lowered from the sky, bringing new evidence along with a surefire plan to entrap the bad guys, of whom we both believed Frank Trusdale was the worst. But if he wasn't the mastermind, who was?

Judging from experience, I might not hear from Leon for months. He possessed the G-man mindset, always reluctant to communicate except with new information — and then judiciously filtered based on need-to-know.

Which comes first — anxiety or depression? Does it matter?

Now that I'd witnessed the consequences of Trusdale's scheme, all my notions and sermons about why there is evil in the world seemed trivial. Yes, imperfection spurs creativity. Ignorance craves insight and innovation. The countervailing forces for maliciousness are generosity and forgiveness. But here was a force inexplicable in its utter senselessness. Brutality in war has a purpose because wars seek geopolitical gain, even if it only invites retaliation. The ego of a cult leader must be nursed by the promise of some great glory. If Obadiah didn't expect his reward from God — then from what earthly power?

Such insanity in the man I'd met was unbelievable. He seemed in touch with reality, capable of reasoning, chatting, and even joking. Perhaps Ida had glimpsed his mean streak. I had no hint of it.

What scared me most and shuddered me to my bones was the possibility that this man might believe sincerely and passionately in what he'd done. Dictators throughout history have justified horrific means by grand and glorious ends. If Trusdale was indeed a reasoning student of scripture — a messenger inspired by the same book that gave me the lessons in my sermons — what difference existed between us? Simply that he had no doubts and I did? I was not alone among clergymen and theologians in regarding apocalyptic prophesies as myths shared by primitive nomadic people thousands of years before humans ate the apple of empirical analysis. There is no room in a deterministic universe for much of what the ancients believed. Presumably, those stories still prevail because they can give us comfort. But what comfort did Trusdale's followers find? Those people in his sanctuary did not appear to be suffering.

Everything I perceived in this world convinced me Trusdale's mission could not possibly be God-given.

And yet he'd been allowed to prevail. Evil had won the incident, if not our era.

41

My longing at times of doubt is for affection. The teachings tell me God's love heals and sustains. But feeling it on the skin is surely one of the blissful ways it gets delivered.

Loretta's old mobile number was still in my contacts. I had no excuse to call, and there was every reason to suspect she'd disposed of that phone. But when we were together, we'd turned the Find My app on for all our devices, which was one way I confirmed Melissa and Luke were in Boulder, Colorado. So it took me less than a minute to learn that Loretta was in Christchurch, New Zealand at a facility named the Holistic Healing Light Center. It was doubly ironic that she'd fled the life of a minister's wife to go to a distant town with such a worshipful name, as well as seemed to be frequenting this New Age meetup. She'd be a counselor or coach there, not installed on a yoga mat. You can take the teacher out of the Sunday school, but you can't stop her from ministering.

Not getting rid of that phone suggested that she wasn't worried about being found, at least by me. I'd always had a hard time believing she was the one who cleaned out the safe at the megachurch. The subsequent arson wouldn't have benefited her at all, and my hunch was that both the theft and the fire had more to do with someone else's need to destroy evidence. But what would such evidence prove? I didn't need facts to guess that Shackleton had run another scam, despite his new profession of faith. Simply, he'd embraced God to repair his brand. And I let him do it.

Even though Loretta and boyfriend Mick Heston might be persons of interest in various official inquiries, no charges had been brought against either of them — so far. Heston's involvement in the teen trafficking scheme at Twin Dragons was deniable, and the hotel chain had no doubt offered him the overseas posting as protection and a reward for his silence. A glance at Google Maps showed me the Kiwi Golf Club and Casino was ten miles down the beach from her spa. Her involvement in the theft of donations and then the apparent destruction of the Shining Waters Temple by arson were matters of allegation and surmise. Stuart Shackleton was our principal benefactor, and his investment had been self-insured. So there would be no private investigation into the loss, and since the church charter was dissolved after the incident — along with my dismissal — no one had any interest in opening a case.

For my part, I'd stepped into Shackleton's plans in convenient denial of his ulterior motives. I hoped being the spiritual leader of a televangelist campaign and a megachurch would bring a wider audience to a sincere message. Power corrupts, but looking back on it, I might have gained influence but no power. I was just a face on Shackleton's brand.

And when the enterprise no longer served our backer's purpose, it went up overnight in smoke.

I couldn't muster the courage to call her. Evening in Appleton City would be midmorning the next day in Christchurch. It wouldn't be a rude time to reach her. I resolved I would, but I wanted time to compose my opener, including my apologies and my heartfelt expressions of — no, not forgiveness — but my optimistic belief she'd done nothing wrong. She hadn't stolen money, and she'd simply run from a situation she knew would eventually break her heart and perhaps mine even more painfully. After all, my mistaken path probably extended back as far as accepting the pastoral role at First Baptist when Marcus retired. At the time, I felt I owed it to him and to the community. But I wasn't the man for the job, even though renaming the congregation Evangel turned out to be a joke on my name. Other than visitations from Naomi, which I admit were supernatural enough, I never thought I'd communed with angels. But someone or something watching over me must have a wicked sense of humor.

I HAD to have a reason to get up in the morning. I needed a clear head, a specific purpose, and a plan. I craved the company of a sympathetic friend, and neither prayer nor Jack Daniels would qualify as companionship. I'd tasked Jeremy Bailey, and he was one of the most sensible fellows I knew. Shepherding the Taggart estate through probate would have been impossible without his help, and we still weren't done. It was unfair to bring more grief to his doorstep, but that was what I would have to do.

I set out before breakfast, thinking I'd offer to buy. When I phoned his office on the way, Marcella told me he wouldn't be in until noon. She sounded upset when she informed me he was on the driving range.

I found him straddling a teed-up ball with a hopelessly meager-sized iron firmly in his grip. He was such an expert it was impossible to imagine he'd simply fetched the wrong club from his bag. The grimace on his face betrayed, not the strain of athletic effort, but an uncharacteristically foul mood. He looked up to see me coming before he began his backswing. He halted, exhaled in disgust, and pronounced, "I've got enough shit on my plate, thank you very much."

"Top of the morning to you too, counsellor." I bowed my head, he might have thought mockingly, and muttered to my clasped hands, "I wasn't bringing you more, but I do sincerely hope you've cleaned up the mess I gave you."

He broke his stance, leaned on his club, and managed a smile. "It's early in the day, but the guy in that food truck over there, Gus, will spike our orange juice if we slip him some extra."

"I'm on the wagon, but you tell me whether it's going to be a long conversation, and I'll gladly pay. I was going to ask what, if anything, you've found."

He resumed his stance, focused, and whacked one that flew straight, high, and hard for a precise 150 yards. As he teed up the next ball, he explained, "I'm working on a new program. It's all about discipline, not power. Executive courses, short distances to the green. I get to use just two clubs, this two-iron and a putter. My drive has to get on the green. Then the most I get is a two-putt. Two and two, that's the formula. So it'll be like at-par on a nine-hole with one hand tied behind my back. My perverse idea of a challenge and a good time."

As he whacked the next one expertly, I realized it wasn't the slamming drive of a power-hitter with a big club. No, his stroke was all in the wrist — whip action. I'd never seen anyone hit like that. I certainly couldn't.

When he looked at me expectantly, I said, "I like to watch."

He continued to hit one after another, pausing between strokes to give me his episodic speech, "You will recall the crux of the problem with the Taggart farm was there is no clear title. Going back to Civil War squatters and, before that, there were federal land grants after they drove off the Indians."

"An enlightening lesson in history," I agreed. "Reminds me of that sign in Peculiar. Nothing to see here, just us nice white folks who know nothing about nothing."

"This time the situation is a lot more complicated and downright sinister. If the Taggart deal was like turning over a rock to find a viper, this time you're Indiana Jones in that snake pit, and the whole floor is writhing and hissing. I've never seen anything like it."

"Do tell me more. And don't leave out the part about how you're going to get us out of there."

He straightened up, his face went slack, and he said frankly, "Evan, if we pursue this, we're going to make enemies who are more powerful than anyone you or I have ever faced."

"Trusdale's in jail! Let's hope they find a way to hold him. There's his accomplice Deacon Daniel. They'll find him soon enough. The operation has been shut down. Who's left to care what we do or what we find? This reporter Harry Ardmore might get a Pulitzer out of it, maybe a movie. It's sad the whole thing might amount to an evening's TV entertainment, but at least whatever story there is will get out. I'd like to say 'never again,' but we're both students of history, and we know the losing side won't say that."

"Okay, here it is, as short and sweet as I can make it. There's no clear title to the End-Times farm. The house was a repo. It was in terrible shape, and the bank didn't want to pay to fix it up. So they flipped it to a real estate investment trust. There's a lot of that going on these days. Big money buys houses and apartment buildings and then leaves them unoccupied. They're playing a long game on appreciation, plus in the short term they're driving up prices by making the housing shortage worse. Big banks, insurance companies, and hedge funds. Maybe a cartel or two in there. Billions in cash floating around that has nowhere else to go. The one percent is down to decimal places and getting smaller by the day."

"None of this is exactly news. Granted, we didn't know Trusdale was caught up in it. Maybe he's not, just took advantage. Are you saying he's a squatter on the place?"

"Yes and no. That's how he comes to be there with no title. His group moves onto the land a few years back when no one's looking. Or maybe they request a temporary space for worship from the bank, but then they refuse to leave. They put up a big tent and call themselves a church. They bring their following and grow it, they start generating cash, and they slip some to local officials. Next thing you know, they've got a registered religious charter, tax-exempt. They forge land registration documents and claim ownership. They put up the electric fence and renovate the farmhouse. The property owner doesn't bother to take action because lawsuits cost money, and keeping the property off the market suits them just fine. And, as you say, Pastor Obadiah's advance man makes a circuit rounding up anyone who will come in buses."

"Are you telling me he has no permission from the owners? No lease?"

"I'm guessing here, but I don't like where it's going. I'd say no lease, nothing to associate him with them. But does he have their permission? Hell, I think they're all players in an even bigger scheme. You told me Obadiah was giving big money to politicians."

"That was the rumor, along with the suggestion he'd tied to far-right white nationalists."

"This trust fits in with land grabs on a huge scale. A partner in the trust that holds End-Times is very familiar to both of us — Bates Bank and Trust."

"Shackleton? No, he must have divested when he declared his candidacy."

"That's what the law says, but who's bothering to enforce it anymore?"

"Shackleton's behind this? Okay, I get the land grab part. But I don't see how he benefits from the ugliness at the farm. And he's not some enemy we don't know. He's a public official now, and you can bet his holdings are at arm's length."

"Exactly. More than anyone, we think we know what he's

capable of, and yet you can't believe he'd be involved with Trusdale. Would a state official who hankers for a long and illustrious political career be associated with an organized scheme of larceny and murder? Even if we could come up with some circumstantial evidence, we'd have a hard time convincing a jury anyone who runs on respectability could be that reckless."

"So what powerful interests? Who besides Shackleton?"

"For Shackleton to be involved, the scheme has to be really big, and he must answer to a higher power. Nothing in what I've found points to who that would be or what they want to achieve."

He offered to show me the paperwork he'd found, but I'd heard enough.

"Email me the proof of the bank's land title," I said, "plus whatever you have on the individuals who are inside that trust."

"What more can I do? You should know Shackleton better than anybody. What's the scheme?"

"I've asked you to do too much already. Trusdale proves he can gather a huge flock. But if you slaughter them, where's your political power or your righteous army?"

Jeremy pointed to the target area in the distance. "It's all about precision and patience, Evan. I'm getting so I can put it on the green every time. But three feet from the pin can be a very long way."

42

I wanted to know more about Talker. Of all the potential witnesses besides Anna, he might have witnessed crimes, perhaps participated in them. I couldn't believe that someone who was capable of brutality and worse could ever have been a friend of Birch, who might be the most godly man I know.

Maybe Birch can tell me about Talker Osceola's old habits. I have the feeling they were tight before Winona decided which one of them she would marry.

~

I CAUGHT up with Birch at Myerson, where he worked part-time doing janitorial work. When I'd called over there for him, he insisted we couldn't meet until after his shift at eight that evening. I wanted to take him out for a meal, see him relax, but he wouldn't go. He was a private person, a man to tell you only what you needed to know and therefore a trustworthy keeper of secrets. He might have been my best drinking buddy, but he didn't drink.

I met him in the staff coffee room. He was still in his work fatigues. He wouldn't even let me buy him a soda.

When I asked him whether he'd had any contact with Talker, he frowned then sighed. I was prepared to hear a story, however long. I'd missed meals all day long, and I informed him that, despite his refusal of my courtesy, he'd have to watch me guzzle a carton of milk while I chomped down a few packets of peanut-butter-filled cheese crackers.

Does anyone eat these when they are not killing time in a hospital?

Birch began, "Winona, Talker, and me was friends. Years go. High school. I told her then, I'll look no further. But she wouldn't have it. Her parents said she had to marry in the tribe. She didn't know Osceola was no more Indian than I am."

"So you weren't close to him? You must've wanted him to come back to care for her."

"Nobody was close to him. Not even her. Strong, silent type impressed her. She probably figured he'd be different when he settled down, that he'd open up, but he never did."

I had to tell him, "Birch, I've been running around like a chicken with its head cut off. I said I'd find him, and instead I stumbled into this End-Times mess. It's like a nightmare and I can't wake up. I was intending to come here, to visit Winona when she got better and could talk. I should have been here and at least held her hand when she passed."

Tears were running down his face now. "I did."

"Oh, Birch." I tried to take his hand now, but oddly he pulled it back. I thought it was a rebuke. "I didn't know her well, and for sure I didn't realize how much she meant to you."

"Even with the medicine, that one is a rough way to go."

Dying of lung disease is drowning, I knew that much. Even loaded up with sedatives and painkillers, the body fights desperately for air.

Before I could ask, he told me, "She didn't say nothing. She was out of it most of the time. Weak and on the respirator."

"But I'm sure she knew you were there. An angel at her side."

"There's evil in my heart, Pastor."

I smiled at that grizzled face. His close-cropped hair and beard had turned white. "Fudge your income tax? Roll through a stop sign?"

As he'd told me about attending to his lost love, his eyes had become bloodshot, wet to overflowing. He sobbed as he blubbered, "When I find Talker, I'll kill him."

I DIDN'T REPLY to Birch. There was no counseling or consoling him. I was too upset, and he was boiling over with rage. I got up and raced into the restroom. I couldn't make it to the stalls, so I retched into the sink. My distress was the consequence of poor diet and the shock of coping with an impossibility.

I'd known Fred Birchard since childhood. Farm boys knew how to kill chickens, usually by wringing their necks rather than chopping their heads off with an ax. But when I'd used the old figure of speech, he'd winced. The idea of harming any animal, then and now, made him cringe. Granted, I'd been finding out how deserving Talker Osceola might be of brutal justice. And I could imagine that Birch had decided not to wait for me but to hunt him down himself.

But kill? Not Birch.

I simply didn't know what to say to him. Back in my trailer, throwing myself onto my cot, I tried to slip into the ignorance of the unconscious, but I slept fitfully. My stomach had been upset even before my vending-machine meal with Birch and then quickly voiding it, but now I had no appetite whatever and fortunately no whiskey to further irritate my inflamed guts.

If Talker turned up dead, he would be one key witness who now couldn't be flipped to admit Trusdale had given him direct orders. I feared Ida would hold out, wouldn't betray him. Anna had seen a fit of jealousy in her, so the bond between Ida and the preacher could have been more carnal than spiritual.

I'd bet Deacon Daniel had seen it all, probably had a hand in most of it. But he'd be unlikely to cop a plea. With bonds of gold or threats, the Trusdales would have made sure that their right-hand man would be forever silent.

43

F red Birchard knew Anna's car. He was reporting to his usual night shift when he saw her Honda pulling out of the Myerson lot. He didn't see the driver. He'd hoped he'd see the girl on one of her visitations. He'd always been fond of her, and now he was worried how she was dealing with the doctors' prognosis that Winona didn't have much longer.

For years, he'd been in Winona's emergency contacts for the family and had Anna's number. But until now he'd been reluctant to call. They'd never been close, and he didn't know whether it was proper. What would she think of some old guy calling out of the blue?

He called, and she answered.

"Anna, were you over to the hospital tonight to see your mom?"

"No, why? Has she taken a turn?"

"They say she's resting comfortably. I been checking in on her. Reason I call, I saw your car there, figured it was you, thought we'd have a talk to see how you're holding up."

She gasped, "My car!" She went silent then muttered, "It's regis-tered to my dad. If they didn't sell it, I bet they let him have it."

"Sounds like could be Talker slipped in there to see Winona on the sly."

"If he did, it was to say goodbye. He won't be back."

44

I persisted in believing that Stuart Shackleton was amoral, not evil. Imagining that he was somehow involved with Frank Trusdale was like watching a witch's brew erupt in a violent froth and boil over. After a series of scandals and skating past allegations of not only fraud but attempted murder, before his new political career, he'd declared himself to be born again. He'd sponsored the expansion of my ministry, and I'd let him. He was behaving himself — at least in his public performances — and when our governor's deputy had keeled over from a heart attack, Shackleton was appointed lieutenant governor to fill the vacancy until the next election two years from now.

After my meetup with Jeremy, I'd lost whatever appetite I might have had. I retreated to my trailer, thinking meditation might suggest an answer. But my mind wouldn't be calmed. Thoughts spun, set in motion by Jeremy's discoveries.

Am I ready and willing to confront Shackleton again? He might be corrupt in ordinary kinds of ways, but I thought he'd renounced evil.

I harbored no ill will toward Shackleton, even congratulating myself I was capable of forgiveness of such scope. I'd welcomed his sponsorship in the beginning — but like Caesar putting by the crown and then accepting reluctantly. So I blamed only myself for how things had turned out. I'd overreached, and I'd mistaken my vanity for an inspired mission.

I didn't have trouble imagining that he could still be involved in crooked schemes. What daily compromises were necessary in his political life? But *this?* Trusdale's role in the End-Times scheme might be explained by either insanity or megalomania. But knowing his methods, why would any sane person risk being associated with him? Here was the same question I'd faced about Bob Taggart's suicide. He'd taken his own life, as so many innocents at the farm seemed to have done. But if Trusdale had driven his followers to starve, what did he hope to achieve? And how was it kept secret for so long? Those bodies had been in the ground for months, at least.

Sleepless, I was tempted to phone Harry Ardmore right away and give him the scoop of his career. I doubted he knew of any connection to Shackleton. But what did I really have to say? All that could be proven was that Pastor Obadiah didn't own the farm. While the sitting lieutenant governor might still have financial ties to the landowner, and breaking the story might be embarrassing or even scandalous, I had no proof Shackleton had known that people lost their lives there, let alone whether he or his cohort should bear any responsibility for it.

The world is waiting for the medical examiner's findings. Did they all die of starvation?

I'd been following Ardmore's column in the *News-Leader,* which by now had been syndicated all over. I had my own online search agent set for any breaking news that included Ardmore's byline, Trusdale, Obadiah, or End-Times. According to those reports, the sheriff had so far taken twenty-four survivors into protective custody. They were housing them at the Sisters of Mercy Children's Home, a place fraught with unpleasant memories for me. The diocese had been planning to close the facility after the earlier unfortunate events there. So far, none of the survivors of End-Times had been willing to talk. To a person, they vowed their devotion to Obadiah, and some were still refusing to eat.

Except, perhaps, Anna.

Reverend Bingham had told me that Anna was no longer staying with her. The deputy sheriff had picked her up, deposed her, then transferred her to the convent for care. I had to assume Anna had told the investigators as much more than she'd shared with me. But I'd seen no news of it.

It was two in the morning. Someone knocked ever so lightly on my door. My heart jumped, and after a moment of panic, I guessed it must be Olivia, sleepless and demanding answers. I hadn't been trying to keep her in the dark, but I didn't want to burden her with suspicions when I had such scant evidence. I knew she regarded Trusdale as a fake but probably not as a murderer.

The gentleness of the rap suggested this person was no threat. Despite all my misadventures, I was still a trusting soul.

Nevertheless, I grabbed my utility flashlight, its long, black tube filled with three D-cells, making it weightier and potentially more lethal than any club. I'd never used it that way, wondered if I could.

On my doorstep was Anna Osceola, looking demure but more vital than when I'd seen her undernourished self at the farm.

She was staring down at the flip-flops on her dirty feet as she muttered meekly, "It's me, Pastor."

She'd referred to Obadiah as "Pastor," not that she was a follower but perhaps because that was how everyone at the farm had referred to him. But now, addressing me that way, I wondered whether she now thought of me as her minister and protector.

"Anna, I thought you and the others were in care at the convent."

When she looked up, I could see the tracks of tears on her face, which the full moon made silvery and oddly beautiful.

"I slipped out. No one saw me."

"Come in. We'll figure out how I can help."

She put her foot on the threshold, but then she announced before entering, as if her news were so frightful I'd send her away, "My mother's dead."

I set the flashlight aside and beckoned her in. "Oh, Anna," I managed to say. I was about to give her a hug but then held back.

She sat down on the rumpled bedding of my cot, and I busied myself putting the coffee on.

She watched me intently, as if she were waiting for me to be the first to speak. When I was pastor of Evangel, I'd never counseled her. After I hadn't been able to help her at the farm, she might not think of me as someone who could make matters better for her, which made her greeting doubly confusing.

As I sat in my only chair beside her, I said simply, "Tell me."

The night was hot and humid. All she had on was a T-shirt and cutoff shorts. She smelled of stale sweat. Hygiene at the convent must not have been a priority.

I was still wondering whether she expected a hug. My withholding it might seem just as awkward. She sat stiffly, perhaps defensively, and I was acutely aware that counseling a young girl in my little closet home in the middle of the night would be judged by any prudent person as unwise. I was already thinking about where I would be taking her to spend the night.

I didn't yet know why she'd come. If she was here to seek physical comfort, this would be a brief meeting, but then what? Back to the nuns? She wouldn't want to stay there, perhaps might even face consequences for running away the first time.

I was desperate for more information from her, but I had to comfort her first — if I could manage this sensitive situation like a man of the cloth rather than a defrocked boozer.

Is she the only eyewitness who has talked? She might be in jeopardy now. At least I'm wide awake. My insomnia was a blessing.

She said softly, her head bowed again, "Before she went, the hospital tried to reach my dad, but of course they couldn't find him."

I couldn't help asking, "Do *you* know where he is?"

Does she know the sheriff still wants him for a hit-and-run? She must've been asked.

Here came the sniffles. I found a paper towel so she could blow her nose. She shook her head, saying, "I'm sure he's hiding, and he's good at it. I have to tell you about him, about the last time I saw him, but there are things I haven't told anyone. Then you have to let me leave."

"You'll have to tell the sheriff, put it on record."

"No, not this part," she insisted. "I'll tell you, then you do whatever can be done."

"Anna, I'm not your jailer. But you need help. And a lot more than I can manage on my own. How can you make me promise before I know why you came, what you need? Is anyone making arrangements for Winona?"

"I don't think so."

"The church has a fund for such things. I'll speak to Pastor Bingham. You won't have to worry. Is that why you came?"

"Thank you, but no. I have to tell you about that place. You can't say it was me who told you. They kill people who talk."

How does she know this? Threatening harm in itself is a crime.

"Who? Who kills? Give me a name, a description."

A stony look. No answer.

I insisted, "I have to tell the investigators. Otherwise, why would you want to tell me? Trusdale and his people are in custody. What's needed now is to find out what crimes were committed and who's responsible. They can't hold him or any of them indefinitely without proof."

"You can do what you want, whatever you have to do. But you can't say it came from me."

"How are we going to do that?"

She was defiant. "You figure it out. I'll take care of myself."

"Anna, you're not being —"

"Not being a victim anymore!" She glared at me as she demanded, "Now, do you want to hear what happened? I don't have to tell you anything."

In a lowered voice, I tried to calm her. "Of course, I want to know. But losing your mother? Don't you want to talk about what you're feeling right now?"

"No. No, I don't. She was lost to me a long time ago, even before I took her there. I was stupid to think she'd get better, but right away they took her to be with the others. I didn't get to see her until that phony healing stunt. Then we were kept off to ourselves with the sick people. Before the cops took me to the nuns, I was allowed to see her in the hospital. That's when the doctor told me there was no hope, they'd make her comfortable."

"You loved Winona. I know you did."

She assumed I was telling her what she needed to hear. "How do you know?"

"Because…you cared enough to take her to the farm. Even though you didn't share her beliefs, you went. You put yourself at risk. Maybe you intended to leave her there, but then they shut you in as well. You almost laid down your life for her. If that isn't love…"

"They didn't lock me in at first. They said I'd get to see her after she was better. That's why I stayed. Never happened, of course. Then when I knew more, I was trapped."

"But when she was finally getting good care at Myerson, did you have hope again?"

"No, when I saw her there, I knew she'd be gone. The doctors were straight with me after that. What I feel now is relief. She's not suffering."

"You'll go through all the emotions, like a roller coaster. All of us go through the stages of grief, and not just once."

I should be counseling her loss, but she's in denial, for now.

I was desperate to know what Trusdale had done to her and the others. Once I had the information, perhaps we could agree on the next steps.

I took a deep breath, squared my shoulders, and told her, "You're putting a lot on me, Anna. And you're putting yourself at risk — again. You could wait, don't give me anything. I can drive you to the sheriff's in the morning, and you can go on record. Then they'd know how to protect you."

She stiffened. "They'll lock me up. It won't be jail, but it will be like the convent. I don't know where, but it will be as bad or worse. Now that Mother is gone, I get to have a life."

The coffee was ready. As I handed her a cup, I said, "Anna, I'm so sorry. Shall we pray about this?"

She was defiant. "No!"

The coffee was black. She took a sip and made a face.

I offered, "Sugar?" I had no milk or creamer. No food in the house.

"Lots, please."

As she put a couple of teaspoonfuls into it and stirred, she blurted out, "All this religious nonsense got her killed! She listened faithfully to the guy's broadcasts. She wouldn't take her meds, wouldn't eat. No school for me. He preached all that. Then she insists I take her to that awful place."

I was considering all the ways I might trick her in her best interests to tell me everything before she raced out the door. I had to keep her talking.

Some time ago — I couldn't remember when — I'd been involved in so many evidence-gathering sessions that I'd set up a shortcut on my phone. Triple-click to record. It might be unethical, and I should have told her, but I simply shoved my hand into my pants pocket and turned it on.

Whatever she told me wouldn't be admissible in court. My thought was I would share it with Ardmore if he'd accept it from an anonymous source.

I risked asking, "Winona didn't expect to die at the farm, did she? She was thinking he'd heal her."

"I don't know. Either get well or see Jesus. People came thinking they'd get a meal, maybe get his blessing, and leave. Yeah, I'm sure there were some who wanted him to put his hands on them to magically cure whatever, but I don't know who else he claimed to heal besides Mom. Maybe the other people with us in the sick ward, but they weren't talking. Sure, the new folks got food, but then they found out they had to stay, and they were expected to fast until they expired."

"When I saw you — when Trusdale let me see you — you were a recent arrival. Were you still allowed to eat then?"

I never told her I knew of her text messages about starving and puking.

"I didn't see everything. New people live apart from everyone else, and the farm is organized according to levels — each group in a separate building. Building One holds arrivals, the New Faithful. There you're told — Ida leads the sessions — about the program of fasting and worship. On this level, you get food and water, but over time you get less and less until you're down to one piece of fruit a day. When you begin to starve, you feel dizzy and weak. You get headaches. When you're showing signs of suffering, you're a Decider. That's when he says you need to take courage, stick with it. You know you're on the right path. If then you commit to eating nothing at all, fasting until you meet the Savior, you join the Purified Souls in Building Two. But the Deciders who can't commit, they become Doubters. Those noncommitted folks are put in Building Three. They get some food and a lot of group sessions.

While they are on that level, they become either Repentants or Deniers. The Repentants — the ones who've decided to commit — they join the Purified Souls who are fasting, waiting, and praying."

"And the Deniers?"

She gulped. "They're prisoners now, pressed into…hard labor."

"Doing what?"

"Maintenance."

"What? Swabbing out latrines?"

"Sure." Then she added quietly, "Also digging graves."

Here's the story. If only there were proof!

I asked the next question carefully, "Did you actually see anyone do that?"

"No," she admitted. "I never got out of Building One. I never saw what happened to people on the other levels. It was all gossip, after lights out. Talking among ourselves about anything but our faith was forbidden. If we'd been caught repeating rumors, Ida said they'd put us in with the Deniers. But you can't keep people from talking — especially when we're scared."

"Where was Trusdale through all of this?"

"Like I said, none of us ever spoke to him. We didn't hear him give orders to anyone. You were in the sanctuary. It's a big barn. They rigged it like a rockstar stage. Sunday mornings and Wednesday nights, they'd take us there — people from all levels but seated separately. But the night you were there, it was only people from the first level, New Faithful. He did his healing act with all the effects, but he was careful not to preach about the fasting. Other times, he would give the same messages my mother heard in his broadcasts — emphasis on starving so you can meet Jesus. The promise was for us to get to the level of Anointed Ones. Building Four. None of them attended services. He said they didn't need to. They were in a state of grace. No one I talked to knew exactly what went on in there. He preached that they didn't eat, but they got what he called *miracle manna*, spiritual food that sustained them without hunger. They breathed it, somehow. No one ever spoke of the anointed dying, but there must have been some because they needed all those gravediggers."

"So did you ever speak with anyone who had contact with a gravedigger?"

"All I know is no one wanted that job. No one called them gravediggers. They were Toilers in the fields of the Lord. Some could manage it for one day, maybe a few more. They'd get food so they could keep up their strength, but then they'd be retching it up while they worked. Sooner or later, a Toiler would claim to lose their doubts and become a Repentant. For those, Pastor would hold a special ceremony — the three C's — Confession, Contrition, and Cleanse. But those were broken people. They'd rejoin the Deciders. I did see some of them later at services. They were brain-dead, terrified. They wouldn't speak. Their choice was to commit and follow the rest to their deaths — or go back to digging graves."

"Do you think any of the gravediggers had to be murderers? I mean, do you think all of the deaths were from starvation? You said the ones who gave in looked terrified. Maybe they witnessed what happened when some changed their minds or didn't cooperate."

"Rumor. Like I said. Enough people believed, and gossip wasn't a constant thing. You got the facts in bits and pieces. People were too scared to say much. Somehow everyone knew, if you couldn't manage enough faith, you'd end up digging graves, especially the men. Many of them feared that more than dying."

"Let me ask you, and you needn't answer. Did Trusdale ever abuse you personally?"

She smirked. "I wasn't there long enough. I'd get looks from him, and I figured he wanted me. He'd get that lech look, you know? That day I saw you in his office, he took me aside and said I should come to him for a private session. We'd pray together. But Ida wouldn't allow it, so he never got the chance with me."

"Was she jealous of you? Because maybe she was close to him?"

"Let's just say she's the type who would do whatever it takes to get what she wants. She had him on a short chain."

"Didn't anyone try to run away?"

"Oh yeah." There was a glazed look in her eyes as she stared again at her toes. "But you never saw them again."

Here's the urgent question!

"Anna, who were the enforcers? The cops could only find a few security guards. They seemed like day workers, about as threatening as parking-lot attendants."

Unaccountably, she started to sob. She gasped, "I ran into one of them."

I took her hands in mine. I hoped she didn't think I was coming onto her.

She squeezed back as she told me, "I tried to run away once. At the fence, I get this bright light in my face. There were dogs. He had a crossbow aimed at my chest. He marched me back to the dorm and said if I ever spoke of it, some other guard would kill me."

"Did you recognize him? Why did he let you go?"

As she burst into tears, she whimpered, "I lied when I told you I never saw him there."

45

I could see she was exhausted. She had put her faith in me. If I had a squad car pick her up now, she'd have to endure intake before she could rest. So I let her stretch out on my cot. I told her she could lock the door from the inside. I went out to sleep in the Egg. I slept sitting in the passenger seat with the windows rolled down a crack to relieve the heat. I could've cranked them down all the way to catch whatever slight breeze, but even out here in no-man's land (but for Olivia), we might worry about prowlers, but none had ever come around.

Even with all that coffee, I must've fallen asleep as soon as I leaned back on the headrest.

I woke by force of habit at six, soon after the sun was up. I was stiff from sleeping curled up like a possum in a hole, but other than the persistent crick in my back, I was better for the rest. Anna's story had the facts I'd been seeking, if not the essential evidence to nail Trusdale. But if I could get her to go with me to the sheriff now, perhaps a case could be made for child endangerment, even kidnapping.

But I found the door to the trailer unlocked. She was gone.

ACTING ON MY CALL, Deputy Crandall put out an all-points on Anna Osceola and Curt Carper. It was a fair guess he'd been the one to drive her to my place, probably stopping some ways off to let her out so I wouldn't hear the car. He might've waited there for her the whole time. Perhaps she hadn't slept at all. Or he came back there at a time they'd set. Perhaps they'd use a borrowed vehicle or one with stolen plates.

I couldn't see why she would think running away would keep her any safer than letting the cops protect her. They must've both wanted a new start, many miles from here.

I BRIEFED Otis in his office before I'd had my breakfast, and I was thankful for generous refills of his watery coffee and a couple of his sticky, sugar-glazed doughnuts.

This sugar high will drive me crazy, but it's a short trip.

Fully aware that the recording of Anna's story didn't have the weight of a sworn statement, I summarized it for Otis anyway. Then, without asking permission while I was sitting in front of the sheriff, I emailed the audio file to Ardmore stipulating the source must be confidential. I didn't worry about what was honorable under the circumstances. Okay, I'd made a promise to Anna, but I'd betrayed it the minute I pressed record. For the sake of all those people who laid down their lives — especially for any who didn't do it willingly — I felt the truth had to come out, and soon.

Otis sighed, "Oh, they'll get picked up. Can't get far these days. Problem is, even if the girl gives us a sworn statement, we still got a shitload of accusations but no proof. She didn't see anything! Sounds like this Ida coached the people. If Trusdale's keeping his hands clean, she or somebody else was giving orders. But who? I guess we like Talker Osceola now more than ever. If his job was chasing down runaways, maybe he did follow Gropius, saw an opportunity."

"I'd assumed Gropius was on his way to End-Times when I met him. But now I'm wondering whether he was an escapee."

Otis nodded. "Gives us motive and opportunity, truck was the means. And not just manslaughter."

"The old guy had this notion about a plot to fake the Second Coming. At the service they let me attend, they had some high-tech gear. When Trusdale acted out a healing, I saw a spectacular vision, and I think the rest of the folks did too. Like VR without goggles. When Gropius worked for the government, he designed advanced display systems."

Otis managed a grim smile. "Once again, Preacher, I hate that you're so damned useful. Those victims over at Sisters of Mercy are refusing to talk. How about you head over there on one of your compassionate visits? Anybody starts to share, get it recorded. Maybe that way we get some leverage on Ida or Trusdale. They're both in custody, but time's running out. We're gonna have to charge them with something or let 'em go."

ON LEAVING the sheriff's office, I alerted Leon with our text code. Surprisingly, he replied right away from a new number:

Sup?

I have news. And I think I know what's next

Can it wait till tomorrow?

Victim witness now a fugitive

What's next?

Second Coming

Joke?

No

In DC. C U soonest

46

When Anna lit out of Evan's trailer at two in the morning, Curtis was waiting for her, parked at a meeting place down the road. He'd bought a camper van from a friend and loaded it with minimal baggage for each of them and supplies. He had no idea where they'd be going, but he was content for her to be the navigator and the brains. It impressed him that she could look at every challenge like a thought problem. Must be the scientist in her.

As she climbed in, he asked her, "He give you a hard time?"

"Like how? He looks at me like all men do, but he insisted on sleeping in his car. I'd have swiped some food, but he has nothing."

"Where are we going?"

"Long term, I don't know. Depends how we get along. Short term, we're going after my father. He has my car."

"It's an old model, not like you can track it."

"I think I know where he'd go. I have to try."

229

BIRCH MIGHT HAVE CALLED Evan or the sheriff to let them know where the fugitive was last seen and what he was driving. Instead, he waited, hoping to spot the car again and have an opportunity to confront the driver. But he didn't see the Honda again, and then Winona died. Talker would have no reason to return.

Rather than alert the authorities, Birch decided to set out on his own.

He had an old Toyota 4Runner he'd kept in near-perfect condition by doing repairs himself. He'd bought it back when he was scoutmaster and Talker was his assistant. This was before Winona had decided which of them to marry.

He knew Talker was wanted for the hit-and-run, and he preferred to believe it was an accident. The man he knew was running as much from his past as from the present. Talker had killed a man in a fistfight back when his name was Henry Walker.

Talker was never widely traveled and, considering his background and reconstructed identity, never wanted to venture too far from home. Over the years, the Osceola family vacations were no more than weekend car trips. Talker had chosen their habitual campsite — the same one where he and Birch would take the boys in the troop.

So Anna and Birch shared the same hunch about where her father would be likely to go.

THE DAY before cops had raided the compound, Ida had warned Daniel that, if Talker ever ran, he must be hunted down. For the assignment, she'd given Daniel a battered Jeep Wrangler, which because of its high mileage and sad state of repair was less reliable than he would have wished.

Daniel didn't want the job. He'd have preferred for Talker to get caught, then it would be his unreliable word against Pastor's. Daniel couldn't shift the assignment to Philip Hart because the fellow had fallen gravely ill and might soon be in need of burial himself.

When the armed convoy was on its way to close down the farm, Daniel was on the same road, returning from running an errand. Seeing the threat from a distance, he'd executed a U-turn and sped way. Deacon Daniel was now on the lam. Not knowing whether there would be anyone now to take his side, he had no choice but to find Talker and silence him.

Daniel had his own affairs to attend to first, including retrieving a stash of money and survival gear he'd left with an ex-roommate in St. Louis. He could have wished he could retrieve a firearm, but all he had in the truck was an old crossbow he'd kept handy for perimeter security at the farm.

It took him several weeks to take up the search. But he figured he was in no rush. He had an advantage over Anna and Birch. He'd affixed a tracking device to the Honda before they'd given it to Talker.

47

I found Reverend Mother Bernadette in her office on the second floor of the former children's home. The suite had been stripped bare, leaving only a metal desk and two utilitarian wooden chairs. She was in her expected place behind the desk. In preparation for closing down the place, most of the staff of the convent had been let go. I couldn't imagine there was much paperwork left to do, but she was riffling through a considerable stack.

Her expression was grim.

She looked up briefly and nodded for me to sit. "Reverend Wycliff, I prayed for better circumstances."

"I can't imagine what could be worse."

She didn't look up. She was filling checkboxes as her pen moved down a form. "Come now. You're a student of history. There was more than a hundred years of evangelism during something called the Inquisition. Murdered millions more people than the Holocaust. Then, another *H,* we had Hiroshima. Should I go on?"

"I should have come before all this. With a birthday cake or something."

Her expression hadn't changed. Finally, she looked up to explain, "The abrupt dismissals were during Covid. No doubt the diocese judged the liability would have been too much, not only for the staff but also for the children. There's typically no formal retirement plan for nuns, but, living on donations, some of them set up a communal home outside of Springfield. I'm still here, as you see, presumably to lock up after our present wards have been healed and sent home to their loved ones."

So there must still be children in her care.

I remembered there had been some with severe developmental disabilities, others with devastating illnesses, such as TB that had infected the spinal cord and left them doubled up for life.

This is getting profoundly depressing. Time to change it up.

"Sister, shuck the habit and I'll buy you a drink!"

Her face flushed red, and she bowed her head again and clasped a hand over her mouth. Her chest heaved, as if from sobs, then I realized she was shaking with giggles.

"Evan!" she gasped, letting her hand fall so she could breathe. "What a wicked thing to say!"

"Glad we cleared the air. It was getting kind of stuffy in here."

She frowned with mock severity as she informed me, "This habit is about all I have left of my pride and my station." She was wearing the formal habit of her high office. On previous visits, I'd seen her in casual clothes, most often in the coveralls she wore when she was tending the roses in her garden. She went on, "The uniform also seems to have an effect on our patients — possibly imparting an air of authority, perhaps even fear. It's one more thing I can do to motivate them to cooperate and eat. Most of them are refusing."

"And I believe the law says you can't force-feed them."

"The nurse attaches an IV if they are delirious, unconscious, or comatose. Otherwise, yes, forcing a tube down their throats — or noses — is considered torture if they have the ability to say no. For the others, we offer them a high-protein smoothie at least once a day. If they refuse to drink, I will permit a bit of a ruse. The sister who is working as nurse-practitioner will show them a hypodermic. The syringe is an antique — you know, the kind with the long needle? They're told they'll be anesthetized, then the nurse will administer the IV. So far, few refuse the drink. It's no surprise they'd be terrified of needles wielded by strangers."

"So you trick them?"

"We do what we can. Two of the retired sisters have come over to help and once again have taken up residence so we can provide round-the-clock attention. At least one sheriff's deputy is assigned to be on the premises at all times in rotating shifts."

She explained that, despite the feeding regimen, some were so sick on arrival that they grew steadily weaker and thinner. Doctors from Myerson had to be summoned at times to deal with the complications, which progressed into pneumonia. Those patients had to be segregated because their coughing could spread the infection. Bernadette had appealed to state family services for more help, but the reply was they were short-handed already serving clients who were on authorized public assistance. An emergency court order would be needed to provide funding for the needed care in this special circumstance, but the paperwork wasn't moving fast enough to save some of Obadiah's faithful. They'd likely suffer the fate they'd willingly sought.

I said, "I'm here to visit and pray with anyone who wants to see me."

She scoffed, "They don't, believe me. They're either brainwashed or terrified, probably both. But we do have one refusenik who is in a bad way. Philip Hart. He told the nurse he wants to confess."

"Is he Catholic? You know I can't do that."

"He's not, so I'm not supposed to hear him either. We might as well learn what he has to say."

THE OLD MAN had been moved to a private room. Before we entered, Bernadette slipped on a paper face mask and asked me to do the same. I was surprised when she suggested conspiratorially that I turn my phone on to record, which I did and slipped it back in my pants pocket. Then she showed me into the darkened room. It was a hospice setting.

The fellow once had the body of a brawler, now withered. He was lying on his back, propped up part-way in the bed and hooked up to a monitor that displayed his vital signs. A tube connected to a tall oxygen bottle on the floor was thrust up his nose.

I was surprised to see that he'd been lashed to the bed with terrycloth straps. I'd have thought he'd be too weak to become violent, but there must have been a reason. It was almost as if the nuns feared he'd pull a Lazarus and walk out of there when they were looking the other way.

Seeing us enter and Bernadette's form looming before him in black, the patient wheezed, "Have you come to hear my confession?"

I replied, "I'm not a priest, Philip. I'm a Baptist minister. I'm here to pray with you, if you wish. And to hear anything you want to say. I can't give you instruction, but perhaps I can offer some comfort."

With obvious exertion, he turned his head and gasped, "Preacher said if we don't eat, we'll see Jesus. Will I, Pastor?"

How can I say this? In all the times I visited deathbeds, no one asked me the question.

I took his hand. "No one can say what you will see. I believe God will touch you."

Bernadette turned to look at me. The hint of a smile and a nod told me she couldn't disagree.

Philip closed his eyes. I didn't think he was in the throes because his chest was pumping. His short speech had cost him precious breath, and now he was gasping for more.

The Reverend Mother had advised me we shouldn't linger in there. It wasn't only because of the contagion. She worried any excitement would be trying for him.

His eyes still closed, he summoned the strength to whisper, "Please, don't bury me there. Tortured spirits. Some of 'em didn't want to die. It's no place to rest in peace!"

I leaned over him to ask, "Philip, how do you know they didn't want to die?"

The nun was standing behind me, and the man's reply was so softly spoken, perhaps she didn't hear him say, "Because I had to help them."

I let go of his hand. I wanted to offer my prayer, the one I believed to be true always, simply affirming the power and presence of God.

But I couldn't manage it.

I CALLED Otis on his mobile as soon as I had a private moment back in my parked car outside the convent.

I played the recording for him. The grabber was barely audible but undeniable. I told him, "It was a deathbed confession, not a sworn statement. But it's the first evidence we've had that at least some of those folks didn't go willingly into the dark night. And now we know some of those gravediggers had to be the killers."

Otis wanted to know, "Did the sister hear it?"

"I'm sure she will testify the recording was made in her presence."

"Maybe we could type it up, have him sign it."

"He didn't say someone ordered him to do it. It's not like you'll be charging him."

There was a long pause during which Chet Otis uttered a low groan, the complaint of a man with a nagging ulcer or no sleep.

"Evan, I got a coroner's report here. Me and the Feds got it, no public release as yet. Autopsies on the first ones they took out of there. More to come, and it won't get better."

"So — cause of death? No surprise."

"Causes. Multiple."

"What?"

"Starvation, yes, sure. Most of them. But some? Blunt-force trauma to the head. Strangulation."

We'd all feared as much, but now the cruel facts are undeniable.

I muttered, "Now we know at least one who did it to them."

Otis choked before he could say, "There's more."

"Chet! What?"

"Some of those bodies with the injuries? Children." He found new strength to growl, "Trusdale? We gotta hang him alive by his heels. Get a mad dog to chew his privates off. No way that bastard can suffer enough."

I was still on the phone as I watched the ambulance pull up in front.

I FOLLOWED the paramedics back in. Moments after we'd left him, Philip Hart had gasped his last.

I called Harry Admore right away. I let him know I'd heard a deathbed confession from a gravedigger who'd killed faithful who wouldn't go through with it. I gave him the name. He told me he was finishing editing the transcript of Anna's story but hadn't yet published it. This new information I had to give him would not only add credibility, but it would also protect Anna.

Like me, he's eager to burn the evildoers.

Bernadette was distraught she'd lost one. I think she'd hoped all of her new wards would make it out of there alive. Her remorse made me think she hadn't heard Hart's confession, but she hadn't asked me what he said.

I stood aside while the crew loaded the gurney bearing Hart's body into the van, got back in my car, and called Otis back right away.

I asked him, "When are you going public with the report?"

"The coroner's giving a press conference tomorrow morning. Lucky me, I get to stand behind him. He won't be naming victims because the corpses are in such a state we still got no positive ID. He'll take a lot more words to say pretty much what I just told you. He'll add he's not taking questions at this time."

"Anna was worried if I told you or anyone that Trusdale would figure out she's the one who betrayed him. But now that I've leaked the story to Harry Ardmore, he'll have to say it's an unnamed source. Then he can let it be known that I visited the survivors today at the convent and Philip Hart confessed he was one of the killers before he died."

"What does that do?"

"The story gets out there, and it protects Anna. Ardmore will be implying Hart was the source for all of it. And, God bless him, as of a few moments ago, the guilty party is nicely dead."

Now the sheriff's reply was more of a grunt than a growl. "Preacher, I thought you were a man of God. *Nicely* dead?"

"Pray the Almighty won't smite the messenger."

48

Ardmore filed his breaking story with the *Kansas City Star* and WDAF-TV. That day, it was all over the national news and social media. As I'd told Otis, the reporter had managed to imply that his source was the remorseful but deceased gravedigger Philip Hart.

I hoped Anna would see the news and stop running. She was still missing, as were Curt, her father, and Deacon Daniel.

Matters became complicated — and heated — rapidly. The server that hosted the registry of missing persons crashed because thousands of relatives — and not just from Missouri — feared their loved ones might be among the victims.

Incensed citizens flooded state legislative offices with demands for closer government scrutiny of all churches. Petitions were drafted to require churches to submit their charters for review — including new provisions banning not only hate speech but also admonitions for self-harm. Revoking the tax-exempt status of all kinds of places of worship was once again a topic of nationwide debate.

Church leaders of all faiths and denominations insisted in

opinion pieces and interviews that responsible believers shouldn't be punished for the horrific sins of a cult led by a madman.

Frank and Ida Trusdale were still being held in custody, both of them, along with the End-Times Foundation, represented by Bertram Harrison. The attorneys had filed a writ of habeas corpus, demanding they be either charged or released.

Influencers among Obadiah's followers posted that holding him without due process abridged freedom of speech, freedom of religious practice, and his ability not only to sustain financial support for his mission but also to save souls. Some innocent souls would surely face hellfire because they'd been deprived of his preaching before they died.

The state attorney general convened a grand jury to determine whether crimes had been committed and, if so, which persons might be charged. The announcement emphasized this investigative process would take time and that during the proceedings persons of interest would be freed, subject to subpoena for their testimony.

The End-Times leaders were barred from returning to live at the grand End-Times farmhouse, where the entire property had been roped off as a crime scene. Trusdale promptly took up residence in a nondescript apartment building in Springfield, within walking distance of the courthouse. The address wasn't made public, and it looked for a time as though he'd be adopting a low profile until the grand jury deliberations were over. As he'd no doubt expected, he was presented with a subpoena to testify. That obligation, at least, forbade him — but did not restrain him — from leaving the state.

Released from custody, Trusdale intended to resume his sermons. But the television network that carried Obadiah's end-times broadcast abruptly canceled his show, issuing no press release or public explanation. His website, which had included a prominent donation button, disappeared, disabled by the hosting service.

The authorities must have debated whether he was a flight risk, but he had his own reasons to stay. He began a series of podcasts, hosted on a site that dished conspiracy theories. He peppered his messages with appeals for contributions to his legal defense fund.

His messages were now more explicit, urging fasting, disparaging the practice of medicine, and advising followers to renounce their possessions, sell their assets, and donate the proceeds to his righteous cause. Now he was again saying the Second Coming could be any day.

To conclude each session, he said, "My friends, during the time I was so wrongfully incarcerated, I was told that bodies had been unearthed from the farm. I have trouble believing this. You know how the media and the forces of darkness are arrayed against us. Destroying faith is their business, and lies are their currency. If any of our followers fasted to the point of their demise, it was their personal decision to end their suffering and see Jesus. And if any of your loved ones are missing, my dears, be comforted that there are no earthly remains to be found. They have been borne up!"

Rumors circulated, unconfirmed by the medical examiners, that some bodies showed evidence their organs had been harvested. Obadiah's supporters labeled these reports and the actual findings of trauma as fake news, going on to repeat that all the deaths at the farm were unsubstantiated, the video evidence of the exhumations nothing more than staged events performed by actors and super- vised by government operatives. The coroner was compelled to issue a press release stating that none of the autopsies showed evidence of removal of organs, and it was clear from lack of medical facilities at the farm that harvesting would not have been possible.

Other reports claimed that, even though there were children at the farm, none had died. They had been trafficked by a cartel or abducted by UFOs. The proliferation of these wild theories may have made some people conclude that stories about corpses were equally unbelievable.

Investigative reporters had no trouble tracing Trusdale's generous contributions to politicians. His critics alleged the purpose of the End-Times farm was not to save souls but to exert power over the masses to further a populist authoritarian agenda.

Obadiah's followers claimed to see through the Deep State's campaign against the prophet. As he was now preaching openly, the Second Coming was imminent — any day now. When it happened, the atheist-communist leadership of our nation would claim it was a cleverly manufactured hoax. The faithful believed Obadiah would be anointed, rise up, and crush the false prophets and the evildoers.

Prominent spokespersons — claiming to be objective and moderate — urged hands off the popular evangelist. Unless evidence was brought forward that Pastor Obadiah had killed — or directly ordered the killing — of his followers, he'd committed no crime. These voices echoed the legal position Harrison was taking.

According to the doctrine Trusdale claimed was divinely inspired, he'd urged his faithful to fast, which they'd done willingly, some to their demise.

And among those urging tolerance of Pastor Obadiah was Stuart Shackleton.

49

The campground where Birch and Talker took the troop every summer was inside Ha Ha Tonka State Park, a five-thousand acre preserve located at the southern tip of Lake of the Ozarks, not far from Camdenton. The odd name meant *big laugh* in Dakota Sioux, despite the fact that the tribe never lived in the area and, even if the origin were truly indigenous, no one remembers the joke. Nevertheless, the site is known today for a cruel irony, which took place long after the Indians of Southern Missouri were driven east to reservations. In the late nineteenth century, a white tycoon from Kansas City erected a European-style mansion there on a high overlook. But he died in the state's first automobile accident before the grand home was completed. His sons carried on, one moved in, then the place was devastated in a fire.

The sandstone-block ruins of the Snyder mansion were open to tourists. Its stone water tower was intact, and being the high point of the locale, offered a stunning view of the lake and lush woodlands from its parapet.

Besides the attractions of the lake, another tourist magnet to the region is its profusion of caves. One of the most visited has been Bridal Cave, an immense cavern often used for wedding ceremonies, located to the north on the other side of the lake. The cliffs around Ha Ha Tonka are riddled with caves, and some openings are accessible by boat from Ha Ha Tonka Lake.

When Talker took off from End-Times, tourist season was nearly over. It was still hunting season, but the park was closed, as were the caves. The Department of Natural Resources was perpetually short-staffed, and the caves were dangerous places. Experienced spelunkers could apply for permits, but apparently there were other sites more fascinating to them than Ha Ha Tonka.

Although Talker had not a drop of tribal blood, as far as he knew, he was a wannabe-Indian. Besides his manner of dress and the headband he wore around his long hair, he prided himself on his ability to absorb and master native lore and skills. He'd considered taking the name Tracker instead, but he thought Talker implied a communion with spirits, which he never practiced. As assistant to scoutmaster Birch, he'd worked with the boys on their merit badge tasks. He knew fire building, cooking, how to pitch a tent against a storm, and several stories from the Osage Nation, which the normally taciturn fellow could be prompted to tell to rapt faces huddled around a campfire.

There were too many caves for Talker to know all of them well, but he was familiar with one. It was large cavern, accessible by small boat or canoe from the lake. There was a broad entrance, spanning about thirty feet, at water level. Springs inside the cavern fed its underground pools then flowed into the lake. But the boys never knew of this way in.

As a rite of initiation and the culminating experience of many camping trips, Talker would lead them in through a shoulder-high opening in the hillside above. The pathway in from that point narrowed, requiring the young explorers to crawl on their bellies, each holding a flashlight with one hand. At the narrowest point, the access opening was about the size of two basketballs. If the kids were claustrophobic, none had ever let on. Emerging from the narrow passage and that test of grit and manhood onto a ledge above the huge cavern was an unforgettable experience, winning Talker the reputation of intrepid adventurer and wise leader to secret haunts known only to his warrior ancestors.

Setting out in the early evening, he drove from the farm near Taberville to the AllUNeed store in Bolivar. He stuck to two-lane state roads. He'd swapped license plates with one of the confiscated vehicles Daniel would be selling for scrap. He'd never been to that store, so he assumed he wouldn't be recognized. And Anna's car was so nondescript he doubted anyone would notice it, especially if he didn't park it in one of the employee spaces.

Back when she'd begun to work there, Anna had given him a gift card for his birthday. Two hundred bucks — a lot for a young working girl. It was too much for a young person who had to pay for rent and groceries, which made him worry she hadn't found her own place and might be shacking up somewhere. She'd also bought her mother a portable oxygen concentrator, and he knew those weren't cheap. At least, he was glad that the gift of the breathing machine had been his daughter's priority. Winona had used it pretty much all the time.

He bought a small propane stove and gas canisters, a one-man tent, thermal underwear, and two sleeping bags so he could double up. He was cheered to see solar-powered LED lanterns. He bought three of those and two flashlights so he'd have spares. He wouldn't have to worry about stocking up with kerosene.

He had to worry winter was coming. He didn't plan to stay there forever, but he wanted to be able to hole up in the cave until he got news that Trusdale, Ida, and Daniel were at least indicted if not convicted. He was not about to give himself up or offer testimony. He couldn't risk that no one would believe him, and even if they did, the manslaughter warrant for Henry Walker had his fingerprints. He felt he'd changed his likeness enough to be safe.

From the store, he drove east toward Camdenton, following the narrow roads at the edge of the Niangua arm of the big lake. He expected that the guard shack at the main park entrance would be closed and barricaded, and he hadn't planned on entering that way. When daylight was almost gone, he pulled onto a dirt fire road that ran to the shore across from Ha Ha Tonka Island. He parked the car in a copse of trees and explored the muddy shoreline. It didn't take him long to spot an abandoned old dinghy tied up to a tree. There was no one around.

He decided he'd sleep in the car tonight then at dawn would use the boat to ferry his supplies over to the cave entrance.

50

Curt prided himself on how slow he was to anger. Holding it all in often made him surly, if not down-right grouchy. He was beyond annoyed that Anna had shared so little with him about why they had to get away just now. But he knew she'd been through an ordeal at the farm, which she refused to say much about, and now she was dealing with her mother's death. He too wanted a clean break and a fresh start. And when she'd given him instructions about when and where to pick her up down the road from the preacher's place, he'd simply complied.

When they set out in the moonless predawn darkness, she'd told him to head south and then soon nodded off to sleep. She didn't wake until after the sun was up and they were headed down SR 13 in what had become a torrential rainstorm. Even with the wipers going at full speed, it was difficult to see the road, adding to Curt's annoyance.

He finally had to ask, "Where are we going?"

She helped herself to big gulps from a water bottle he'd brought and smirked. "Now or in our life's plan?"

"C'mon, Anna. I don't expect you to spill your guts about everything that happened on that farm. And I can understand why you'd want to get far away from those folks. But there has to be a plan for us. We want to be together, but where? And how? Both of us broke? With no jobs?"

"I gave the sheriff a sworn statement, told them everything I know. I saw people fasting, but I never saw anyone hurt anyone. So I'm not much of a witness for the things they really want to know. As for us, we'll have plenty of time to talk about it while we're on the road, but there is something I really have to do right away — find my father."

"Excuse me, but this is sounding pointless! The cops want him. They'll find him or they won't. What can we do?"

She studied her phone. "I know exactly where he is and why he's there."

"You're tracking his phone!"

She mused, "We set it up when he bought me mine. He thought he'd be able to know where I was, but I don't think he ever learned how to use it. And I bet he hasn't thought to turn it off. Or maybe he doesn't know how. And even if he shuts the phone off, he'll have to turn it back on to get the news. He has to keep up with what's going on."

"Do I get to know, or are you just going to keep giving me directions?"

"Ha Ha Tonka park. It's his getaway place. There are caves, and it's the off season."

"That's ridiculous! A person can't expect to live there."

"No, he needs to hide out long enough for the people who want to kill him to get locked up. Same as me, except he knows more and must've seen more."

He couldn't help growling, "I still don't understand why *you* have to be chasing after him. Or what this has to do with me — I mean, *us.*"

She turned her head to look directly at him, and the tears were starting to come. He looked back but then made an effort to keep his eyes on the slick road. "I need him to tell me whether he hurt anyone," she said. "He won't lie to me, and then I can decide whether I ever want to see him again."

"Is that so you can decide about us?"

She blew out a breath. "Oh, I've decided. I thought you had too, but maybe not yet. You see, the other reason I need to see him is to tell him he'll have a grandchild."

51
———

The lieutenant governor was only a tap away on my phone, but my finger never found the courage to touch the speed dial. I still had one of his personal mobile numbers, presumably because his biological son Luke had been my ward. I was one of the few people in the world who believed the young man's schizophrenia bestowed not only anguish but also spiritual insights. When his girlfriend Melissa had been trafficked and then abducted, he helped me devise the plot that had brought down mob boss Dmitri Churpov before he could take her out of the country.

I called Shackleton because by now I had few answers but a mental notebook full of penetrating questions. Financially, at least, he must be inside Trusdale's tent. I shuddered to think he might be at the center, but I didn't yet understand whether Pastor Obadiah's fundamental motivations were spiritual or earthly. Despite Shackleton's recent professed conversion and sponsorship of my ministry, I'd never thought of the former banker as anything but a political animal.

I never thought he was evil. He's amoral. He's self-centered, not deliberately vicious.

So I hit the button and got voicemail. I terminated the call right away because from the ID he'd know it was me, and some assistant might be screening his messages. But inside of five minutes, he called me back.

"Evan! I hope everything is all right."

In the past, the reasons for my calls most often had to do with the welfare of Luke, Melissa, and toddler Buzz. Shackleton would expect it was a request for money to help them, which he would willingly provide without question. Not understanding what to buy, he'd never been much of a giver of physical gifts, and showing affection was not in his makeup.

I told him, "I believe you know Luke and the family are living in Colorado. I've had no word in a month, which means they're at least maintaining happily on their own."

"You should be more involved. You're my eyes and ears."

"Benign neglect, that's been my plan. I'm not much of a role model these days." He knew I'd fallen from grace, perhaps not how far.

"Nevertheless," he said. It was a subtle rebuke, doubly ironic coming from him.

"I'd like a meeting. I need your take on recent events of public concern."

He knows exactly what I mean.

There was a brief pause while he checked his calendar or his conscience. Then he said tersely, "Information desk, state capital building, two today." He didn't wait for a reply.

WITH AN EMPTY STOMACH but anticipating an early lunch on the road, I set out midmorning in the Fiat for the two-and-a-half-hour drive to Jeff City. It was a golden, muggy day, and the abundant greenery along M-52 was thankfully exhaling its collected rainwater back up to the blazing sun, giver of all life. Missouri is intensely green and moist in the summer, frozen and either brown or white in winter. If you can't grow it here, you don't need it.

At this time of day, the road was congested, not with commuters but with semitrailer trucks headed to supermarkets and RVs barreling toward campgrounds. I wasn't seeing as many live-aboards out on the highways these days. Gas prices were too high.

Shamed by Shackleton's scolding, I rolled up the windows I'd had open to for the air and called Luke on speaker. I'd better have something to report when I faced the big man. Luke had a job shelving books in a public library, a place where hardly no one went. His most difficult chore, he'd told me, was walking around and nudging sleeping homeless patrons to at least sit up and crack a book.

"We can talk," he said. "There's no one here."

"I'm on my way to see your father. I know you guys must be okay, and I don't mean to pry."

"Yeah, fine. This job is a snore. I stay out of trouble. Melissa has a table at the farmer's market for her jewelry. She's almost supporting us. Buzz is Buzz. Can't stop burping and laughing. Tries to walk, falls over, rolls, and giggles so hard he can't get up for a minute. A future fullback. I'll have to take an interest in football, I guess. Maybe the statistics would be interesting."

"I have to ask, can you guys get your meds? Are you taking them?"

"Yeah, we're mostly okay. Melissa had a fit in a store last week, fell down, vomited, freaked everybody out." I'd heard the story from Walt but didn't want to admit I'd known and not bothered to call.

Melissa suffered from chronic epilepsy, which was controllable most but not all of the time with a drug cocktail that her doctors had to monitor and keep adjusting. This was one reason I worried about their being away from home, especially if they were moving around like nomads. The fits were a fact of her life, not usually a medical emergency. But if an episode took hold of her in public, onlookers always reacted as if it was a heart attack.

Luke went on, "I wasn't with her. Buzz has seen it, giggles like it's a game. Fortunately, nobody thinks we're witches, and they're not running us out of town. She recovered quickly enough before they could call the paramedics. It was just a cleanup on aisle five." Then he asked, "You hear from Mom?" He was asking about Loretta, not his birth mother Ann, who'd passed on during Covid.

"I'm not ready to have a conversation with her. She has my number, so I guess she feels the same." I didn't want to dwell on it. Luke's supervisor might be watching him, and I knew he couldn't engage in a long chat. But his insights often surprised me. I asked him, "You've seen the news about the farm?"

"Yeah, hell on earth you have to say." I waited for him to add, "You know, you had that sermon, God doesn't have to judge? The eternal soul looks back on its life and judges itself. What does that guy expect? A medal? He can't believe a word of it."

"Are you saying his treasure's not in heaven?"

Luke laughed again. "Buried in his backyard, more like."

He might have been joking, but my sense was if Trusdale had anything buried out there, the gravediggers would find it.

But it occurred to me to ask, "Luke, your ESP amazes me at times. Have you picked up any vibes about this guy?"

He thought a moment then said, "If he loves anyone, it's his mother. And if he's terrified of anyone, it's himself."

That's my Luke! Maybe someday I'll figure out what it means. He may not know.

I let him go. He was actually busy converting this old branch of the system from Dewey decimal to Library of Congress indexing. Give a dog a job, give a genius a nasty problem with numbers.

~

AT THE CAPITOL BUILDING, I passed through security, including the magnetometer and a courteous underarm-to-crotch pass with the wand. I was one of the few businesslike people dressed in suits who wasn't carrying a briefcase.

I'd dressed up in the black tailored outfit I used to wear on Sundays. I'd kept it neatly folded, along with shoes, a starched white shirt, and a muted tie, in a suitcase in the trunk of the car. The previous night, I'd put it on a hanger in the trailer so it would be less wrinkled in the morning. The funky humidity helped, and I judged it didn't look like I'd slept in it.

The first floor of the cavernous institution was thronged with more tourists than legislators. The acoustics echoed the shuffling of feet on the marble floor and their excited chatter. The high dome of the rotunda was a breathtaking open space above me, four stories high. I'd never had a reason to be here. When I presented myself at the information desk, the attendant had only to cast an approving look over my shoulder, and there stood a uniformed officer. With a curt nod and no greeting, that young woman led me across the floor to the northeast corner of the building, where she ceremoniously opened a paneled door, beckoned me in, and left.

Lt. Gov. Stuart Shackleton, resplendent as was his habit in a bespoke silk suit, sat affably in the big chair behind his desk, his hands clasped behind his head. He looked like the feature-article photo of a famous man relating his colorful life story to an interviewer.

Shackleton threw out his hands to indicate the limited span of the space. "Can you believe it? When I was at the bank, my admins got bigger offices!"

I put my hands in my pockets and looked around. "Nice paneling, luxury carpeting. All the pride you can't swallow."

He laughed. "You're implying I'm the power behind the man?

Don't count on it. All those jokes about the useless Veep in the White House apply here." He stood and came around his desk to grab me by the shoulders in the manful equivalent of a hug. "Evan!" He pushed back to get a close look. "Your cheeks are sunken, darker around the eyes. And you've shed most of the roll around your middle. You'll need those pants taken in so you don't look like a schlump."

"You look great too," I said.

He threw a comradely arm around my shoulders and walked me out and over to the elevators. As he punched the button, he winked. "We'll take a trip to the top."

As we got in and rode up, thinking I was getting the tourist treatment, I asked, "Top of the dome?"

"Hell no! They call that place the Whispering Gallery. Off limits to most visitors unless you're guest of an official. No, up there anything we say gets heard all over the place." In a dramatic hush, he added, "I'm taking you to top of the food chain."

We got out on the second floor. He unclipped the ID badge from the breast pocket of his coat and swiped it across a reader on the wall. He opened a tall entry door and we were standing in a prestigious circular office, about forty feet around, tall ceiling and floor-length windows in back of the huge desk, facing a paneled wall inset with giant oil paintings of legendary leaders of yesteryear.

"The governor's office?" I asked unnecessarily.

"No one home," Shackleton sneered, "even when he's here."

From the gleam in his eye, he wasn't fantasizing about moving in here. In his mind, the chair was already his.

Hinting at my own agenda, I suggested, "Could it be the scandal is keeping him away?"

Shackleton's expression went blank. He took my arm and led me out a side door. Now we were standing on the balustrade of the north portico, looking out over the Missouri Veterans reflecting pool, a fountain and bronze statuary in the distance. It occurred to me my great-uncle's name should be engraved in stone somewhere in that memorial.

Were World War I and the Spanish Flu so different in scale or destruction from the crises that beset us today?

"We can talk frankly here," he announced, also unnecessarily. We were alone on the parapet.

I announced frankly, "Some digging discloses your investment group owns the End-Times property."

"Evan, that's a real estate investment trust. It's blind. I have no part in its activities."

"So you must have been surprised as anyone with what some other diggers found there."

By now, anyone who hasn't heard Ardmore's news is deliberately refusing information.

Shackleton's face went blank again, a look some might have interpreted as sincerity. "Of course. Horrible. Like some third-world nightmare. Witch-doctor stuff."

"Would you be as surprised to learn that the End-Times Foundation has made several significant contributions to your campaign committee?"

"It's a PAC! Citizens United? I'm not sure, but I bet we've got Saudi princes and Chinese manufacturers."

"You and your staff don't solicit? Play golf? Drop into some country club for a chat, a cigar, and sipping-whiskey neat?"

"Is that all you have?"

"What about Trusdale's lawyer? Harrison represented you, as I recall."

He scoffed, "Bert follows the money. And Trusdale must have a pile of it. Should I give you a list of Alan Dershowitz's clients? Everyone has a right to competent counsel. It's the law, and a good one."

Shackleton pursed his lips in frustration and gestured expansively toward the horizon. A few hundred yards off, at the edge of the bluff, the Missouri River flows listlessly and inexorably. Some things were reasonably certain. A hedge-fund guy once confided to me that, for the last few centuries, Missouri-to-Mississippi barge traffic had always been one of the surest and sweetest ways to make money while you slept.

He pointed. "The statue on the left, that's the Louisiana Purchase Treaty. There have to still be French aristocrats who rue that day. Then on the right, the Ten Commandments. How many of those are we keeping these days, Preacher? How many have we ever kept?"

He can't expect an answer. Where is he going with this?

I confronted him with, "You've defended Obadiah in public statements. How can you do that?"

Shackleton turned back to me and growled. "I haven't defended the man, nor what he did! Without a trial — and you know that will drag on for years — God knows what he did or what he's responsible for, legally or morally. I'm defending religious freedom and his right of free speech."

"If that's the only rule, the guy could walk free of all this! There are actually serious people saying it was all a hoax, that there are no corpses, just body bags full of stuffing and actors. Doesn't that worry you? How about the truth? How do we call ourselves Christians if someone can do this in the name of God?"

"Evan, you may have noticed there's a tidal wave of populism in this country — hell! — all over the world! Do you think these people and their elected leaders are all suffering from some kind of insanity? Are they all brainwashed, racist crazies?"

"I don't understand anything anymore. You sound like you know."

"I do. I understand this much, and so does any so-called public servant. What drove those people at End-Times over the edge wasn't faith. It was *fear*. People are terrified not only of change but of the fearsome pace of it — and from so many directions! How's

the world going to end? It used to be a hypothetical question —
but not anymore! Not just fire or ice — how about catastrophic
weather, water shortages, wildlife extinction, polluted oceans with
poisoned fish, nuclear war, nuclear winter, meteor collision, food
insecurity, race war, all the bees gone, and — yes, political insurrec-
tion, internment camps, and firing squads. But who will be firing
and who against the wall? Is it any wonder these fearful folks crave
strong, authoritarian leaders? Pastor Obadiah's message is *shut up
and follow!* Get on the bus or you'll be left behind!"

"Surely you know he's a fraud. Does he want political influence?
You can't be thinking he'd run for office himself."

Shackleton came close to say, "What motivates the guy? I can't
guess. But when he sells them a story, a hundred people buy it and
lay down their lives. The folks who push the big brands hire some
big agency, spend millions of bucks, and they can't get anyone to so
much as switch their toothpaste. However, when Pastor Obadiah
does it, he commands power. That's the right stuff in anybody's
language. A smart man doesn't fight a gale-force storm. The wind's
blowing the other way."

I can't, I won't, say more.

Finally, he asked, "So how are the kids?"

"Maintaining, which is saying a lot, considering. They send
their love."

"I know they don't. Listen, this morning I transferred funds
into Luke's account. A lot more than he needs. You still decide how
to spend it. Get yourself a haircut, some decent clothes, and get
back on the air."

"Why would you want that? What do you expect me to say?"

"You want to do battle with the guy? Go ahead. First amend-
ment. Say anything you like as long as you don't tell them to vote
for the other party."

ON MY HURRIED WAY OUT, I wasn't thinking clearly. I was so angry I had to find a way to calm myself before I got back behind the wheel. I picked up a tourist brochure from the information desk and read that this glorious building was finished fairly recently, in 1917. The previous three structures had burned to the ground. The historical note didn't mention how the first one caught fire, but the second had been struck by lightning.

Perhaps those lawmakers had also been heedless of the consequences of sin.

When this structure was new, the war to end all wars and a pandemic were still raging.

The French have a saying. Maybe it's in the Bible somewhere: As much as things change, they remain the same.

WHEN I WAS GROWING up on the farm, the question of why there is evil in the world bewildered me even then, although I didn't frame it that way. When there was an illness, an accident, or brutal unfairness, I'd ask my dad, "How come?" And he'd say, "Son, sometimes God goes fishing." Back then, I had no idea what he was trying to tell me, but it was as much explanation as he would offer. Reflecting back on it now, perhaps he meant that the Creator expects humans will always screw up, and sometimes we have to wait for the consequences to play out, the hysteria to die down.

At such times for me these days, Naomi will show up, my spiritual paramedic. I was strolling aimlessly in the meticulous landscape of the capitol when she appeared by my side on the footpath. I was still too upset to drive. No one was close by, but lest anyone suspect I was insane and having a conversation with an unseen person, I kept my head bowed. I might be praying, rehearsing my speech on the Senate floor, or speaking on my phone.

I glanced over furtively to see she was wearing navy pants and a colorful, African-themed silk blouse with bright red beads around her neck and hoop earrings to match. She looked like a society lady headed to an afternoon garden party. The pants would be a statement, not a coincidence. It was her bossy look. The festive rest of it told me, no matter how dark the funk I was mired in, she'd have none of it. She was ready to party.

"You walked right into that one," she sneered.

"Do I get to say I go where the spirit leads?"

She was amused. "What was it they used to tell kids? If your friend told you to jump off a cliff, would you do it?"

"Obadiah told those folks to starve themselves."

"You know he's going to say he preached the gospel, and they made their own decisions."

There were ducks fluttering and quacking in the water fountain. They were having a good time, perhaps playing a mating game.

I asked her, "What do I do now? I could sell cars at Zed Motors, cut my hair, and get the suit cleaned and pressed, like he said."

"He gave you money."

"No, he gave Luke money."

"No, he sent it to *you* so it wouldn't go on the books as a bribe."

"I don't have to take it."

"You took it before, back when you thought the good you could do would be bigger than the sin."

"And how did that turn out? Are you saying I should repeat the mistake?"

"Hanged for a sheep, hanged for a lamb. Another cute old saying." I was going to press my argument, but she added, "Gotta run. I have to decide whether my drink is vodka tonic or Mimosa." And she was gone.

~

THE DAY I CONFRONTED SHACKLETON, the news was all about Trusdale's expected appearance before the grand jury. Some news commentators speculated he might defy the subpoena. Others opined he was a flight risk and some rich benefactor could sponsor his residence in some country that wouldn't extradite him. But Trusdale must have been confident of his safety and protection from a higher power, whether earthly or heavenly, all along.

The court proceedings were being held in secret, and his attorneys advised him to cease his podcasts and any public statements. But he was not to be warned off his message or his mission.

Ida and the other staff members had also been set free, released without conditions but advised they were likely to be subpoenaed eventually.

As I drove back from the capitol, I decided I didn't have to make a decision right away about Shackleton's compromising donation to my welfare. After all, he hadn't given me a message to deliver or a position to press. Ever the politician, he was playing both sides, betting I'd find a way to serve us both.

Still no word from Leon. I worried he had other priorities. If he did, he might never close the loop on this one, especially if the law continued to have trouble hanging any offense on Trusdale.

52

As if in answer to prayer, Pastor Bingham came by the next morning with a basket of her carrot-ginger-raisin muffins, still warm. I put on the coffee, and even though she'd intended some of that batch for Reverend Thurston, we consumed all but a few right then.

But it was not a social visit. Apparently, questions she might have put to Anna had been resolved by too much information made public since. Today, she was fretting about something else. She lamented that the Southern Baptist Convention was considering expelling all female pastors. She'd requested a meeting with Marcus this morning and wanted me to go with her.

Marcus had his own repast laid out for us — banana bread, plums, yogurt, and local black walnuts. It was a righteous presentation, even though his coffee was weak as ever.

I kept my mouth shut through Olivia's plea. She wanted to convene the board of deacons and pass a resolution for the church to register a formal objection, backed up with a petition from the membership, along with a provisional threat to dissociate from the national organization if the policy became mandatory.

Marcus didn't ask for my opinion but gave me that wide-eyed look, as if it were all up to me, which we all knew it wasn't, at least officially.

I replied, "Baptists are prone to run off their pastors eventually, be they male or female. The excuse is usually doctrinal, but I'd say it's more like our little communities can't find enough to fret about. And every time there's a new legislative agenda, we have to get our tails in a twist, if only to show our fellow citizens we're still relevant. But this time I think it's about the horrors at the End-Times farm. Churches all over have grown understandably defensive. So naturally we'd rather argue about anything else until people forget what the question was."

Marcus asked me, "So — what? We do nothing?"

I nodded. "As little as possible. Then, if they're still harping about women in the pulpit, yes, we send the letter. We don't need to get the congregation riled up with a petition. The deacons can sign a letter from our board. No threat for the church to quit. Then we wait some more for a reply, which might take time, if it ever comes. Meanwhile, Olivia, you might be shopping for some other health insurance we could buy for you. It also might be a good idea to find another pension plan, no matter how this turns out."

Marcus looked over at Olivia. She smiled and shrugged. I worried I'd made it all sound like no big deal, and I knew she was justifiably angry. Whatever our next steps, it would be important for her to feel we were ready to fight for her.

Marcus chaired the board, so he said he'd draft the letter. He insisted he'd make our objections firm and unconditional.

Then he leaned back in his rocker and heaved a deep sigh. "Evan, what are we going to do — what should we do — about this awful farm? We can't have people thinking Trusdale's craziness is the essence of what it means to be a Christian. I wonder myself, but here's another dangerous place literal interpretation of scripture can take you. Back when I was pastor, if you'd told me the end of the world was a real possibility in our lifetimes, I'd have paid no attention. But now? The Earth might be still be here, but extinction of the human race seems not only possible but likely. What do we tell folks? What do we believe ourselves?"

I answered, "It's not advice for us as a church, but I've been expecting Trusdale would be charged with some kind of endangerment, maybe even murder, and put on trial. When the facts come out, people will see him for the fraud he is and for his preaching to be wrong and malicious."

Here came my mentor's meaningful look again, as he said softly, "Evan, I would have told you to stay out of all this, but I know you wouldn't and can't. If you hadn't been nosing around, maybe it would have taken a lot longer for these evil deeds to come out. My worry is this guy will wriggle free somehow. The church has to stand for its freedom, and yet, years back, if he was one of ours, we'd tar and feather him and run him out of town."

I wasn't about to share my concerns about Birch, but I felt I had to tell them about Shackleton. Neither of them would have suspected his connection to the farm. And now that I'd met with the man, I couldn't hold back, especially since he'd already advanced the funds for me to resume my ministry. No matter how I did or didn't follow through, if the community or even the public at large thought me a hypocrite, I had to be ready to withstand criticism. But here were two people whose opinion about the sincerity of my beliefs mattered most of all.

I told them I'd discovered financial relationships between Shackleton's investment trust and the End-Times Foundation, along with the suggestive fact that money had also flowed from Trusdale's accounts as donations to Shackleton's campaign PAC.

Marcus knew of Shackleton's professed conversion after not one but a series of scandals that found him plotting with opportunistic gangsters like Churpov. And after seeing light on the way to his own Damascus, the banker had funded my televangelism ministry and a megachurch, both ventures to my (hopefully not everlasting) shame. I summarized as much for Olivia, although she'd undoubtedly heard it all as gossip already.

News to both of them would be Shackleton's urging me to use his money to get back in the game. I shared as much with them, careful to emphasize that this conversation took place only yesterday, and I was still wondering what to do about it.

"It's not surprising he's trying to play both sides," Marcus observed. "And if Trusdale goes down, he'd want his opponents to look like weaklings. For it to look like a fair fight, you'll need to make a comeback first and become a worthy rival. Then you can have your rematch. And win."

I hadn't expected unperturbed candor, nor an astute lesson in political gamesmanship. "Marcus, am I to understand you're encouraging me to do this?"

He was holding a handful of grapes and hesitated before he popped the next one past his wide grin and into his mouth. "You know, I've really enjoyed my retirement. And I plan to continue to do so — as the old folks used to say, as long as I'm spared. Evan, in case I never said as much, it wasn't lost on me how brave it was for you to step in during Covid and follow through with all those visitations. I regret the burden your being minister put on Loretta, but I'd say the final chapter on you two hasn't been written yet."

He couldn't resist chomping down a few grapes, as if he needed the energy for the rest of his speech. With a wink in Olivia's direction, he went on, "Now, I don't believe God decides each time a sparrow falls. I'd think there's a divine plan, a pattern, and things play out as they must. But I do believe in providence, and I do most certainly believe in prayer. And I've been praying night and day you'd come out of your funk — understandable as it's been considering all we've put you through. So here we are.

"Olivia has brought our attention to a doctrinal issue that requires we speak out — forcefully. As well, here's this charlatan

Obadiah running around, spouting nonsense, claiming it's biblical and raking in cash for himself. The law might get him or might not. But from the viewpoint of our ministry, somebody's got to stand up to him."

Pastor Thurston leaned forward to rest his elbows on his knees, leaned in my direction, and like a coach concluding his half-time speech insisted, "What we need is a voice. You know more about apocalyptic theology than anybody, even though you don't hold with it. Debate the guy. As to Shackleton, I'd say, I can't think of a better use for his gold, ill-gotten or otherwise."

Olivia smiled, nodded, and must have hoped her "Amen!" sounded reverential, not like sucking up to these men.

53

The process of exhuming bodies from the End-Times farm, performing autopsies, and processing evidence took time, and grand-jury proceedings went slowly. To keep Trusdale back into custody and under control, and possibly to silence his podcasts, state prosecutors wanted to book him on something, such as child endangerment or assisting suicide, but they couldn't find sufficient grounds for either charge.

As the exhumations were taking place, public interest had been keen. Each day's news report increased the body count, appealed to loved ones to register missing persons, and lamented the agonizingly slow process of identifying the deceased by forensic and DNA analyses. The forensic team working at the farm announced they'd finished all exhumations at the farm after seven weeks on the job, but processing and matching DNA samples took much longer. Despite redoubled efforts, federal investigators had found no illegal weapons. One by one, the refrigerated mortuary trucks had departed until there was no one but a small contingent of state troopers onsite. Yellow tape ringed the property, woven into the chain-link fence, but the power to the electrified fence hadn't been restored since the day the first bodies were discovered.

At this point, no one imagined anyone would still want to go there.

Through all this, twice a week, Obadiah released new podcasts. Now I was subscribing to research my opponent. His rant became bolder and more explicit.

"My dear brothers and sisters, I have been defending you! You may not know it yet, but more than ever in our recent history the forces of evil are arrayed against us. The unbelievers have coalesced into an insane mob, and they are powerful. I mean the Communists, the Jews, the Catholics, the impure races, the progressives, the big-money interests, the shadow government, the naysayers, and all their fellow travelers. The truth burns their skin! They are saying — and they will keep repeating the lie — that I am a murderer. What, I ask you, have I done?

"I have done none other than to preach the gospel — the literal truth: If you believe, when you die, you will join our Maker in Heaven. How is this not the truth? Am I the only voice proclaiming it to a new generation? I have preached that Big Pharma poisons us, that public education poisons minds, and that licentiousness infects us with ugly sex diseases and poisons our souls. How many other preachers and prophets of other faiths are free to teach the same? And yet they are persecuting *me?* No — they intend to persecute all of us! And if we don't obey, if we don't bow down before their golden calf, they will assuredly round us up, line us up against the wall, and mow us down!"

My blood pressure rose every time I listened, but I knew I couldn't ignore him. There was such a tide of emotion swelling in his favor, I was bewildered about how to counter his awful message without sounding like a bitter evildoer myself.

I'd stayed in touch with Harry Ardmore. I could seek counsel and comfort from Thurston or Bingham, but alone among my friends, this journalist had the latest information I needed to stay in the game. Granted, I could drop out. What business was it of mine? Trusdale was mired in the legal system now, and as Ecclesiastes 8:10 tells us about God's justice, the United States system of jurisprudence "grinds slow and exceedingly fine."

And that was what Trusdale would be counting on. By the time there was sufficient evidence to charge him, try him, and render judgment, he'd have united his backers and his followers would have anointed him a king, answerable to no one.

I'D APPROACHED Ardmore soon after Birch's confession to me. You could say I was in denial, but I refused to go to Otis with this. Without disclosing what my old friend had told me, I wanted any news from the reporter about Osceola's whereabouts. I still believed fervently Birch wasn't capable of harming — much less, killing — anyone.

Ardmore didn't want to meet at his apartment, which he feared was bugged. He didn't trust his girlfriend Petra either, saying she had "big ears." He worried she secretly worked for a rival news network, but she was nevertheless a friend with compelling benefits.

I told him my trailer might be likewise wired, but we could take strolls around its environs, where we risked being overheard only by rabbits and squirrels.

He didn't like walking out in the open. Presumably, he feared dish audio pickups or snipers. I didn't want to ask.

He liked the idea of my favorite meeting place with Leon — sitting in the bleachers overlooking the playing field at Appleton City High School. I'd learned a lot already about not only soccer but also field hockey and lacrosse. Sack races were difficult to watch without breaking down into debilitating fits of laughter.

"You could at least bring popcorn," he quipped.

I told him, "Hey, I'd have brought a flask, but I'm all out. What's the scoop? We needn't take all day. Maybe you don't want to be seen with the likes of me."

"You?" He sniffed. "I'd be in a lot more trouble if you were back on the radar."

"What do you mean?"

"You used to have your own podcast, right?"

"Yeah, podcast and TV. It was kind of dry. Sunday-school lessons for Bible thumpers, agnostics, and backsliders."

"Are you ready to go again?"

Has Olivia or Marcus put that idea in his head, or is it that great minds think alike?

I pretended it was a new thought. "Are you serious? Who's talking here?"

"Me — and any intelligent person who wants to hear the other side. The legal arguments get talked to death. But someone like you who knows scripture should be calling this guy out and talking him down from inside the revival tent, so to speak. As of now, there's nobody challenging him except news readers on the left-wing channels. They like to debate the legal proceedings like it's the statistical baseball league."

"Since when are you not a leftie?"

"Who me?" He laughed. "Last Democrat makes it out of Missouri alive, please turn out the lights."

"Are you seriously suggesting I should go back on the air?"

He smirked. "If you don't, I'll write nasty things about you until you do."

It irked me that he had nothing new to tell me in this meeting as if I'd agreed to see him under false pretenses. But it turned out he was the one with a full flask, and watching teenage girls disporting themselves was worth the trip.

54

I guessed the librarian at the Mid-Continent branch on Oldham Parkway was first-generation East Indian. "Darshana" was on her name tag, there was a red caste mark on her forehead, and she spoke with a lilting accent. The exotic vision would have been complete had she been wearing a sari, but hers was an Under Armour workout jacket and deliciously tight jeans.

As I handed her the three books Monica had let me take, Darshana smiled sweetly to ask, "Returning?"

I assume she means the books. Her flirtatious look makes me wonder whether she means me. Vain much?

"Yes, for a friend," I said. "Are they overdue?"

She passed each barcode over her scanner, glanced at the computer display, and replied, "Indeed, yes. Your friend owes us five dollars and seventy-five cents."

It was hardly enough to buy my next sandwich, but as I searched in my pocket for cash, I did regret the expense. I found a ten and laid it on the counter. As she took it and made change, her smiled broadened. "Your friend, the old fellow, he's not ill, I hope?"

Ah, this could be a stroke of luck.

I was so pleased by the coincidence, I had to summon a sober expression to tell her, "Sadly, he passed away last week." I didn't want to upset her with details that would have us in the usual chat about cause of death, surviving family members, and condolences.

"Oh, I'm so sorry," she said softly. "He was a charmer."

"You knew him?"

"I saw him almost daily for a while. He was a diligent student."

"Theology?"

She shook her head to say, "From these books, you'd think so. But he had me doing online searches for technical white papers."

"Do you recall the topic? I knew he was involved with fascinating stuff, but he wouldn't tell me much about it. Simulations and displays? Sensors?"

She said proudly, "I can recall specifically. Holographic telepresence. Studies from the optics departments at the universities of Arizona and Osaka. Not recent. From 2010 to 2011."

"I'm impressed but don't know the term."

"Projection of 3D images on clouds or steam. The student experimenters in Japan called their invention the 'Osaka fogograph.'" She was amused to say it. "He wouldn't tell me much either, but he did say he'd done work in aerospace, so I surmised his interest had something to do with projecting phantom images of fighter jets on clouds to confuse the enemy in aerial combat."

Or manifesting a pair of lions out of thin air?

"Wow," I said, "I can understand why he couldn't talk about it."

"Now, perhaps you can answer one for me. What is this book by Bruno? Why do you think he was interested in it?"

"The Expulsion of the Triumphant Beast. By *beast,* he meant the Pope and the Church. The Inquisition burned him at the stake for saying that blind faith in anything, including Christianity, would keep people from asking questions to learn truths about the universe. In effect, he was arguing in favor of scientific experiment,

although it would take another century or two for the idea to catch on."

She thumbed the book, "I read some of it, but it made no sense to me."

"It's long, poetical story with mythological characters. The god Jupiter is trying to purge the universe of evil. Hence the reference to expulsion. It's amazing Cardinal Bellarmine's scholastic monks understood the story well enough to despise it as heresy."

As she turned the pages, a scrap of paper I hadn't seen fell out. She glanced at it and asked, "Do you want this?"

"Is that the overdue notice?"

"Yes, but it has writing on it." She handed it over.

The printout from the library system showed not only the doctor's email address but also the crusty fellow had scrawled "4the-Beast!" in a shaky hand. His security clearance would no doubt have forbidden him from writing down passwords, but judging from the public web domain, this was his personal email, and perhaps he'd been growing forgetful.

I folded the slip and tucked it into my shirt pocket. If I hadn't told her he was deceased, she no doubt would have been sharp enough not to let me have the personal data.

I asked her, "Do you know if he used your computers here?"

She replied, "I expect he searched our catalog and databases like WorldCat." Perhaps she suspected why I wanted to know when she added, "We don't allow personal log-ins. Patrons share a guest account."

Nurse Monica said he'd used a computer there.

It occurred to me to ask, "Did he tell you he was living at John Knox Village? It's quite a drive from here. Do you know whether it was their van that brought him here?"

"I don't know how he got here most days. But there was one time when he asked me to help him to the curb and a fellow in a pickup truck was there to take him."

"Did the truck look beat-up? White?"

"That's right. His other friend was Native American, I believe. He had long hair and wore a red kerchief on his head. Perhaps you know him?"

I risked saying, "He was a worker at the End-Times farm."

"Oh," she said with a slight gasp. She must have heard of it but only added, "He never spoke of it. Are you from there?"

"No, no. I used to be pastor of Evangel Baptist in Appleton City. I'm kind of retired these days."

It might have been good customer-service training or my sheer attractiveness that made her ask, "Is there anything else I can help you with?"

"Actually, why don't I check out the Bruno book myself? We looked at it in divinity school, but it's a dim memory. You've made me wonder why the doctor was interested."

Darshana patiently helped me register for a new card, copying information from my driver's license and, perhaps ignoring the formal rules, accepting only my reverend business card as proof of residence.

As I thanked her on leaving, I asked, "Your given name. I'm not familiar. What does it mean?"

Big smile. "One who observes and understands!"

55

Since I had Gropius's log-in credentials, I was tempted to dive in right away on my laptop. But I worried I'd get caught up in a double-auth loop. I didn't have his phone, and as far as I knew he didn't have one. Otis said none was found on his person the day of the accident.

Darshana had as much as told me he couldn't log in or check his email from any of the terminals in the library. Nurse Monica had let me know that their facility had a workstation the residents could use. She'd already confirmed he didn't have his own computer. So my thought was, if I could log in from there, it would likely show up as the same IP address he'd used. If his email account had previously trusted that address, there was a chance the password would be enough by itself to let me in.

Monica seemed pleased to see me, but she could tell I was preoccupied and not wanting to chat. When I asked to sit down at the computer in the solarium, she took me right there, flashed a smile, and walked away, taking with her a guest chair that had been beside the desk. She didn't go so far as to ask me what I was doing, but she must have sensed I needed to avoid onlookers.

I got through, and "4theBeast!" was still the key. Checking his email account, I was quickly reminded how cautious he was. Confirming my suspicion, he didn't have or had avoided using a phone, many of his emails were about logistics, making arrangements that might otherwise have been handled in texts. He corresponded with a catchall address at Obadiah Ministries to arrange for Talker to pick him up. I could see no messages of substance. He'd either deleted them or didn't use email for other purposes.

It was initially disappointing. I'd made a special trip to Knox only to find out what I already knew about Talker's driving him between the home and the farm and the library.

But then it occurred to me to check his cloud account, which held a trove of files. From the filenames alone, I could tell those were mostly scholarly articles. But there were other documents he may have written himself.

One was named *For_Evan_* followed by a long string of sequential numbers and the extension *gdoc*.

Even though no one was looking over my shoulder, I chose not to open the file there. I had a thumb drive in my pocket and copied all of his files.

I passed Monica at the reception desk on my way out and must have still looked hurried and worried. I stopped long enough for her to ask me, "Did you get what you need? I'm sure you're the only one who's bothered."

"He wrote me a note," I confided. "But I haven't had time to read it."

"He spoke of you fondly," she said. "Even though I believe you hadn't met him until that day. You might be the only one who could understand what he was about. I don't think he was deranged or demented, just someone who spent all his time in his own head."

"You're right," I told her. "That's me."

She could see I didn't want to linger, but she offered, "Anytime you want to share."

As soon as I was back in my car, I uploaded the contents of the drive to my laptop, and I opened the file.

My eagerness to read the personal note gave way to immediate frustration. The screen was filled with alphanumeric characters and not a single intelligible word. The text was neatly arranged in columns of eight-character groups. It was some kind of code, but how did the old cuss expect me to know how to make sense of it?

Right away, I called Walter for his technical diagnosis. When I described to him what I was seeing on the screen, he chuckled and asked, "Evan, don't you read anything but Bible stuff?"

"Like what?"

"Spy novels? One of them famously has the answer for you in its title. Ken Follett's *The Key to Rebecca*. This type of code is called a *book cipher,* and it's at the center of that plot, but it's also mentioned in any number of espionage stories, particularly British ones set in World War Two."

"How does it work?"

"The codes in the text specify words by their locations in a source text — by page number, paragraph number, line number, and word number. Or you can encode down to the level of characters. But if you don't know which book was used as the basis of the code — right down to which printed edition — you're pretty much out of luck. The plotters in Follett's story used the novel *Rebecca* by Daphne du Maurier as the source."

"Let's say for the sake of argument I know the source. But I can tell the coded file isn't some short message. It's more like a long letter. What can I do?"

Now he laughed, "Rev, these days, there's an app for that!"

EVEN WITH SOFTWARE TOOLS, the file Gropius had constructed was cussedly difficult to decode. I was twice tempted to pick up the phone and ask Walter to guide me, and when nothing I'd tried on my own worked, I considered asking Leon to engage some expert from some three-letter-agency cyber team. But if I involved third parties, I feared disclosing the old fellow's confession, if that was what it was, could risk getting some other living persons in trouble.

The solution came when I asked myself how the doctor would approach the problem. His hints to me and my discovery of the book strongly suggested that *The Expulsion of the Triumphant Beast* was the key. And since the code would be based on the page numbering and layout of a specific edition of the printed work, I had to assume the copy he'd borrowed from the library was the right one.

When I began to think about how I'd go about making a text secret, I realized how, even though the choice of a book cipher was clever as a ruse, it wouldn't support a lengthy contemporary message. The Gropius document contained many pages of encoded text. The messages in the old spy novels, when finally "unbuttoned" through tedious manual lookup, were more like brief telegrams, taking hours to decode by hand. But even with a computer to automate the decoding, building a longer message composed of words from Bruno wouldn't be practical. The old book wouldn't likely encompass the vocabulary Gropius would need to convey modern thoughts. The encoding scheme would have to be character- rather than word-based.

I was beginning to think the *Expulsion* book was a poor choice, but I had nothing else to go on.

With the file open as text, I noticed it was broken into two sections. The first was brief, having only a few columns and rows containing groups of fixed length. Each row contained a series of five-digit groups, separated by spaces. With reference to the book, I guessed the five digits in each group represented: page number, paragraph number, line number, word number, and character position in that word. Decoded, each group could be one character of the message text. I saved the first section of the Gropius document to a separate file then used Walter's app to decode it as a character-based book cipher using Bruno as the source.

The result was a string of garbled alphanumeric text.

Okay, it's a result, but how useful?

I wondered why the Gropius encoded-text document had two sections. I reasoned that the longer section was some lengthy document, presumably some secret explanation of why he'd come to see me. Since I'd guessed that the Bruno text would be a poor book cipher for such a message, I guessed that the first section was an encryption key — a brief, coded message, based on Bruno — that would tell me how to unlock the rest.

File-transfer methods that use public-key encoding—a method used routinely on the Internet — requires two keys, one public, knowable by all potential recipients, and one private, disclosed only to the intended recipient. The key I decoded must have been the private one. I had the other when I realized the document's file name contained exactly the required number of characters to be the matching public key.

Now I input those two keys not to the book-cypher app but to a file-transfer utility and applied it to the whole document.

The result was clear text but in German. It took another translation pass with an online translator app to make it understandable to me.

My dear Evan,

If you are reading this, I have stepped out of the movie. If we should ever meet in another dimension, we will have much to discuss.

Clever of you to decipher this. Wise of me to hide it.

This is not so much a confession as a warning, but I must first tell you what I did for O. My motivation was simple. I needed money. I feared I would eventually become sicker than I was, and you know it is easier and less expensive to be admitted to a care facility if you are not yet in failing health.

I was also intrigued at first by the technical challenge. My work for the military had included battle simulation imagery, and I wanted to pursue the idea that virtual reality scenes could be induced in an audience without viewing devices. For his part, O wanted to create believable illusions to support his healing ceremonies. At the outset, this seemed innocent enough. I became more concerned when in my research I came across Project Blue Beam, which as far as I know is fantasy. However, it chilled me to think that, should such an operation ever be undertaken for a nefarious purpose, someone with my skills could achieve the result.

I was aware that 3D holography has been impressive when projecting images into water vapor. I searched for a medium that would be more reflective and therefore more realistic. Into a cloud of steam, in various experiments, I tried injecting silver iodide, potassium iodide, dry ice, and liquid propane. The results were messy and not sufficiently persistent. Reasoning that clouds form around dust particles in the atmosphere, I next tried smoke, and the kind produced by incense lent a nice, aromatic touch. O may have given you a chance to see the convincing result. His ego would delight in your amazement.

Originally, O wanted to manifest a host of angels to attend his high moments. I convinced him that, ancient imagery to the contrary, today's audiences won't believe that angels propel themselves on avian wings. We settled on the idea that glowing, androgynous humanoid bodies with halos could be convincing. Then I came up with the idea of rampant lions. When I stressed that such imagery through the ages has conveyed the divine right of earthly kings in crests and badges, O eagerly embraced the idea to support his healings. I explained that his audience needn't understand the symbolism. It is embedded in the collective unconscious.

I was aware that he lured hungry people to the farm with promises of food. I assumed his intention was to build a small army of the faithful. I later learned that he was receiving subsidies from political organizations to take homeless people off the streets. The combination of religious retreat and homeless shelter seemed to me, at first, as innocuous as his ministry. Then problems arose when the population grew so rapidly that he realized the situation was not sustainable.

They kept running out of food. They could manage deliveries, but even providing meager bowls of rice regularly to hundreds proved impractical without hiring more cooks and crew from the outside. The residents themselves became too weak to work, and disciplining them with physical punishments would also require staff recruited from outside, along with potentially criminal behavior. O wanted minimal staff because he feared outsiders could be disloyal. Secrecy was always at the core of his plan.

So he hit on voluntary starvation as the solution. During the time I was there, the crew did not yet include enforcers. If someone asked for food, they received it, but furtively and away from the others, along with warnings about violating their vows. I suspect that, as time goes on, more stringent discipline will be required. Then the place will become a concentration camp.

I do not know what they do with the bodies of those who have expired. They are careful I do not see that, but I hear things. The plan is malicious and clever. The children are to die first, followed by the women. The men are to remain strong enough to bury their dead. Then, if they do not die when they weaken, their neighbors will help them, then expire themselves. By this method, few must be executed at the hands of nonbelievers, perhaps none held accountable. Presumably, O and his sister are to die last, but I suspect they will survive no matter what.

I have drawn a parallel to conspiracy theories about government plans to fake the Second Coming of Christ. How could we ever conceive of an image of Christ that all nations would accept? But I should emphasize this was not O's plan. Doing so could put an end to his operations and subvert his earthbound intentions. No, he will not claim to be Jesus. He will instead array himself as a glowing John the Baptist. He will then announce that the next president of the United States will be the Antichrist. O will predict that the man will rule for forty-two months. During that time, he will become allied with other dictatorial leaders in a corrupt world government.

O will gain credibility from the fact that other evangelists and cult leaders have already made similar predictions.

O plans to be the Antichrist's Rasputin. And his farm model will be used to build concentration camps to house marginalized groups and dissidents. The beauty of this plan, as he sees it, is that the victims will commit themselves voluntarily, perhaps even to the extent of their demise, lured like lemmings to the precipice.

In some versions of prophesy, the Second Coming will then occur at the end of the Antichrist's rule. However, O does not believe it will, nor does he wish it. His plan is about worldly power for himself and his co-conspirators. Once they have what they want, and even after the interregnum has passed without incident, they will simply announce that some human shortcomings caused God to postpone the event.

I hope when you are reading this that the direst events have not yet transpired. O must not be allowed to use the technology I have developed to pose as anyone but his pathetic self.

If O is not stopped and yet his ambitions fall short, I suspect that, like other cult leaders before him, he will order some form of sudden mass suicide.

Which, even knowing him as little as I do, I believe he expects to survive.

Evan, please carry my story to whoever will listen and act. You once had a powerful and persuasive voice. I pray you regain it.

Your friend in this world and the next,

Hans

56

Birch knew the cave nearly as well as Talker did, and that was where he suspected his friend would hide out. It was an uncomfortable prospect, but he knew the man was daring enough to risk it. With luck, Birch would spot Anna's Honda first then could surveil it, expecting Talker would have reasons to return to it occasionally. He wasn't looking forward to chasing Talker among those cold, slippery rocks.

He didn't think Talker was stupid — just single-minded. The man was stubborn, insisting on his own way, not someone to be reasoned with. Still, Birch had to try to confront Talker. Of course, he'd always resented Winona's preferring the guy. And it was doubly unfair because the couple had pretended to her parents that his heritage was Osage. The old folks and their neighbors knew enough about their own Kiowa background to know he wasn't one of them. But finding any full-blooded man who respected the old ways was a challenge these days. They liked the lanky, swaggering look of him — and most of all that he'd come to them to ask permission to join their family, along with his suggestion that it be a Kiowa ceremony.

It wasn't for those reasons Birch thought Talker was the wrong man for Winona. That judgment crept up on him over these recent years when she'd fallen ill and then grown steadily worse. Talker was not a caregiver. He had to be moving and doing. And because his hands always found work, he was a good earner. But when Winona had informed him she wouldn't take the medications or even submit to the doctors' care, Talker's money was useless, as if her devout religion somehow castrated him.

True, as the disease progressed, she'd had no energy for affection. But Birch was sure he would never have left her side.

BIRCH'S SUV was equipped with GPS, which helped him get to the site, but he was unaware of any digital methods he might have used to stalk Talker, and he was likewise unaware that others were engaged in the pursuit.

It never occurred to Talker that either Birch or Anna would follow him. He didn't think himself that important, and in many ways he felt he'd failed both of them over the years. He'd taken the job with Trusdale because he hoped one day Winona would get desperate enough or sick enough to finally accept medical care and when that happened he'd be able to pay enough to get her some attention. Then after he'd served at the farm and endured its humiliation and frustrations, he thought that time wasted, especially after Winona showed up there with Anna.

That place was no solution, he knew, for anyone. It was like his wife was slitting her own throat, and it disgusted him, but what could he do? And Anna? Shouldn't she have known better? It showed how desperate she was to do anything for her mother, toward the last.

Talker was smart enough to fear Daniel would be going after

him. First because he'd witnessed what the others had done. And, most crucial for Daniel, Talker was the only one who knew for sure who'd been driving the truck that fateful day. With Talker dead, the cops would close the case, figuring either way the matter was as settled as it could be. They had no reason to suspect Daniel unless Talker turned himself in and told the truth. Then a lot of them would be in trouble. All the more reason they'd want him dead.

Talker couldn't have suspected that Daniel had planted a tracking device in his car. Talker wasn't clever technically, but he expected Daniel was no better. It was Ida's idea to let him have his daughter's car, which was really his, as if making up for ordering Daniel to torch the truck. If Talker had reflected on it, he would have realized that Ida didn't do those kinds of things out of kindness or guilt. It must have been her idea to put the thing on the car, planning all along she'd be sending Daniel after him if he ever took off.

So the convergence of all the players on Ha Ha Tonka Park wasn't a coincidence. Daniel had tracked him there. Even if Anna hadn't known how to track his phone, she could have guessed where he'd go, as did Birch. Talker didn't have much imagination.

It wouldn't have been a surprise to anyone, but Talker soon decided he couldn't hold out in the cold, damp cave for longer than a few days. Ferrying supplies in there via canoe was too risky in daylight and difficult to navigate at night except during the full moon, which wouldn't show up for weeks yet. Even with the double bed roll, his teeth chattered, and his back ached when he tried to stretch out on the slick limestone.

He gave up his plan and decided to sleep in the car, reasoning that he'd parked it where it was sufficiently camouflaged, and it was the off-season after all.

Birch, Anna, and Daniel all spotted the car on the same day. Each held off, unaware of the others, watching to see when Talker would show up.

Talker had been on the lookout continually. From almost the moment the scoutmaster pulled into the Ha Ha Tonka campground, it was Talker who was stalking Birch.

Daniel already had Talker in his sights and was waiting for the opportunity. But then he spotted Birch and hesitated while he worried about how to deal with this complication.

CURT HAD WANTED to be the voice of reason for Anna. What did she expect to do? To achieve? After enduring years of her father's irresponsibility and neglect, did she expect him to finally step up? Do the honorable thing?

"Let's think about this," he urged as she scanned the scene through binoculars. "Assume he's guilty of something — the hit-and-run or worse at that farm. What do you expect him to do? Jump in the car and let us drive him back to face the music? Or — what if he's totally innocent? What if he never hurt anybody? Will anyone back there believe him? What I'm asking is, how can we help whatever happens next for him? Don't tell me it's the baby."

"Why not?"

"He wasn't much of a father. How will he behave any different as a grandfather?"

"Because he knows Mom's dead, that's why."

"What are you telling me?"

"He doesn't have to try anymore. He knows I can take care of myself. He doesn't know you at all, but he'll know I can take care of you too, if I have to."

"Give me more credit than that."

"I do." She smiled. "Not much, but I do."

TALKER HAD BOUGHT a hunting knife but nothing else he could use as a weapon. He imagined he might be skinning rabbits, although he hadn't thought ahead about how he would manage to kill them.

Talker didn't expect to stay away indefinitely and wouldn't be running to Mexico. He'd read that poor Phil Hart had confessed and then courteously expired. That guy was an eyewitness, and Talker didn't know of any others — who'd survived. He had to hope that Trusdale, Anna, and Daniel would be permanently behind bars sooner or later. Then he could show his face and answer their questions. He hoped his outstanding warrant from years ago would be unimportant then. There had never been a conviction, he'd never meant to hurt the guy, and after so much time had passed, there would be no one to contradict his version of events.

He worried about Anna, but whatever she was doing he couldn't help her now. It saddened him she'd taken her mother to the farm. He knew the girl hadn't expected to be detained there. But Frank and Ida were sharp enough to know that Anna would never be one to keep her mouth shut.

BIRCH HAD FIGURED that Talker's car wouldn't be far from the boat dock. The caves would be an ideal hideout, however uncomfortable. Birch parked his SUV a hundred yards above the riverbank, then early in the morning he crept cautiously on foot down toward the water, careful to move as silently as possible by stepping on soft earth instead of dry brush.

From a distance, he didn't see anyone in the gray Honda. Talker was either curled up sleeping in the backseat or off in search of food or a hiding place.

Daniel got out of his Jeep a half-mile away from where he last saw a live signal from the Honda. He couldn't risk driving closer because the damn car was so noisy. He was carrying the crossbow. Here there could be questions about the license, the wrong hunting season for archery, and his presence in the park itself. If he suspected anyone in authority was approaching, his plan was to toss the weapon quickly away and hurry back to his car. Then if he was accosted empty-handed, he'd be an angler from up north who'd returned post-season to pull his rowboat out of the water.

He meant the crossbow for Talker. It would look like an off-season hunting accident, another anonymous hit-and-run. Problem was, Daniel had not been trained to use the thing. At the farm, he'd worn a sidearm openly, more for intimidating display than for actual use. He liked the idea of silent killing, but the crossbow he'd taken with him hastily hadn't been maintained.

It was badly corroded and had a manual hand crank for the cocking mechanism that was difficult to operate. Cocking should engage the safety catch automatically, but it didn't always, especially with Daniel's clumsy handling. Anticipating he'd need to take his shot as soon as he spotted his prey, Daniel had cranked back the string and loaded the weapon with a foot-long carbon bolt. He counted himself a fair marksman with pistol or rifle, so it never occurred to him he'd need more than one shot.

Birch approached the gray sedan cautiously. He was unarmed. If he encountered Talker, he didn't expect to be threatened. He mostly wanted to know whether Talker had hurt anyone. If the man had sold out to those hustlers at the farm, he wouldn't be deserving of Fred Birchard's friendship or support. Would he have stuck by Winona if she hadn't passed? Birch would have been a more attentive husband, would have taken better care of her. But she'd made her choice. Birch couldn't blame Talker for wanting her.

Daniel was on the high ground, looking down at the big black man as he circled the car. Talker was nowhere to be seen. This guy could well be law enforcement, more to be feared if he were running down Talker than simply citing trespassers in the park. His presence was a complication Daniel couldn't abide. He certainly couldn't attack Talker with this guy around, and he couldn't risk being questioned or apprehended for any reason. He'd have to leave without being seen and come back before sunset.

As Birch tried a door handle on the empty vehicle, Daniel accidentally betrayed his presence as he shifted position to see more clearly, reached out to steady himself, and the dry limb he'd grabbed cracked loudly.

Birch wheeled around in the direction of the sound, and assuming the figure was Talker, yelled, "Hey!"

Daniel panicked and, turning his back on the man below, took off at a run. Having been seen, he couldn't simply throw the crossbow aside. So he clutched it to his chest, the width of the bow being narrower than his shoulders, hoping the lawman hadn't seen him holding it.

It was a long way back to the Jeep and cumbersome to carry the weapon, but Daniel dared not leave it behind, and he was still expecting he'd need it. He didn't dare return to the farm if he hadn't completed his mission.

Birch took powerful strides up the hill. He stopped to catch his breath, intending to call out to Talker he meant no harm, when the man he was chasing tripped and fell.

It should be nearly impossible for a properly cocked crossbow with a working safety to fire unless the marksman pulls the trigger. Loading the bolt should be deferred until the target was in sight and in range. But as a matter of habit, even when unloaded, carrying a crossbow with the nose end pointed toward the ground should be mandatory procedure.

The bolt had been pointed instead at Daniel's chin. It shot through his gullet, through the roof of his mouth, and into his brain. If he had a moment's lucid thought before blacking out, it might have been, *Stupid!*

Even before he bent over the body, Birch knew this wasn't Talker. The man was slight of build, his hair close-cropped. Birch reached out, depressed the neck with his forefinger, and found no pulse.

Anyone happening on the scene would conclude this was a freak accident. Birch tipped the body toward him far enough to see the man's face, and he didn't recognize him. But it was pretty obvious this was someone else who had been stalking his friend, and with evil intent.

As Birch was considering what if anything he should do, the van carrying Curt and Anna pulled up behind the Honda. Anna had no fear of confronting her father. They jumped out and were peering into the car as Birch came back down the hill.

Birch called out, "He ain't here!"

Anna shouted, "Birch! Have you seen him?"

Out of breath again, Birch couldn't help hugging her. "Nope. But there's a guy up there come to kill him who's killed hisself. His karma done run out."

Anna was explaining Curt's presence, and Birch was telling them what had happened when Talker strode up as if they were all meeting up for a family picnic. A skilled stalker himself, he'd seen everything from a higher vantage point.

Finally seeing Talker again, Birch's hatred evaporated. Old resentments might linger, but the emotion that washed over Birch was relief that his friend — and Anna's father — had not been murdered moments ago.

Talker professed his innocence. He'd never hurt anyone at the farm and hadn't even been riding in the truck when Daniel drove it into town following Gropius.

Anna announced her glad news, which Talker took as a new reason to believe his life need not be pointless. Birch called the sheriff's station in Osceola, where later that day they all gave sworn statements about the circumstances of Daniel's demise. For an hour and a half longer than the others, Talker's statement included why he'd gone into hiding in the park and everything he'd done and witnessed at the End-Times farm.

57

I emailed the decoded and translated letter from Gropius to Harry Ardmore. I was aware the public might perceive it as another wild conspiracy theory, not only unbelievable but also totally unsubstantiated. And perhaps because there was so little proof of crimes, some people were still alleging that even the reports of abuses at End-Times were fake news. Phil Hart's confession to me confirmed some of it, but what he'd told me on his deathbed wasn't admissible.

Now that Deacon Daniel was dead, the authorities didn't have enough to charge anyone, and as a result there were no cooperating witnesses. Talker's testimony was suggestive, but even though he knew Hart was an enforcer he'd never seen him engaged in a criminal act. Anna had heard a lot of gossip when she was held there but hadn't seen the worst of it.

I finally relented and gave the name Kenny Pulaski to Sheriff Otis along with my strong suspicion he'd been trafficking in the stolen phones. Since I'd seen him at the controls in the sanctuary the night of Winona's supposed healing, I hoped he'd be able to describe how Pastor Obadiah intended to use those special effects in future plans. But it turned out Miller was little more than a button pusher. Gropius hadn't shared anything with him about the engineering, and he had no details other than what was required of him to follow the order of service in the church. Because he knew what he had to do to produce the effects, he suspected Trusdale's healings were fake. So did many people, but Miller had no inside information to share.

Nevertheless, Ardmore ran the full text of the letter in his story. It was a testimony to the craziness of the post-truth era that its predictions were not more sensational.

Within just three weeks of starting, grand jury proceedings apparently came to nothing. Jurors were dismissed and no one was charged. Hoping to find any grounds to put Trusdale and Ida in custody until more evidence came to light, state prosecutors charged him with operating a cemetery without a license. The result was a fine, no jail time, and an unnecessary cease-and-desist injunction.

Grand jury proceedings were secret in Missouri unless someone was indicted. Prosecutors could permit exceptions, but in this case testimony might have been deemed privileged, possibly on religious grounds.

One would have expected the grand jury process to take months, at least. Close observers like Ardmore and me suspected someone in authority had pulled the plug. It was an election year, and public discourse was heating up. Trusdale was not running for office, but he was spouting off about everyone who was. Shackleton was in the race for a Senate seat. Trusdale had endorsed him, and Shackleton had not repudiated him. Neither had any officials of the major Christian denominations. Evangelicals in particular had responded to the End-Times news by pushing back against any proposals for closer government oversight of churches. The few spokespersons who dared to be critical of Trusdale wrote him off as another wacko, claiming the body of believers did not deserve to be tarred with that brush.

I'd seen so much from the inside, playing a role in uncovering Trusdale's abuses, and at least for now the End-Times Retreat Center was no longer in operation. But I continued to worry what might happen if his enablers gained political power and found his methods useful.

Shackleton, of all people, had encouraged me to go back on the air, and he'd given me the means to do it. One thing I could still try would be to debate Trusdale in a public forum.

58

I titled the show *News of the Second Coming with Reverend Wycliff.* The topic was a popular draw, highlighting all manner of end-times prophesies, including cult leaders through history, mass suicide pacts, faith healings, and conspiracy theories, including the anti-Castro plot cited by the Church Committee, as well as the more recent stories about Project Blue Beam. My purpose was to demonstrate to the audience that Trusdale's plot was nothing new. And it was as corrupt and false as Jonestown, as misguided and tragic as Waco.

Guilt by association was not justice, but, the legal system having failed to charge, much less convict Trusdale, showing him to be ridiculous might be all I could do.

Not surprisingly, he eagerly accepted my invitation to be interviewed live on camera.

I OPENED the telecast with a recap of discoveries at the End-Times farm, including footage of workers in hazmat suits exhuming the bodies wrapped in white sheets. I could see that it annoyed Pastor Obadiah that I called him by his given name, so that was how I addressed him, despite the video.

"Frank, surely you don't deny that you operated this religious retreat where many people ended up starving to death. Some people have alleged no such thing happened."

Trusdale looked untroubled. He'd rehearsed and delivered these responses many times in other venues. My being so familiar by using his first name backfired when he used mine as if to include me in his cohort. "Evan, my dear colleague, needy people came willingly to the End-Times Retreat Center. We fed them, we counseled them, we encouraged Bible study, and we shared prophesies of things to come with them. To a man, woman, and child, they were desperate. They thought they had nowhere else to go. They sought solace and received it, such as we could give. Our teachings, as divinely revealed, counsel that fasting purifies the soul. Many came to us because they were weary of this world, and they fervently believed, according to prophesy, they would soon see Jesus. This is why we encouraged them to fast. Naturally, if any asked for food, we ministered to their needs."

"So, many *did* die? Do you admit there actually were bodies in the ground?"

"Yes, Evan. Some expired, as they intended to do. This was their relief from suffering, their deliverance from their cares and woes. They are with God now."

"Isn't suicide a sin?"

"There is a debate in doctrine about this, Evan. Each will be judged by a golden rule that is not within our mortal powers to apply."

"I'm sure you know the state medical examiners have done autopsies on each of the recovered bodies. Their findings were that not all of them died from starvation. Some apparently were strangled, some died from head trauma as if they were bludgeoned."

Trusdale sighed patiently and said, "Reverend Wycliff, believe me when I assure you, I witnessed none of this. I condoned no acts of violence. If such was the case — and I emphasize I only have the opinion of the coroner on this — some people no doubt assisted one another at the end. Families stayed together in their resolve. It's human nature after all to fear the moment of death, strong as our faith might be."

"The first two bodies exhumed were an infant and its mother."

He shook his head morosely. "Sadly, the woman died in child-birth, and the infant lived only a short time. Again, I was told this. She was a new resident, reportedly in late-term pregnancy when she arrived. I did not know her, and I was unaware of her condition until after she'd passed."

"Shouldn't the baby have been taken to a hospital?"

"There was no time, I believe. We had limited resources, and many of our residents declined medical care. I really don't know the specifics of the matter."

"Do you claim to do faith healing, Frank?"

"My ministry and its practices give people hope. Evan, as I know you believe, healing, like vengeance, is the Lord's."

We'd kept Shackleton in the green room outside the studio. Now I brought him on with a brief introduction, reminding the audience of his Congressional campaign. Trusdale looked mildly surprised to see him but not upset.

I led with, "Mr. Shackleton, in your capacity as lieutenant governor, a high office of this state, are you disappointed no one has been held responsible for the deaths at the End-Times farm?"

The arrangement of chairs on the studio set had him seated alongside Trusdale, facing me. It occurred to me the impression was they were both on the same team.

Shackleton began congenially, "Evan, thank you for this opportunity to comment on these unfortunate events. And, Pastor Obadiah, I'm pleased to join this discussion. It may be stating the obvious, but this is fundamental. Religious freedom and freedom of speech are irrevocable rights in America. Whether or not we agree with the convictions of people who chose a fatal path at End-Times, we mustn't react to these circumstances by limiting basic freedoms for everyone else. As I understand it, Obadiah's message has not been substantially different from that of many other reputable evangelists. How any believer chooses to respond to that message must be a matter of individual conscience. Some say this farm was a cult, and perhaps it was. But its practices do not continue to this day. As I understand it, the initial intention was to welcome the homeless and the disenfranchised, to minister and provide care. To get people off the streets! We might guess that many of these folks faced mental health challenges. Suicidal behavior would not be inconsistent. In my campaign, I propose new initiatives to address homelessness, malnutrition, and mental illness."

Addressing Shackleton, I asked, "Stuart, if the pastor is correct in claiming these people all did it to themselves, and perhaps no one is to blame for their fatal decisions, would you say that in other respects the End-Times farm was a benefit to society?"

The politician nodded. "Were these deaths unnecessary? Preventable? Perhaps. But to the extent that Pastor Obadiah was providing services that the government should have undertaken, yes, I'd say there was a contribution. Homelessness has been on the decline our state, not only because of his efforts, of course. But I will say that it is significant that these needy folks went there voluntarily. No one had to round them up. Such voluntary approaches deserve examination."

"In closing, I'll ask both of you. What should become of the End-Times property?"

Trusdale responded first, "My intentions have been misconstrued, and in any case I don't have the resources to continue. However, if I can assist our future senator here in his innovative programs to deal with homelessness and despair, I will gladly join the effort."

Shackleton smiled, gratified for the endorsement, then sat back as if to say the dark clouds had passed over. "Evan, it's too soon. End-Times is no longer in operation, and justly so." He shrugged. "No doubt, books will be written, scholarly papers. Psychiatrists and social scientists will form their opinions. I daresay religious leaders will hold to their faiths and rightly resist efforts to regulate or supervise their legitimate practices. But, you know, looking back on history, after we have some distance from this, at scenes of great tragedy, today there are memorials. Museums to educate, to remind."

I smirked. "You mean, turn End-Times into a religious theme park?"

"Evan, you're teasing. But, seriously, we mustn't forget the lessons of history."

59

I'd succeeded in getting both Trusdale and Shackleton to admit to the facts on the record, but I felt they'd both scored on me in the contest of public opinion. Unless someone with hard evidence of a crime turned on him, Trusdale would be free to continue to preach his toxic doctrine. Or he could take whatever riches he had buried where no one had yet found them, buy an island somewhere, and crown himself king. Shackleton was widely regarded as a popular, even moderate, conservative. Next year he'd be a federal officeholder and policymaker, and with his background he'd probably serve on some finance committee. He'd retain support from Evangelicals, not because he'd defended Trusdale but because he would defend all churchmen against Trusdale's critics.

I was languishing on my cot in the trailer, musing about my topic for the next episode — or whether there would even be one — when I got a belated visit from my favorite G-man. Leon looked haggard, and his usual gray suit needed pressing. It was beginning to spit snow outside. To ward off the chill, I'd flipped on the space heater. Now my enclosure was overheated to stifling. Leon removed his coat, loosened his tie, sat disgustedly in the only chair, and accepted a finger of whiskey with no ice, no water.

He took a big gulp and felt the burn before he greeted me with, "Sorry I couldn't help. The guy's getting away with murder. It wasn't your job to stop him, but as far as it goes, you did."

He'd read Ardmore's pieces about the technology from Gropius and Trusdale's plans to use it.

I pleaded wearily, "Tell me there isn't some other government agency that will use this for some nasty false-flag operation. Or maybe Putin wants to resurrect Lenin."

He chuckled, "Not that I know of, but the whole point of Secure Compartmented Information is that it's compartmented. Even if it were happening in my bailiwick, I might not know the scary parts. It's called look straight ahead, stay in your lane."

"I almost called you for help on the cyber stuff. It was pure dumb luck I managed to make sense of that confession from Gropius. The technology is real, the results are convincing, and he didn't have much help. Put one of your departments on it, give them a budget, and who knows where it could go?"

He gestured for a refill, which I willingly provided with what was left in the bottle. I was already ahead. He chugged it down this time then muttered, "I thought I had a solution, almost brought it to you."

"Now you tell me!"

"I was thinking about that time you conned that Russian hood. Got him to think he'd gone back on his deal with the devil. Then I wondered, what's Trusdale's weak spot? From what you told me, besides his sister, who is a hard case, it was his birth mother. She was sweet as pie, and he doted on her. She died recently enough we could probably pull some phone conversations from the archives and sample her voice. We could fake a recording, have her telling him from the grave he has to fess up and repent or he's bound for the fiery furnace."

The bright spots of the day would be sharing a meal with Leon and flirting with Cora. I assured him, "Wouldn't have worked. Trusdale is a sociopath. I don't think he believes in heaven or hell. The power he craves is in this world, not in the next. That's what has me worried."

"Whatever his plan was, you stalled it."

"The doubter in me would say you can't prevent what won't happen anyway."

"Reverend, are you telling me you don't actually believe Jesus will be coming back one day?"

I answered soberly, "I've always thought — and you're not to be bandying this about — that the Second Coming, if it ever happens, will be a universal dawning of Christ-consciousness. That's the thief-in-the-night part of it. Only believers will know it's occurred."

He teased, "Happening any time soon?"

"Look around us. What do you think?"

FOR FURTHER READING: CHOKE HOLD

SAMPLE FROM AN ELI WOLFF MYSTERY

It is significant that the year was 1981 – before smartphones and pocket video, even before personal computers and the Internet. The location – the city and state – could matter to parties who might not wish this story to be told. Let's just say we're talking about a large metropolitan area somewhere in North America.

This is a work of fiction. You may think you find truth here and there. But guilty parties will take comfort in believing that what you want most is not justice but entertainment.

Putting a law firm above a funeral home might seem an unwise marketing decision. But the price was right on the rent. Luther "Bones" Jackson Jr. gave Lazer "Eli" Wolff a break. Originally, it was because they both liked progressive jazz. Or maybe it was because they both followed basketball, made friendly bets on games, and Bones often lost. But Eli reasoned that he only needed the place for meeting new clients, which so far wasn't all that often. He was a litigator. He belonged in court. Win a few cases and he could afford more impressive digs.

That was the plan, anyway. Until all the rest of it happened.

As for Bones, maintaining a mortuary as a storefront also had its pluses and minuses. On the plus side, having a picture window on the street was a great way to show off caskets, like so many shiny new cars. On the negative side, the clientele might think of the establishment as a kind of revolving door. If you thought about it, life was like that. But no one wanted to be reminded. Also, because Bones offered informal counseling services above and beyond those of an undertaker, locating his business on a busy street emphasized his role as an unofficial public servant.

Indeed, Bones was the godfather of the local community of color.

But the only control he had over the criminal element was what you would call moral persuasion. Eli could offer his own advice on occasion, and as with too many of his other clients, those services ended up being rendered *pro bono.*

Bones did it to keep up what you might call commercial goodwill. He was a standup guy not only for stiffs but also for their living, breathing survivors. Which, in numerous cases, included a warm widow who suddenly had control of the family checkbook. Not that he would hit on that right away. He knew how to court a lady. And Bones was a patient man.

As for Eli, his practice of law needed practice. He had no delusions about that. Collecting from a personal-injury case also required patience. It took one or two years, typically, and he did have a couple of big scores on the horizon. But meanwhile, an upstanding member of the bar had to stay out of the bars, as they say. So, Eli took on some pathetic cases. Which often came to him from Bones.

But today, Eli was expecting a paying customer in the hot seat.

Divorce. Not his strong suit, but, if not too complicated, it would be mostly a paperwork hand he could play.

From the weight of her day jewelry, the silk of her too-tight top, and the prominent bulges of what surely must be silicone implants, Eli judged this babe must have some powerful reason to come to this side of the tracks to find counsel.

Eli was poised to take notes on a yellow pad, but so far all he'd jotted down was a phone number with an area code from the tonier part of town and the first name Chrissy. He guessed she had met Mr. Cadillac at a gentleman's club or perhaps a sporting event. Maybe she'd been a basketball cheerleader and he had one of those expensive courtside seats. She'd been looking for a sugar daddy, he for a trophy wife, and they'd both had sticky hands. Hers were groping in his pants for his credit cards, his inside her blouse for those artificial but perfectly shaped boobs.

Which in her aristo neighborhood was not always a recipe for true love but could be a mutually beneficial marital arrangement.

Chrissy was sobbing.

Uh oh. Here's the first danger signal, Eli thought.

Whenever they turned on the waterworks, he could feel the size of his retainer shrinking. There was bound to be a temporary problem with her cash flow. That was probably the reason she'd come over to his side of the tracks – to find a cheap lawyer. If the guy's wealth was into the millions, there were all kinds of high-toned attorneys on the right side of the tracks who would take her case on contingency. Even if her legal position was iffy, they'd at least take her on retainer, and what Amex account couldn't withstand a ten-grand hit? Answer – a card that has already been maxed out, or one that hubby was quick enough to cancel already.

So, here she was – no cash, no credit – and probably (and this was the real challenge) with no idea whatever where chubby hubby had his assets hid.

Here comes the sob story.

And Eli could decide either to walk away from the case or accept what she could scrape together now and hope he could find the loot on discovery and get enough of the settlement to not only make it all worthwhile but also top off his fee. Just now, considering his own problems with cash flow, he was inclined toward the more expedient course.

A more prudent man might have been concerned that his law practice did not focus on family law. Eli was a competent personal injury man. He knew enough about fractures, soft tissue damage, rehabilitation time, painkiller addictions, chiropractic and acupuncture alternatives, and all the gut-wrenching, subjective issues surrounding pain and suffering.

And what is divorce but an acute personal injury?

If Mrs. Cadillac could do a reasonable job helping him fill in the paperwork, he should be able to float her boat through the sewer of the county court system. It was a job-creation thing. And wasn't this part of town a bona-fide enterprise zone? Besides, Eli's pain-and-suffering antenna was picking up the strong signal that, although Chrissy might be fed up with tit squeezing, what she craved and eventually would pay dearly for was good, old-fashioned handholding.

But, as it turned out, Eli was wrong. She wasn't here about divorce at all. Since she'd walked in without an appointment, she'd been complaining about her husband's performance. Eli had made an understandable assumption about what kind of performance she was talking about. He further guessed that her litany of disappointments would culminate in her wanting to end the marriage and cash out her share of the community property.

"Mr. Wolff," she whimpered, "Since that awful accident, my husband hasn't been able to do *anything* for a long, long time." She licked her lips and started to unbutton her blouse.

She's really overdoing it.

He'd have to get the facts straight before he could decide what to make of her come-on.

"Wait a minute," he said, gesturing to red-light her striptease. "What's this about an accident? I thought we were talking about a divorce here."

"He was injured on the job," she said. "But his employer went bankrupt."

It's personal injury after all? Hey, insurance claim or maybe work-man's comp. Someone should have deep pockets. Maybe we're back in business.

And he asked, "Do you have any health insurance? If they're not paying up, we can fix that."

She sighed. "We got behind on the premiums." Then she added, undoing another button, "Please, I'll do anything."

Eli was getting a time-honored ploy for reducing the amount of his retainer. But something about this woman didn't add up.

She's dressed upscale, but somehow she and hubby failed to keep their insurance current?

Eli had trouble picturing Mr. Cadillac as the groveling employee of a company that was managed so badly it ended up in the toilet.

Unless it had been his company.

And he'd been planning to deep-six it all along.

"Let me get this straight," Eli said. "The company your husband worked for is totally defunct? Is that right?"

"Yes, I'm afraid so."

"And there's no way you could make good on that insurance? No grace period? I mean, they usually give you, like, ten days after the due date."

"No," she said. "It's lapsed. We got the letter."

"And it's not a divorce action you wish to bring?"

"Who said anything about divorce?"

Eli was still trying to figure her angle. There was a long-established Department of Labor procedure for filing workman's comp claims if the responsible company no longer existed. It was a paperwork chore, involving no court appearances, not the kind of thing he'd prefer to take on. What she needed was a paralegal at a clinic or perhaps some social worker. He had no direct experience with this type of claim, and he'd have to do some research to either get the job done or get Chrissy a referral.

But just to be sure, he asked, "Am I to understand there's no one to sue? And it's not your husband's resources you're going after to maintain your own lifestyle? You *do* plan to stay with him?"

"That's right" was all she said. Then she added as she unbuttoned still lower, wetting her lips mid-sentence, "Can't you think of any way you could, ah, waive your usual fee?"

Now, it wasn't that Eli wasn't horny. His last sexual encounter had been about as intimate as a clammy handshake, months ago with a supermarket clerk who craved a hormone flood even more than he did. It was remarkable that they'd taken precautions in the heat of the moment, but they had. He didn't even have that kind of regret to pepper the memory.

He gave her his best, insincere smile.

To which, unaccountably, she started to laugh.

"What's so funny?" he asked.

"Why," she said, "you lose! You've just been punked by Luther Jackson Junior. He was sure, if there was no money, you wouldn't take a case for love or lust, no matter how much I poured it on. Now, if you'll excuse me, I'm running late. I've got an audition for a recurring role on a soap. Bye now."

And she grabbed her purse, stood up, and hurried out.

He yelled after her, "How is that a bet? I would have stipulated as much!" But she was already out the door.

Eli didn't see the humor. And worse, as an attorney, he was

particularly offended there had been no binding wager to begin with. But when in his righteous fury he tried to call Bones, all he got was the mortuary's answering service.

"Bones," he said to the recording in a low growl, "you are one sick, sorry, son of a bitch."

ACKNOWLEDGMENTS

For me, this fourth book in the Evan Wycliff series has been the most difficult. Describing such horrific events emphasizes the age-old questions: Why is there evil in the world? Why do bad things happen to good people?

There have been cult leaders and secretive compounds throughout history. In today's world, it might not be surprising that such events could occur in the remote areas of developing nations. Imagining them taking place in rural Missouri posed challenges but proved to be just as thinkable.

Thanks to my editorial team for their diligence and professionalism. Joan Cate performs background research and marketing administrative tasks. Clare Baggeley prepares impressive graphics. Jason Letts edits, and Lu Ann Sodano pitches my interviews.

Colleagues who kindly read early drafts and lent their wisdom include William Anthony, John Rachel, Pamela Jaye Smith, Ryan Tyler, Damian Andrews, Dana Yarrington, Gabrielle Dahms, and David Drum.

My wife Georja Umano supports and nurtures me. She understands the old joke that her husband may be doing his hardest work when he's gazing out of the window.

Gerald Everett Jones
Santa Monica, January 2024

ABOUT THE AUTHOR

GERALD EVERETT JONES is a freelance writer who lives in Santa Monica, California. *Preacher Stalls the Second Coming* is his fourteenth novel. He has been a longtime board member of the Independent Writers of Southern California (IWOSC) and host of the GetPublished! Radio podcast. He holds a Bachelor of Arts with Honors from the College of Letters, Wesleyan University, where he studied under novelists Peter Boynton *(Stone Island)*, F.D. Reeve *(The Red Machines)*, and Jerzy Kosinski *(The Painted Bird, Being There)*.

Find out more at geraldeverettjones.com, and read his Thinking About Thinking blog posts at geraldeverettjones.substack.com.

ALSO BY GERALD EVERETT JONES

Fiction

Harry Harambee's Kenyan Sundowner: A Novel – Multiple awards in Literary Fiction

Preacher Finds a Corpse (Evan Wycliff #1) – Multiple awards in Mystery

Preacher Fakes a Miracle (Evan Wycliff #2) – NYC Big Book Silver 2020

Preacher Raises the Dead (Evan Wycliff #3) – Multiple awards in Mystery

Preacher Stalls the Second Coming (Evan Wycliff #4)

Mick & Moira & Brad: A Romantic Comedy - Multiple awards in Romantic Comedy

Clifford's Spiral: A Novel – IPA Silver in Literary Fiction 2020

Mr. Ballpoint – Page Turner Award in Fiction Finalist 2022

Christmas Karma – WGA Diversity Award (Screenplay) 2016

Choke Hold: An Eli Wolff Thriller

Bonfire of the Vanderbilts: A Novel / *Bonfire of the Vanderbilts: Scholar's Edition*

My Inflatable Friend (Misadventures of Rollo Hemphill #1)

Rubber Babes (Misadventures of Rollo Hemphill #2)

Farnsworth's Revenge (Misadventures of Rollo Hemphill #3)

Stories and Essay *Boychik Lit*
Nonfiction

How to Lie with Charts - Eric Hoffer Award Finalist in Business 2020

The Death of Hypatia and the End of Fate

The Light in His Soul: Lessons from My Brother's Schizophrenia (with Rebecca Schaper)

Searching for Jonah: Clues in Hebrew and Assyrian History by Don E. Jones (Afterword)

Made in the USA
Las Vegas, NV
18 January 2024

84545002R00194